Thanks of work Caryn

Otherwhens, Otherwheres: Favorite Tales

John Dalmas

John Dalmas

Silver Dragon Books

Nederland, Texas

ISBN 1-932300-00-7

First Printing 2003

9 8 7 6 5 4 3 2 1

Cover design by Brian Vigue

Published by:
Silver Dragon Books
PMB 210, 8691 9th Avenue
Port Arthur, Texas 77642

Find us on the World Wide Web at
http://www.regalcrest.biz

Printed in the United States of America

This book is dedicated to Frank Kelly Freas, the dean of science fiction illustrators, and to the memory of Jack Gaughan, another memorable illustrator. To Jim Burk, who urged me to collect these stories for book publication. Jim's first novel, *High Rage*, will soon be published by Silver Dragon Books.

To the memory of Jon Gustafson, writer, artist, and godfather of science-fiction fandom in the Inland Empire of the Northwest, constant support to artists and writers, and personal friend for twenty-two years.

And, to Jimmy McClain, fireman-oiler-watertender, who helped me grow up right.

— John Dalmas

Gullikksen and the 500-Pound Hallucination

Introduction

Once upon a time I lived in a different universe, one without space ships. Ships, but not space ships. Intermittently, from 1947 to 1953, I made my living on the last great merchant fleet to draw its power from Scotch boilers, stoked with coal by men with shovels. Many of the stokers (we called ourselves "firemen,") were immigrants or their sons: Game-leg Paddy, Onni Hietala, Nuts and Bolts, Bumboat Charley, Firedown Gallagher...some of them great storytellers. Young and impressionable, I enjoyed knowing them, being one of them. And I loved the boiler rooms, dark, brooding, and hot. Big as haybarns, they extended from the bilge plates all the way up to the lifeboat deck. Most of the lower half was filled with the great boilers, enough room being left for stowage, and for the stoke hole where the firemen wielded their tools. Above the boilers was little more than railings, the six-foot induction fan, the smokestack that disappeared through the overhead, and along the catwalks, wires strung by the firemen to quick-dry their laundry.

The boiler room: a realm of ash dust, stinking fumes, and especially *heat*; your dungarees stuck to your thighs from the sweat.

Years later, with the old coal-burning ships replaced by behemoths burning oil or diesel fuel (not a shovel or slice bar to be found), I told myself I'd someday set a science fiction story on one of those old-timers, and eventually I did. This is it.

There's also a story about the story: I'd written it with *F&SF—the Magazine of Fantasy & Science Fiction*—in mind. I knew it wasn't "an *Analog* story." Nonetheless, my wise old agent of the time, Larry Sternig, sent it to Stan Schmidt at *Analog*.

I was right, sort of, but so was Larry. Stan replied, "I can think of two or three good reasons we don't use stories like this, but I'm buying it anyway."

Stan has been cited as saying (approximately): "Don't decide I won't buy something; let *me* make that decision." I now believe him. Meanwhile I'm still surprised—and delighted.

* * *

I knew right away there was something peculiar about him. I mean, who ever heard of a Norwegian heaving coal in the firehold? Swedes—Swedes by the scores. Finns by the dozens. And Irish beyond number, as witness myself. But norskis sail on the deck or in the wheelhouse, not in the firehold.

Except for one: Ingebritt Gullikksen.

We did have some strange crews on the Great Lakes during the war. After enlistments and the draft took their shares, big bonuses to be made on the salt water took part of what was left.

Meanwhile the steel mills were running round the clock. Gold was lovely and silver was nice, but *iron*! Iron was *important*! So every old hull that would float—some of them rusting at the dock since 1930—every hull they could find was more or less reconditioned to haul iron ore down from Lake Superior. An example was the steamer *Henry K. Anibal.*

And every old sailorman that could stagger into the hiring hall was sent out on a job. Then, if they could make it up the ladder from the dock, they were signed on. On top of that, they were shipping out fifteen-year-old kids who were so green they thought "binnacle" was a card game and a bunker was somebody sleeping. A strange and lively time.

Gullikksen came aboard in late September 1943, at Duluth of course, a gaunt old man with great big bony hands, thin white hair, and face the color of blotchy bread dough. I was on deck at the time, and I remember wondering if he could possibly do any useful work. It looked to me like the hearse would have to meet us when we arrived at the Soo.

That was because the sun was shining, and I couldn't see all there was to him, or around him, or with him, or however you want to put it.

I had nothing against age. My grandfather was old, and my father was getting that way, and I knew if I was lucky I'd be old myself someday. And old Inge might have been one hell of a man, thirty years earlier when he was maybe fifty.

But you never saw the firehold on one of those old hand-fired buckets, or felt the heat! The heat! In front of you the tall faces of two great boilers, and at your back the bunker doors, with ten frieghtcars of coal feeding down through them. With a couple of number six scoop shovels, known for good reason as Irish banjos, and other tools of ignorance. Ignorance—but skill.

You'd average shoveling about seven tons of coal a day, plus a ton or two of wet ashes. But that wasn't the hard part. The hard part was cleaning fires. In 110 or 115 degrees of heat. A hundred and twenty on the *Henry K. Anibal,* which was nicknamed "The Hungry Cannibal" for the way she ate up coal and firemen, with the lagging falling off her boilers and all.

And Mickey McKinney, the chief engineer, didn't help any, with his love of free whiskey. Any bandit at a coal dock could sell him a shipment of the worst slack, or even overburden, telling him it was number one bunker fuel. All he needed to do first was pour two or three drinks of good whiskey down him.

The whiskey had to be good, though; you couldn't fool him on that. The best trips I made on the Cannibal was when someone tried to slip him cheap whiskey. That got his Irish up, and we'd sail with the loveliest nut coal you could ever put shovel to.

But we were burning twenty percent slate when Gullikksen came aboard—Gullikksen and his—well, I'll get to that. It was the worst coal I ever saw.

Now I'm a man of principle; I am now and I was then. There are those who call it stupidity. When I signed on a ship, I stayed with it as long as they treated me like a man. I didn't quit just because the weather turned hot and sent the firehold temperature out the top of the glass, or the cook turned ugly and went on a baloney strike, or we'd docked at South Chicago or Conneaut— one of those real fast docks—and I was struck with terminal thirst and no time to slake it.

I was a homesteader. I'd fit one out when the ice was melting in March and lay her up when she froze to the dock in December. Almost without exception.

But with a steamer like the Cannibal, and the kind of coal we had, if I'd realized that Gullikksen had come aboard as my firing partner, I'd have quit then and there. I'd have known for sure I couldn't keep steam up working with a stove-up old wreck like him.

Which showed how much I knew about Gullikksen.

We were out on deep water when I went to go down on watch. I didn't realize old Inge was my new partner until I found him at the head of the ladder, waiting to go below. Then I got so mad I couldn't even talk to him.

But he went down the ladder lively enough, and in the dimness of the firehold he didn't look as frail as he had. There was that about him, you see, that only showed up when the light was poor.

The first thing we had to do was clean the fires, the hardest, hottest part of the watch; and to my surprise it went okay. I'd been afraid I'd have to clean his too, but he cleaned his own, whipping out the glaring, fuming, stinking piles of red-hot ashes and clinkers as fast as I did mine. And in the flame and smoke and steam, he actually looked burly and stout.

When we'd shoveled the ashes into the hopper and out into the lake, and blown the flues, I got my next surprise. "Vy don't you go up and cool off till five?" Inge said. "I vill handle it alone and then ve can svitch."

Well, there was nothing unusual about that; it's what firing partners usually do. But I hadn't thought I'd be able to with him. Still, I left by way of the engine room, to let the oiler know that old Inge was down there alone. He nodded; he'd come out on deck and get me if I was needed.

When I went back down at five Inge was perched on the water barrel, watching the steam gauge, which was sitting right on 200 pounds' pressure where it was supposed to be. And I couldn't believe how big he seemed in the weak light down there. Big enough that I looked him over carefully.

When I looked carefully enough, though, I saw a gaunt, used-up old man. It was as if he had a kind of shadow that, at a glance, made him look bigger. He grinned a toothless grin, stood, and went up the ladder two at a time. Then the needle started flickering and I picked up my shovel, hit some fires again and forgot about him.

The rest of the watch went fine too, with long breaks on deck cooling off. After a shower I went in to hit the rack. Inge was already in bed, reading a copy of *Duluth Skandinav*. I wondered if he had his sea bag in there with him. He bulked the cover up as if he weighed 500 pounds.

"How'd it go?" I asked him.

"Yust fine," he answered cheerfully.

"To tell the truth," I said, "I was afraid at first you might not be able to take it down there. How old are you?"

He chuckled. "It don't matter. I'm seventy-eight, but it don't matter. I got a friend that does the vork for me."

"A—friend?"

"Ja. Didn't you see him down there? I t'ought maybe you could see him."

Oh my God! I thought, *I've got a bughouse for a partner!*

"You t'ink I'm nuts," he said, and chuckled again. "Oskar, I vant you to meet Yimmy Mahan."

I looked around for Oskar, but all I could see was me and Gullikksen. Until the covers raised up off him. Even though he was just laying there. Then something like an arm made out of smoke reached out, with a gray hand bigger than Inge's on the end of it. I could see right through it.

Hesitantly I reached out and shook with it. The only time I'd done anything like that before was after two weeks of heavy drinking. It shook hands firmly, and I knew it was being careful not to break my fingers.

"Wirra wirra wirra!" I said, and crossed myself. "What is it?"

"I don't know. I mean—I know but I don't know how to tell you. I don't know the vords."

"What do you mean—you know but you don't know the words?"

"Vell, he don't talk. You yust sort of know vhat he's t'inking. You can do that vit' him." The old man's eyes twinkled. "Go on; try it."

"Some other time," I said, wagging my head back and forth. I watched the "arm" disappear back under the cover. It didn't seem to fold back in. It was more like it just flowed back in on itself.

Then I hung up my towel and went to bed. But not to sleep; not right away. Instead I lay there and thought for a little while. Then I spoke quietly, hardly more than a whisper, so that if Gullikksen was asleep it wouldn't wake him.

"Inge."

"Jaha?"

"Where did you get him?"

"You mean Oskar?"

"Is that what you call him? Oskar? Where did you get him?"

"It vas yust after New Year's, and I was cookee at Mando's Camp T'ree, a logging camp up in Koochiching County. And the cook sent me out vit' a horse and sleigh to haul up a load of stove wood one of the cutters piled up for us. But before I got there I had to pass this little lake, and I could see that somet'ing had vent t'rough the ice. There vas a big place of new ice in the middle, vit'out no snow on it yet, and all around I could see vhere vater and pieces of ice had splashed up.

"And I t'ought, Yesus Christ, vhat could have done *that*? Because the ice vas about t'ree feet t'ick, you know.

"And then I felt him."

"You *felt* him?"

"Sure. You can't see him in the sunlight. And he vas veak and sick, you know, from the explosion and the crash. He vas in a ship, you see, like a small boat really, that come from some star.

"The stars is like the sun, you see, and got things going around them like Earth, vhere people live."

"Planets," I said helpfully.

"Jaha, planets and animals and everything, yust like here. But different."

"Did he tell you all this?"

"Not in vords. He yust kind of lets me know stuff. It's easier than talking."

"What—what does he eat?" I asked. "Or does he?"

"Vell, not exactly. He kind of gets power from t'ings, you know. Vhen I told him it vas all right, he kind of touched me and the horse and got a little bit from us. That saved his life. He vas veak and hurt from the crash, and then he'd been making do vit' spruce trees for a couple days. But trees don't really have much in vinter; he vas yust about dead.

"Besides, it's hard on him to not be connected vit' a person."

"A person? Are there human beings where he comes from?"

"Ja, pretty much. There vas vun that vas pilot on the ship he vas on."

"So Oskar wasn't the pilot then."

"No Oskar vas the enyine."

The—engine. I just kind of lay there. It was all so strange, I couldn't even think much about it. Too strange for thought.

"Uh, Inge, does he still take energy from you?"

"Huh? Oh, a little bit. It's kind of like he needs that—vhat's that vord again?"

"Energy?"

"Ja. He needs a little of that from something live. But he gives me a lot more back. Mostly he gets vhat he needs from the boilers here. He vas so veak, you know, vhen I found him, and I bet he didn't veigh more than a couple ounces, but he got stronger fast vhen he could be by the stove. And vhen ve vas on vatch together, me and you, I could feel him getting stronger and stronger. Those boilers are good for him."

Inge chuckled. "He *loved* helping me clean fires. Maybe tomorrow ve can clean yours, too."

Clean my fires! Wirra! Cleaning fires is the worst job on the ship, and him seventy-eight years old.

"It ain't hard on me," he went on. "He does the vork; I yust chip in the know-how."

"Why doesn't he just stay in the boiler room? Instead of coming up here with you?"

"He likes company, and I'm kind of his pal, you know. Maybe he'll go down vhen I'm asleep. Vould you like to do that, Oskar?...He says he's going to. And he is learning about my body so he can fix it up good for me."

Then I heard Inge yawn, and the talk petered out. I went to sleep thinking about Oskar lying on the boilers getting bigger and bigger.

* * *

Even on a tough steamer like the Cannibal, and with the worst coal I ever saw, the trip went surprisingly good with someone else cleaning the fires. In fact, he'd even clean them an extra time, which made it easier to keep steam.

Pete the Leech was second cook, and he didn't like old Inge: bad-mouthed him and gave him a bad time. Accused him of having the world's biggest tapeworm—that it was indecent for someone that old to eat so much, especially in time of war. Gullikksen did stow the chuck away, all right, but there's nothing wrong with that. And he didn't eat much more than some of those hollow-legged teenagers aboard.

So I decided that when we docked in Ashtabula I was going to catch Pete on the dock and slap the snot out of him. He wasn't going to talk about my partner that way! But when I mentioned it to Inge, he said not to. He said that everyone knew what Pete was like and that no one believed what he said, which I had to admit was true.

We were lucky in Ashtabula; we had to wait for a dock, which gave us more time to go up the street and wet our whistles. It was ten in the morning when we got to Turpeinen's Anchor Bar. If it hadn't been so light, what happened there might not have. But with the sunshine flooding in those big front windows, and us sitting in front of them, there was nothing strange to be seen about us.

I figured we were in trouble when I saw this big guy look at us from the bar. I'd sailed with him—Jailhouse Olson. He was about six-two and more than 200 pounds, with red hair and fists like cannonballs. He should have been Irish. Friendly enough, ordinarily, but give him one drink and he turned mean. He seldom finished the second drink, and I don't think he ever drank the third. He always got in a fight before that. He knew the inside of every jail from Lackawanna to Allouez.

He was looking at us, and I could tell he didn't like what he saw. Pete the Leech was sitting next to him, grinning, and I'd have bet he'd been telling him lies about us. Olson scowled, stood up, and came over.

"Which one of you is Inge Gullikksen?" he asked. I knew it wouldn't make any difference; I was the one he was going to beat up. He'd never hit an old man, whatever Pete had said.

"I'm Gullikksen," old Inge said with a friendly toothless smile. He got up and pushed his right hand out, as if to shake hands, and Olson was so surprised, he let it wrap around his before he could do or say a word.

I never saw anything like it. At first he looked startled, then puzzled, as Inge pumped his hand. Then he got this kind of absent, pleased look, smiled, nodded real friendly at Inge, said he was pleased to meet him, nodded to me and walked back to the bar.

I saw Pete whisper something to him. Olson stared at him, took the cook by the front of the shirt, punched him right in the face, nodded to the bartender and walked out. Pete sat on the floor, blinking, and bleeding all over his shirt, then waited a safe interval and left, holding a handkerchief against his busted mouth.

We never did see him again; he went back to the ship, packed, and paid off before we got back. Which made him luckier than most of the crew. Meanwhile I was beginning to appreciate Oskar more and more.

But it was four days later that I really came to appreciate him. We'd left Sault Sainte Marie about twenty-four hours before, running against the first storm of autumn. It was blowing hard when we left Whitefish Bay, but far from dangerous. We had a chance to take cover twenty hours later, in the lee of the Keweenaw Peninsula, but there didn't seem to be any reason to. It was just another storm; nothing to worry about.

It was a couple of hours farther along that it got really bad. I realized *how* bad when the seas started sweeping the deck one after another and slamming against the deckhouse so that we dogged down the deadlights. And how I got to the crew's mess was, I waited till I heard one wave hit and then ducked out onto the deck and ran for it before the next one came along. Of course, it helped that the seas were coming from the starboard beam and the galley was on the port side.

But as I ran, I saw something that really hit me hard: less than half a mile to port, rising on the top of a wave like some giant reddish-brown log, was the bottom of a ship's hull—another long freighter like the Cannibal had capsized. In the mess, everyone was pretty quiet; I guess we all saw it.

If anything, the wind got worse, and after lunch, when I went back to the room, I saw something that worried me really bad. Some of the hatch tarps had ripped loose, and one of the hatch covers amidships had started to tear up from the coaming, and was buckling. Guys were out there on safety lines trying to hammer it back down with sledge hammers. Lose even one hatch cover, and we'd take a lot of water fast in those seas.

It took only a second or two to see all that. Then the next wave was ripping along the deck, and I ducked into the firemen's quarters. "Inge," I said, "we're in trouble," and told him what I'd seen. "Can Oskar do anything about that?"

He put down the dog-eared copy of *Duluth Skandinav* and sat up with a belch. He'd eaten earlier and more than me. "I don't know. I vill ask him." Then he got this intent look on his face.

Oskar had grown a lot and didn't come in the room anymore. He just lay on top of the boilers, kind of spread over them like some kind of thick cloudy blanket. Knowing what to look for, I could see him when I was on the catwalk, and I'd think *hello* to him and he'd *hello* back. He even said/thought my name: *Hello Jimmy*, he'd say to me. But he always kept a tentacle to Inge when Inge was up in the room, steel bulkhead not withstanding.

Anyway, Inge nodded, and about then the biggest sea yet slammed against the deckhouse. Oskar better come up with something good, I thought, or we'd all end up in Superior's eternal cold storage.

"What did he say?" I asked.

"He said don't vorry about it," and with that, Inge picked up his newspaper and lay back down like we were floating on a mill-pond.

That's easy to say, I thought, *but these old buckets weren't meant to take beatings like this, even when they were new.* And the Cannibal's engine had *Glasgow 1901* stamped on it.

Just then the door flew upon and this kid fell in, dripping wet, his safety line in his hand. He was sobbing "Oh my God, oh my God." Right away I guessed what had happened: a wave had taken him over the side, and only the safety line had saved him. He was probably sixteen years old.

"It's okay," I said, "it's okay."

"No it ain't! No it ain't! She's taking water forward and the hatch cover ripped clear off!"

Oh Jesus! I thought, *don't let her be coming apart!* I looked at Inge, who'd put his paper down and was sitting up frowning. It looked like he was talking to Oskar like a Dutch uncle. Or a Norwegian grandfather. Then he gave a little nod.

After the next wave, the kid ducked out the door again, to do God knew what. Right after that the whistle started to blast, one after another, to abandon ship. There really wasn't much to choose between. If we went down with the Cannibal, we were dead. If we tried to swim in that icy water, we were dead. And I leave it to you what we'd be if we took to the lifeboats.

But orders were orders in those days. "Let's go, Inge," I said.

He smiled and shook his head. "It's going to be all right."

In spite of how ridiculous that sounded, it got my interest. "What's he going to do?" I asked.

"He's going to lift her out of the vater."

Oh for chrissake! I ducked out the door and went up the ladder to the lifeboat deck. From there, the bunker lids being closed, I could see out over the length of the ship to the pilot house up forward. The ripped-up hatch cover had torn completely loose and gone over the side. The hatch, some fifty feet across and maybe fifteen feet fore and aft, was gaping wide, showing wet coal shiny black in the cargo hold. She'd swallow a ton of water with every wave, or maybe four or five, and a couple more hatch covers were buckling. I didn't know what other damage she might have taken. Guys were hurrying aft from the forward end, heading for the lifeboats, sliding their safety lines along the weather line that ran the length of the cargo deck.

Then I realized the next wave wasn't sweeping the deck; it

was just licking along the edge. And as I watched, I could see the deck start to bow downward!

"No Oskar! No!" I shouted. "Put her back in the water, for the love of Jesus!"

By that time several other guys had come up on the lifeboat deck, and they looked at me like I was nuts. So I didn't yell out loud anymore, I just yelled with my thoughts. *This ain't no spaceship, Oskar. She's got to be in the water or she'll bust in two. She ain't strong enough to float in the air, even without 9,000 tons of coal in her hold.*

* * *

I got this response that felt kind of like *damn*! Then I realized the twelve-to-four watch had come up out of the boiler room, leaving no one down below to keep steam up. And somehow that seemed important to me. Another wave hit the deckhouse so I knew Oskar had put us down again.

Two more guys were coming up the ladder, so I jumped the eight feet down to the maindeck and ducked into the firehold door. Below, in the deep cavern that was the firehold itself, I could hear the scrunch of someone shoveling coal, the ring of the shovel heel on the deadplate of a firedoor. Inge, I realized, was down ahead of me.

When I got to the bottom of the long ladder, I found him firing without Oskar's help, his gaunt old form bending, driving the shovel into the coal, straightening, pivoting, striding with the left foot, the shovel swinging into the furnace door, again and again. I guessed Oskar was too busy with other things to help Inge now. The steam pressure had fallen to 185, but it was holding. I picked up the other shovel and began to feed the portside boiler.

When the steam gauge read 195, I hurried between the boilers into the crank room and up the engine room ladder to check things out. The engine room was deserted, the engineer and oiler gone to the boats. But the condensers were doing just fine, the boiler water levels about an inch below the tops of the glass, and best of all, the pumps were running, including the big centrifugal pumps. Then I checked the journal temperatures and a few other things and went back to the firehold.

Inge was holding up good, and the gauge was at 197. The biggest problem was that we hadn't been able to shoot the ashes since

Whitefish Point because of the seas, and the place was half buried with ash piles. We waited for the needle to start flickering and hit three more fires with coal. Then I went back up onto the lifeboat deck to check things out.

There was no one there. I saw one of the lifeboats rise on top of a wave behind us, then disappear into the trough. Another big wave hit the deckhouse, the spray drenching me again, and I looked forward toward the pilothouse, some 500 feet ahead. Another wave was running along the deck. There were three open hatches now, and the water washed over them without any seeming to go in, as if they were covered with glass or something. Oskar was working on it!

And someone was holding us into the wind; someone was at the wheel. That was Oskar too, I supposed. Then the safety valves let go behind me; I almost jumped out of my skin. I hurried back down to the firehold again, expecting to find Inge in trouble.

He wasn't, though. He was standing there with all six furnace doors open, their bright fires shining into the dark room. The induction fan was off, and the ash pan doors were closed to cut off the natural draft. The steam gauge read 200 pounds. I had to bellow to be heard over the roar of steam from the safety valves.

"What the hell's going on?" I asked.

Inge grinned at me. "Oskar shut off the enyines," he said, "so the valves popped."

"Holy Christ! We'll broach and founder!" I dashed between the boilers into the crank room again. The great piston rods were still, their booming silenced, the eccentrics motionless; the only sound was the pumps and generators in the engine room above. I scrambled up ladders. Without forward speed—slow ahead at least—we were gone for sure.

Our only chance was if they'd left a life raft; with a raft we had a chance. Maybe one in 10,000. It was incredible we hadn't broached yet. I'd know when we did: we'd start to roll and wallow, and end up capsized like that other we'd seen.

I came out onto the fantail and stopped, bug-eyed. We were moving faster than the Cannibal had ever gone before in all her forty years, leaving a wake behind her like a cruiser or maybe a destroyer.

* * *

And that's how it was all the way to Thunder Bay, where the seas were a lot less and we slowed down. Then I went up the long deck to the pilot house. We must have had some plates sprung, because streams of water as big as my leg were coming out the pump spouts. I found the captain at the wheel; it had been him steering us. He stared at me through eyes at the ragged edge of sanity. He'd not only lost twenty-nine officers and men; he'd seen the impossible happen, alone, and with no idea of how.

He didn't ask any questions, though, and I said nothing. I didn't think he was up to knowing, and neither did he, I guess. He dropped the hook near the docks in Fort William because he had no crew to handle winches or lines to the pier.

And there'd been no other miracles: the crew was never seen again. That great ice-cold lake doesn't give up her dead.

Back in the boiler room again, Inge and I sat talking. We talked to each other and sometimes we talked to Oskar. He told us he was ready to go home, wherever that might be. I guessed he knew.

He'd gotten a bit pooped pushing 560 feet of ship carrying 9,000 tons of coal through a ship-killing storm at about twenty-five knots. But he was recovering nicely. Ordinarily at the dock we'd have been able to run generators and pumps, and winches if necessary, with the fires banked. It doesn't take that much steam. But we had full-length fires, six of them, eight feet long and forty-two inches wide, and Oskar was soaking up most of that energy. By the time a new crew bussed up from the hiring hall at Duluth, he wanted to be all charged up to go back in the bush, raise the space ship out of the lake, repair it and reactivate the power unit, and in general get her ready for the long trip.

"Ja," said Inge, "and ve ain't got a lot of time. It's already the first of October, and in six veeks that lake vill be froze up again."

Something else was bothering me though, and suddenly I knew what it was. "Oskar," I said, "if the pilot was killed, who's going to fly it?" As soon as I asked it, I got this strange powerful glow that made my hair stand up. And it came from Inge, not Oskar.

"You?"

"Jaha."

"But do you know how?"

He was grinning like an old gray wolf. He and Oskar had

been planning since last winter. It was why they'd gone to Duluth to ship out—to build back Oskar's strength. The spaceship, they told me, had everything Inge needed to live. And learn to fly her. It wasn't that hard.

And then they asked if I wanted to go along!

* * *

Inge paid off the old *Anibal* in Duluth on a cloudy day, and walked down the dock followed by a large dim mass that was plain enough to me but that most people wouldn't notice because they'd feel much better not to.

And I probably would have gone with them—I was a bachelor then, and there was nobody would have missed me that much— but I wasn't willing to quit the *Anibal.* I stayed with her and helped lay her up that December at the foot of Genesee Street in Buffalo.

That's the winter I met your grandma, God rest her.

Anyway, these last few days I've been having this feeling: as if Oskar and Inge were somewhere around, maybe in a big orbit around the Earth. Inge must be 120 by now, but I don't think that means much to him anymore.

Anyway, don't be surprised if I go away for awhile. That's why I told you this, so you'd understand and wouldn't worry. Don't tell your mother, though, because she'd get mad and say Grandpa's gone off his rocker. But I'd appreciate your telling your dad when he comes into port; he knows all of it already, except the last part about Inge and Oskar being around somewhere again.

No, I don't think I'll tell him myself. There's not time, you see.

Mary, you know that ship carving you've always liked so much? It's yours now. And Jamie, I know you've taken up smoking lately, and I want you to have that rack of pipes you've always admired.

So why don't you kids take them now and then go do your homework? Grandpa's going out for a nice long walk.

Moonlight Nocturne

Introduction

During the Prohibition Era, the St. Clair River, connecting Lake Huron with the lower Great Lakes, was a significant waterway for bootleggers. But the smuggler's boats didn't go up or down the river; they went across it, from wet Canada to dry Michigan. And although the mobs dominated the racket, any farmer with a rowboat, and money enough to buy a few cases of whiskey in Canada, could go into the business in a small way.

It could be dangerous though, and not just because of the G-men. Which gave rise to stories; I read some of them when I was a kid.

Fifty years after the Prohibition Amendment was repealed, Herb Clough resurrected Leslie Charteris's much loved *Saint* mystery magazine, with Charteris's cooperation. And I decided to try my hand at writing mysteries. "Moonlight Nocturne" was one of the results, and Herb bought it, along with a couple of others. But before "Nocturne" could be used, distribution problems sank the venture, and those stories already paid for but unpublished were reverted to the authors.

I later modified "Moonlight Nocturne" slightly for a different publisher, *Pulphouse*, which published it. I hope you like it.

* * *

My lungs felt ready to burst, but I knew better than to surge to the surface, splashing and blowing. Instead I just kind of slid up and breathed big and quiet through a wide open mouth, hoping they wouldn't spot me.

It would have helped if there hadn't been a half moon riding the sky. I was in luck: they hadn't cut off their motor. I could hear it growling a hundred feet away, and turned to look back at it. I could hear them talking too, loud enough I knew it wasn't English. If it'd been me, I'd have cut the motor and no talking, and listened like crazy. Making that much noise was stupid.

I'd been stupid too. I should have just fallen out of the boat when they started to shoot, instead of diving overboard. Then they could have thought I was dead, same as Art was. It's a wonder I wasn't, the way they'd charged us shooting with Tommy guns.

No way were they T-men, Treasury agents. They were part of the Purple Gang that ruled the rackets down in Detroit, forty miles off south. Especially bootlegging; that was 1927.

Anyway they were idling along with the current, their searchlight poking around where our boat was floating. That hundred feet wouldn't mean much to a bunch of bullets, if they saw me, but just then they weren't looking in the right place. As quiet as I could, I started swimming on my side toward the Canadian shore, maybe a quarter mile away. They'd probably expect me to swim for the Michigan side, which was closer, and likeliest to be my home side.

But closer doesn't mean much if you're shot full of holes. Then the searchlight started stabbing out farther, and I went back under, avoiding any splashing, letting my waterlogged clothes take me down, and stroked on east under water.

I came up again after maybe fifty feet; I was still short of breath from the first time. Gradually I opened the gap, going under anytime the searchlight came my way. I was surprised they didn't spot me without it. I guess they were watching where the lights were; they were using a flashlight in the water close to their boat now, and the searchlight out farther.

When I got far enough away, I shucked out of my clothes and clodhopper shoes, and after awhile I got feeling pretty safe. I wasn't worried about playing out and drowning; I'd swum a lot in that river in my nineteen years.

I was swimming on my right side, facing upstream, when all of a sudden I got this awful fear, and turned. A ship was bearing down on me, an ore carrier upbound for Lake Huron. It looked like a mountain. I took off swimming hard. She had a lookout, watching the water ahead for small boats I suppose, and he seen me without any searchlight. "Man in the water!" he bellowed. The whistle started hooting, and I swam for all I was worth. She passed some sixty or eighty feet behind me.

I didn't stop to catch my breath, just kept going. Them wops in the speedboat had to have heard what the sailor yelled.

They did come over. I had to slip under several times when their light came my way. One of them yelled once. "'ey, sonabitch! Why donna you give up? We don' wanna kill you. Just aska you questions: whatsa you name, who you worka for."

I wasn't having none of it. First of all, I didn't believe him. And second, who I'd been working for was my brother Gus. After a little bit I crawled out onto the bank and into the grass, glad I was suntanned. They were still cruising up and down out there, and I could almost smell their hate, even if I couldn't understand it. We'd had twelve cases of Black Label when they'd hit us; small potatoes. And if they wanted Gus to stop, all they had to do was tell him. He'd have quit right away.

When I got far enough away, I got up and started walking. The mosquitoes were fierce. I didn't really know where I was going, but I'd come to a road soon enough, and follow it. I wondered if there was something Gus hadn't told me. Gus was my oldest brother, twenty-three then. I'd never done a booze run before, but one of the guys that usually did was sick, and Gus asked me to. Now there I was in my underwear, in a big wet meadow with 50 billion mosquitoes.

There was a ground fog forming. The Canadian side was Indian reservation along there, and they raised a lot of horses. Pretty soon I saw a bunch of Percherons, blacks and grays, running around playing, and I couldn't see their legs in the ground fog. It looked like their bodies were floating around on it. They came trotting up to look me over, then I clapped my hands together and they ran off.

I came to a gravel road and followed it, limping because my feet were sore, till I came to a creek, and two Indians fishing over the rail of a little bridge, bullheading. They talked to me as if guys walking down the road in their underwear was common as dirt. I ended up going home with them, and in the morning they took me across to the Michigan side. I was wearing someone's cast-off overalls, and glad to have them.

They let me off at Frank's boat dock at Tiberius, my home town, about forty rod from where I worked at Elwood's auto repairs. Tiberius was one of those little towns—four hundred people—where everybody knows everybody and talks about their doings. Except if it had anything to do with running booze over from Canada. Then there wasn't much said.

I expected to get razzed, limping in barefoot with overalls that ragged, but Jim Elwood glanced around at the couple of guys there whittling and talking, and motioned me to come in the little room he had for an office. He wiped grease off his hands with an old shirt-rag, then closed the door before he started talking.

"Jake," he said quietly, "there was two guys in here earlier asking for Jake Rubner. They weren't anybody I ever saw before, and they were wearing suits. The one that talked sounded Eye-talian." Jim looked hard at me. "I think you better go someplace else for a while. Flint maybe."

He didn't ask why I was late, or what I'd been doing or anything.

I'd been boarding just up the street with Grandma Jennings. She wasn't really my grandma. Everybody called her that because she was so old, her first husband had been killed in the Civil War. Anyway I went home and put on shoes and some of my old clothes, wondering what to do. Then Grandma Jennings knocked at my door and told me some funny-looking gazebel had come by an hour earlier, asking for me.

So I walked to the cheese factory to talk to my brother Gus. He'd been running the place since Pappa got run over and killed by a team of horses a year earlier that got startled when a rock went through the silo filter. The reason I worked for Jim Elwood instead of Gus was partly that I loved working on cars. And partly that, being in the family, I'd be expected to work in the cheese factory for almost nothing.

But Gus and I got along good, for brothers. We even looked a lot alike, except he was blonder and huskier. He could take a ten-gallon can of milk in each hand—around 105, 110 pounds each—and load them both at once on his model-T truck. I needed both hands to put up one can, like just about anyone else.

And Gus had all his fingers. I'd lost the ends off three of mine to a buzz saw, buzzing firewood when I was fourteen. But all that meant was, I picked my nose with my little finger, 'cause the others were blunt and hardly had any nails.

Anyhow I told Gus what happened, and he looked thoughtful for a minute. Finally he looked me right in the eye. "What you been doing that you ain't told me about?"

"Nothing, Gus. Honest to gosh!"

"Well if they're asking for you by name, it must be *you* they're after, not my little rum running business. How much money you got?"

"About $30 in my room and 120 in the bank at Marine City." That was quite a lot in those days.

We ended up him taking me in his chevvy to Marine City, where I drew out my money. Then he took me out to the home place, about four miles west of town. I was to stay there, out of sight, till he could arrange for me to go work someplace far away.

That was long before television, before even electricity on farms. So I played solitaire, and after supper, Ferris, my other brother, played whist with me awhile. By the third day I was so bored, I was ready to pick up and leave. Along about four o'clock, Gus came out and said he'd got a telegram that there was a job for me in Pinconning, at a big cheese plant. He'd come get me about nine the next morning, drive me up to Port Huron and buy me a train ticket.

I wasn't all that happy to be going off like that. I'd been on the farm all my life, or no farther than Grandma Jennings'. Then my cousin Reini showed up just at supper, and I didn't feel so bad about it, because he said he'd like to stay awhile. He'd lived with us when I was ten and he was fifteen, just out of school. He'd given me such a bad time, Pa ran him off, and he'd been a bum ever since. Drifted through every couple of years and stopped a few days.

That night though, after we'd all gone to bed, I couldn't get to sleep—I was homesick already—so I got dressed and snuck out to take a last walk around the farm. There was a cool breeze out of the north, and the moon was about three-quarters full—about as nice a night as you could ask for. The corn was up to my waist. I walked out along the county ditch, where I'd trapped many a muskrat, to the north edge of the woods, the sugar bush. There I climbed this tree I'd climbed before, and out onto the roof of the sugar house. The wind kept the mosquitoes off up there, and I laid down to look at the moon.

Which saved my life, because I fell asleep.

And dreamed. In the dream there were three of us. We were driving west on the Switzer Road. When we came to ours, the Rubner Road, we turned north, and I told the driver to switch off the headlights. Told him in Eye-talian; it seemed natural to me. Going slow like we were, the moonlight was enough to drive by. When we were just coming to our place, I had him pull off in the shadow of a big old sugar maple, and we got out—all three of us had guns—and walked up to the house. That was the first it felt like a proper dream. Whispering in Eye-talian, I told one of them to stay on the porch and watch, and me and the other one went in.

Grandma's bedroom was downstairs. I opened her door and went in alone, and there she was asleep, the moonlight coming in her open window. Her teeth were in a glass by the bed, and her mouth was open and looked kind of caved-in. She never liked people to see her without her teeth.

And I thought: *this is a weird dream.* Because just then, part of me knew and thought just like me, but the other part—it was like it was separate, and I couldn't know what it was thinking. I took out a folding knife with a handle about six inches long, then I pressed a button and the blade snapped out. Then I reached down with my left hand, grabbed her hair, and—*cut her throat!*

I woke up with such a start, I nearly went off the roof. Then I sat up, shaking for a few minutes. I couldn't get the picture out of my head, the dream; it was stuck there in the moment of cutting her throat. Finally I climbed down and started for home along the ditch.

When I got past the woods, I could see fire, and took off running. Either the house or the barn was burning. Turned out it was the house. It fell in while I was running along the cornfield, a great cloud of flame and sparks going high in the air. When I got up near the buildings, I stayed back out of sight because some neighbors were there. They'd got the livestock out and run them into the pasture, in case the wind should shift and burning shingles light the barn off. And the pumper from Tiberius had got there and was hosing down the barn and the sheds. Finally they hosed down the fire to cool it off, and left.

When everyone was gone, I hung around, sort of numb. I half slept a little on the ground behind the barn, shivering with cold and shock. When the moon finally set, the heap of embers had cooled enough, I could go up almost to the foundation. I saw the cookstove, and the potbellied stove in the living room. I could even see all five bedsteads, four of them with bodies that had to be Ma and Grandma and Ferris and Reini. Reini'd come a day too early.

It would have been worse, except I knew they hadn't burned to death; their throats had been cut in their sleep. I knew that without a doubt. I just walked away then, walked west down the road through the night, and never went back for more than sixty years. But I couldn't walk away from how I felt. Whoever did it, it was me they were after, so it seemed like somehow I was to blame. I was too numb to cry, walking down that gravel road. I'd do my crying a few nights later, on a coal car crossing Nebraska.

On the west coast I worked harvests and I mechanicked. That's when I started having the nightmare, the same one I dreamed on the roof of the sugar house. But worse, as if what happened later added horror to it. There was a while there it happened so often, I'd be afraid to go to sleep, afraid I'd find myself cutting Grandma's throat again. I got fired from one harvest crew because I'd woke up yelling something about the knife and the blood. I guess they were afraid to have me around, figured I might be a murderer. I didn't blame them any; somehow—somehow it seemed like I'd done something, and because of it, the mob had killed three quarters of my family. All but Gus. Or maybe they'd got him too.

After awhile I got married and started a family, and only had the dream maybe a couple of times a year, or less. Then World War Two came, and the marines turned me down because of the lost fingertips, so I joined the Seabees and spent the war on the seat of a bulldozer, from Guadalcanal to Kwajalein. I never had the dream the whole time I was over there. There were too many gyrenes and soldiers getting killed.

After that I had a farm equipment sales and service in Bakersfield, California for thirty years. Every now and then I'd have the dream, but less and less. I'd go three or four years without it, then there it would be again. After I'd woke up and the horror faded, I'd feel the grief, that old, unexplained loss, a little like when I rode that hopper car across Nebraska. And I'd wonder what I'd done to make it all happen.

In 1978 I retired, and Betty Lou—my wife—and I did a lot of traveling in our Chippewa Motor Home. We'd visit our kids and grandkids from Houston to Fargo to Charlottesville, or her sister in Idaho Falls. We never went back to Michigan, and by that time she never asked about it any more. In '83 she had a heart attack, and I lost her. After that I played a lot of golf.

This August I visited Dick Batey, an old Seabees buddy in a retirement home in San Diego, and he introduced me to some of his friends there. One was this woman, and after he said my name, she stared at me like she couldn't believe it.

"Jake Rubner? Are you from Michigan?"

Maybe I should have said no. But what I did say was, "Yeah, a long time ago."

"Do you know who I am?" she asked.

I looked at her hard, but I couldn't recognize her as anyone I'd ever known.

"Mary," she said expectantly. Then, "Mary Wocelka." Her voice was like a young woman's.

"Um. Oh yeah."

She concentrated. "You were from some—little town up the Saint Clair River, toward Port Huron."

"Tiberius," I said.

She laughed. "That's it, Tiberius. I was never there, although I must have seen it from Johnny's yacht."

Dick interrupted us. "Look, you two got things to talk about, and I got to go out and get some smokes. I'll be back in a little while." He winked over his shoulder at me as he left, then Mary led me out into the garden, her hand on my arm.

"You were the best," she said to me softly, "the best ever. I thought of you often over those years, Jake. I still do, sometimes. It's hard to believe we had just that one weekend together."

She reached out and took my hands with hers. She was pretty, even in her eighties, but I had no idea what she was talking about.

"You had the best body I ever saw," she went on. "Muscles! When I first saw you on the beach, before I ever went up to you, I thought, 'that's the man for me!' The only problem was Johnny Boccato. We might get away with a weekend, but if we'd kept on, he'd have found out and killed both of us.

"It would have been more than male pride and Sicilian passion," she went on. "Johnny Boccato actually loved me. And I played around on him, which was not only a poor thing to do to someone; in this case it was playing with dynamite."

"Or with fire," I said.

She nodded. "Or with fire." Then she noticed my hand. "Oh! What happened to your fingers?"

"Uh, lost the ends of them in an accident. Years ago."

"That's too bad. I remember thinking how remarkable it was that such strong hands could have such lovely nails." Her eyes trapped mine. "You don't remember, do you?"

"Yes," I lied, "I remember. It was a long time ago. More than sixty years. Did you ever tell anyone?"

"Only Ruth, my chum, the girl I was with when I first saw you. She was full of questions, and I had to share it with someone.

"You changed my life, do you know that?" she went on. "After you, I couldn't stay with Johnny Boccato anymore. He might have been a big man in the mob, and a big man with gifts, but he was no one I could love."

You changed my life too, I thought.

"So a few days later I ran away," she said, "and came out to Hollywood. But I was afraid to get into films. If I made it big, Johnny would know where I was. So instead I married a nice nice man, who ended up making lots of money in real estate. But he wasn't any Jake Rubner in bed."

She smiled again. "I even named our second son Jacob, after you."

After me. Well, I went back to Bakersfield and thought about it a lot for a couple months. I couldn't help thinking about it, because the nightmares came back, every night for a while. But after I'd wake up, it wasn't grief I felt. Finally I drove back to Michigan. Things were a lot different after sixty years. Across the river from Tiberius, where there used to he horse pastures—Indian reservation—there was oil refineries. But some of the same people were still around; I looked up some of them. They could hardly believe it; they thought I'd died in the fire; they thought Reini was me. That's what the papers said; what the sheriff thought. I also went out and looked at the old farm. There was a new house, of course, or it had been new half a century ago. I found I could look at the place without crying.

The cheese factory is a lot bigger, and so are Rubner's Cheeses. But Gus wasn't there. He'd retired, and had already left his big summer home on Lake Huron for his winter home down here in Sarasota.

When Gus answered his doorbell, he didn't believe me at first, didn't believe who I was. So I told him about Reini, and being out at the sugar house when the fire started. Then he hugged me and cried, and grinned through his tears and cried harder, right there on his porch. I'm a little surprised I didn't cry with him.

Then he mopped his tears and asked me and my friend in, and we sat down and he started reminiscing. I almost changed my mind, listening to him, but he didn't stop soon enough. He'd made a nice little pile bringing booze across the river and distributing it to speakeasies as far north and west as Imlay City and south almost to Mount Clemens. "South of there," he said, "I left well enough alone. I didn't want to get the mob after me. I guess"—he sobered when he said it—"I guess even that was too far south.

"Anyway, when they burnt the old home place, I got out of bootlegging. I'd only got into it for money to build up the cheese business."

He looked at me curiously then. "What have you been doing all those years?"

I told him, told him what I've told you. Including my talk with Mary Wocelka. "Why did you use my name?" I asked him. "Why did you do that?"

He stared back at me, looking all caved in, and shook his head a little shake that said he didn't know why. But I knew. It was insurance, in case Boccato found out. And Boccato had.

"Anyway," I said, "that told me why they'd been after me. And why the house got burned down, and Grandma and Mama and Ferris with it, and Reini."

I stood up. "Now I'd like to introduce you to my, uh, my friend here. He understands about things like this. Gus, I'd like you to meet Johnny Boccato."

Boccato had gotten up when I began the introduction, a smallish old man about ninety, still dapper. He didn't say a thing, just bowed slightly, kind of a head bob, pulled out a small flat automatic, and emptied the clip into Gus.

Then, when he'd put his gun away, I took my little .32 caliber out of my jacket and shot Johnny Boccato once, right in the head. Because he'd killed my whole family, counting Gus now.

So that's the story: three old men evening out some scores at the end or their years. I'm sorry if I caused any trouble. And Lieutenant: I don't think I'm going to have the nightmare again; I don't think it's there anymore.

Picture Man

Introduction

Back in the '60s I was a research ecologist for the U.S. Forest Service, stationed at CSU, Colorado State University. Sixty miles south, the Department of Psychiatry, in the University of Colorado's School of Medicine, had an engrossing research project in progress: an investigation of a psychic photographer. A man strange and interesting enough that U of C was inviting scientists of other agencies and specialties to take part in the studies. These outside scientists included a physiologist friend of mine, who brought U of C's Professor Eisenbud to give a slide lecture to a full auditorium at CSU.

Eisenbud's show blew my mind, and inspired this story.

I wrote it with *The Magazine of Fantasy & Science Fiction* in mind, but my agent sent it to *Omni*, which rejected it. Ditto *Analog*, ditto *Asimov's*. Finally it did go to *F&SF*, which published it. And to cap it off, after being rejected by three magazines, it made two of the three SF "best of the year" collections for 1985, so I got paid for it three times.

Which illustrates that, among other things, editors have their own tastes, and magazines their own personalities. And also that persistence sometimes pays.

A final comment: the story's scumball Professor Boeltz *in no way* resembles his real-world counterpart, Professor Jule Eisenbud, a good guy.

* * *

I put down my copy of *Ecological Review* and walked over to the TV. I generally liked to catch the ten o'clock news. The picture popped out to fill the screen; the last moment of the opening commercials was just flashing off.

I sat back down to watch, all by myself in my three-bedroom, one-and-a-half-bath, near-campus, 1950-model house. It got a little lonely at times since Eydie had "dear John'ed" me with Barney

Foster, but it was certainly quieter and less irritating. For example, the house wasn't dominated night after night by game shows, situation "comedies" and TV dramas.

I'd learned the hard way that marrying the best-looking girl in the class and living happily ever after weren't necessarily the same thing.

Several female faculty and staff members had demonstrated an interest in filling the presumptive hole in my life, and there had been some interesting evenings. Maggie Lanning in particular combined looks and physical interest with remarkable level-headedness in every area we'd talked about. Plus, she was willing to hike in the rain, played a great forward in couples basketball (she was an assistant professor in phys. ed.) and even had a collection of old John Campbell editorials cut from years of *Astoundings* and *Analogs.*

Not that she was old. She was thirty-three—two years younger than I.

But marriage? We could already talk and romp at our mutual convenience, and she had one major drawback: ten-year-old Lanny. Lanny was a good kid, we got along fine, and he kept hinting I'd make a good dad and Maggie would make a good wife. But he was going to be a teenager in less than three years.

And I was still enjoying my new independence. I should, I decided, write a thank-you note to Barney, now that the divorce was final. I wouldn't, though. It would be a cheap shot, and I wouldn't feel good about it afterward.

The weatherman joggled me out of my reverie with mention of a sunspot storm. So when the basketball and hockey scores were over, I put on a jacket and went to the door. Sunspots might mean an aurora display, and watching northern lights was one of my favorite spectator activities.

If I'd turned on the porch light before I went out, I might not have seen what I did. A stocky square-looking man was digging in my plastic trash can that sat by the curb waiting for morning pickup. Two steps, and he could have been out of sight behind Chuck Ciccone's privet hedge. He'd dug in to the armpit, setting some contents on the sidewalk for better access, straightened for a moment, then tidily put everything back in the can and replaced the lid, clamping it down. There hadn't been anything edible or valuable in the can.

"Hey!" I said. Slowly he looked toward me, then lowered his

face and started to walk off.

"Just a minute!" I called. "Come on in. Do me a favor; help me eat some leftovers."

The dim face looked at me again for a few seconds, then he walked toward the house, hands stuffed in the pocket of his denim work jacket. For a moment I had a feeling of strangeness as, hunched against the cold and night, he approached. Not a feeling of threat. Just strangeness.

The square, high-cheekboned face, grimy and stubbled, was lined with the track record of late middle age. He looked like someone who'd ridden into town on a freight train, probably headed south. I held the door for him—it was that or wash the knob—and headed him for the bathroom.

"Why don't you shower down while I cook?" I said, then pointed out the guest towel and washcloth and left him there.

Being fresh out of leftovers, I put eggs and wienies on to boil, set a can of beans over a low flame, and put the teakettle on for hot chocolate. When everything was under way, I resurrected an old pair of jeans and a baggy sweatshirt and put them on the bathroom rug. The place was full of steam, like a turkish bath; he must have a remarkable tolerance for hot water, I thought. I announced to the shower that I was going to run his clothes through the washer and dryer, that I was leaving some of mine he could wear, and, getting a faint acknowledgment, went and started the wash cycle. I even threw his black stocking cap in; I'd have to remember not to put it in the dryer.

What in the hell, I asked myself, *are you doing? This guy could be a psycho. He could murder and rob you.* But there'd been nothing deadlier than a small jackknife in his pockets.

On an impulse, and feeling uncomfortable about it, I checked his wallet. It had no money. A merchant mariner's certificate identified him as Jaakko Savimaki, of Calumet, Michigan. Fireman, oiler, water tender. Dated 1951—thirty two years back. The square face in the picture was a youthful version of my man's, the hair blonde and crewcut. His driver's license address was Ironwood, Michigan; I'd heard about the mines up there being shut down.

Opening the bathroom door, I peered into the clouded interior. "You'll find a razor and shaving cream in the medicine cabinet," I said, and turned on the exhaust fan so he could find the mirror.

When he came out, he looked a lot better, although on him, my jeans were a couple of inches too long and a couple too tight. He'd made do by folding cuffs into them, leaving the waistband open, and keeping them up with the elastic belt.

"My name's Terry," I said, "Terry O'Brien."

"Mine is Jake," he answered, "Jake Hill."

Even in those few words, I detected an accent.

"Mr. Hill, I took the liberty of looking in your billfold for identification. It said your name is Savimaki."

He didn't blush or look angry or embarrassed. The strange, soft blue eyes just gazed at me as if examining the inside of my head.

"Savimaki is a kind of hill in Finnish," he said. "Away from home, it's easier to just tell people 'Hill.'"

I nodded. "Got it," I said. "All right, Mr. Savimaki, supper is on the counter."

As hungry as he must have been, he didn't bolt his food. When he'd finished, he thanked me and took his dishes to the sink before I realized what he was doing. Then he turned to me, and again his eyes were direct. I got the feeling that he saw more than other people did. "How do I pay you back?" he asked.

"Forget it. It's on me."

He didn't shake his head—simply said, "It's not all right for me to take something for nothing."

Well, I thought, *that's a refreshing viewpoint.* I wasn't sure I totally agreed with it, in a country where the system was so screwed up that some people found themselves backed up against the wall. But if everyone had his attitude, things would be a lot better.

"O.K.," I said, "what do you do?"

The pale eyes shifted to the fireplace. "You got any wood to split?"

"No. Sorry. I buy it already split."

"Any carpentry you need done? Windows fixed? Locks repaired?"

I looked at the possibilities. "You hit me at a bad time. I've got nothing like that. Why don't we defer payment? There'll be snow to shovel a little later in the fall."

His eyes withdrew for a moment; he didn't plan to be around Douglas long. "Tell you what," I suggested, "why don't you pass it on? Help someone else out when you have a chance."

He nodded slowly. "O.K.," he said. "I guess that's O.K." Then he turned to the sink and began to run water for the dishes while I transferred his clothes to the dryer, remembering to hold out his stocking cap. He seemed to think slowly, but he washed dishes fast. They were clean, rinsed, and in the drainer in about two minutes.

When he was done, he followed me into the living room and stood uncomfortably. I could see he still wasn't happy about not exchanging anything for the bath, meal, and laundry. Then he noticed the pictures on my wall, mostly wildland photos. When Eydie had taken her prints from the house, I'd mounted some scenic photographs on mat and hung them to handle the bareness. He walked over and looked at them.

"You got a camera?" he asked.

"Three of them. A 35-mm Pentax for slides, an old Rollei 4 X 5, and a Polaroid 680."

"A Polaroid." He considered that for a moment. "How would you like if I gave you some interesting pictures?"

"What do you mean?"

"Let me show you. Get the Polaroid."

Feeling mystified, I got it reluctantly. When I came back to the living room, he was sitting in a chair.

"Is it loaded?" he asked.

"Always," I said.

"Then aim it at my face." He closed his eyes tightly, his brow clenched with concentration. "When I say 'now,' shoot it."

Feeling foolish, I raised the camera.

"Now," he said. I touched the shutter release, lowered the camera, and waited. He was on his feet beside me when I removed the print. It wasn't a picture of Savimaki. It was a house, somewhat blurred, an old frame, two-story house with a steep roof, no front porch, and an upstairs door that opened out onto thin air. A ladder was built on the wall up to the strangely placed door.

"Let's do another one," he said. "That one ain't very good. I can get something more—interesting than that."

"Wait a minute," I said. "How come it isn't a picture of you?"

Actually, I thought I knew why. Years before I'd read a book about the detailed, if somewhat ambiguous, studies done on Nick Kopac, the psychic photographer. This looked like the same kind of thing.

"I don't know," he said. "It's just something I can do."

"Strange-looking house. Where is it?"

"In Calumet, Michigan. It's the house I grew up in. It looks like that because they get so much snow there. Some winters you get in and out through the upstairs door."

"My god! And didn't you know that's what the picture was going to be of?"

"No. I haven't learned how to know yet." He sat down again. "Usually I get something I never even seen before. But it's always a house or a ship. So far. Actually, I only ever did this about ten or twelve times before. I found out about it last winter, by accident, when a guy tried to take a picture of me and I didn't know it. I was reading a magazine and all he got was a picture of a lighthouse."

"Are you ready now?" he asked.

I nodded. "Yep."

He closed his eyes, I aimed, he said "now" again, and I shot. Together we looked at the print. This one was sharper, hardly blurred at all, showing a square house that looked stuccoed. It reminded me of pictures I'd seen of French farmhouses, but in the background was a broadly naked landscape with what looked like a high, cliff-faced plateau behind it. As an ecologist with a strong interest in biogeography, I was willing to bet it was an Afrikaner farmstead in South Africa, and told him so.

He shrugged. "Could be."

We took a couple more then called it quits, and I showed him the guest bedroom. But my mind was racing. I didn't have a class the next day until two in the afternoon, and I could always cancel my morning office hours, although I didn't like to. I thought I knew where I could get Jake a job. After he sacked down, I went to the phone and called Herb Boeltz.

I didn't actually know Boeltz very well, although as well as I wanted to. We were both in the faculty jogging club. He was a faculty politician, if you know what I mean, reputedly handy with a knife to the back, a full professor in psychology at thirty-two, and a man who always seemed to have access to grant money.

And he was said to be interested in parapsychology.

It was 11:15, and apparently I had wakened him; he didn't sound terribly friendly. So as soon as I'd identified myself, I put it to him this way.

"I think I've got something that can get you a lot of good publicity. Remember the studies on psychic photography at the University of Nebraska?...That's right, Nick Kopac.

"Well, I've got a guy staying here at my house that does the same sort of thing. I took four shots with my Polaroid; got two houses, a church, and what looks like a commercial fishing boat...

"No, I just met him today. Seems like a good enough guy. Kind of quiet. He needs a job and I knew, or at least I heard, that you had some grant money that might be available. It looks like a good opportunity for research with some media appeal, if it's handled right."

When I hung up, we had an appointment for eleven the next morning.

* * *

At 11:07 we walked into the Education Building, which also houses the pysch department. I prefer to be on time, but Herron's Men's Wear doesn't open until ten, and we needed some presentable but inexpensive clothes for Jake—slacks, a shirt, shoes, sweater, jacket...Actually, on my salary there isn't such a thing as inexpensive clothes. Some just cost less.

The meeting wasn't long. Boeltz admitted to eight hundred dollars in an account for exploratory research, which these days suggests he had something on someone. It wasn't enough to put Jake on the payroll. He agreed to pay him a ten-dollar allowance for "cigarettes and socks," as he put it. Jake was to stay with me, and Boeltz would pay me thirty dollars a week toward his room and board for any week in which Jake's services were used, plus ten dollars for each additional session, which we could split as we saw fit.

I was also to transport Jake to and from local sessions, as the studies would be done at Boeltz's home on the other side of town. Starting that evening at 7:30.

Boeltz had a bad reputation, so I wrote it all down and the three of us signed it, and afterward I got it photocopied. I was surprised that my wanting it in writing didn't annoy Boeltz, but he was genial and cheerful throughout. I told myself he ought to be. He was getting a very promising research project, journal articles, personal publicity, and speaking engagements—all at damned little expense. And none of the expense was his personally.

I, on the other hand, would be an unpaid cook and chauffeur.

But it did promise to be damned interesting. We hurried home, I grabbed a quick snack, and left Jake there while I rushed off to handle the Thursday afternoon lab in Plant Science 101. It occurred to me that it wasn't ideal, leaving a stranger alone in my home while I went off to work, but somehow I didn't feel concerned.

I took time to phone Maggie that afternoon; I needed someone to tell all this to, and she was the closest thing I had to a confidante. She said she'd be at my place about 5:30 to meet Jake and fix us supper; she sounded almost too cheerful to be real. Then I phoned home. Jake sounded sober and had started reading Churchill's memoirs. I told him Maggie would be coming by to fix supper and might get there before I did.

She drove up just as I was opening the garage door, and we went in together. To find supper on the table! Jake had hunted through refrigerator and cupboard and had fixed pork chops, rice, sweet potatoes, and cornbread. He'd walked to the store and bought the cornmeal out of a five I'd loaned him. When I came out of shock, I introduced him to Maggie.

"*Hyvää iltaa*, Mr. Savimaki," she said grinning. I stared at her.

"*Hyvää iltaa*, Mrs. Lanning," he said back. "*Mitä Kuuluu?*"

She laughed. "I just used up all the Finnish I remember. When Terry told me your name, I thought, 'Hey! That sounds like home!' I'm from Duluth."

"So that's where you learned to say *Hyvää iltaa.*"

"Right. My mom is Finnish-American, but my dad wasn't, so I didn't learn much at home. I learned more from the neighbors." She turned to me. "What a treat this is going to be." She gestured at the table. "If I'd fixed it, we'd be having hot dogs and beans."

I knew better than that. After supper, when Jake insisted on washing the dishes, I decided this arrangement was going to be a lot better than I'd thought. And after I took Jake to Boeltz's, I could hurry back to spend an hour or two alone with Maggie.

But that wasn't the way it worked, because Maggie wanted to go along and stay to watch.

That was fine with Boeltz; he liked to play to an audience. He had his own Polaroid, new that day, and took quite a few exposures. The first couple were "whities"—no picture. Not even of Jake. They looked as if they'd been shot into a floodlamp, which was remarkable enough in itself. The third was a blackie—it was as if it hadn't been exposed at all. But Boeltz and I were prepared for that; according to the literature, Kopac used to get whities and blackies a lot.

Boeltz looked at Jake, then, with this knowing smile, went over to a cabinet and poured a whole glass of bourbon. "Would you like a drink, Jake?" he asked. But how it came across was, *Okay, you cunning boy, I know why you're holding out on me.* It irritated me—I felt insulted for Jake—but whether the whiskey had anything to do with it or not, the next picture was of the Taj Mahal, sharp and clear. Then Jake threw down the whiskey like ginger ale.

The next was of a Hilton hotel somewhere. Without saying anything, Boeltz nudged me and pointed at a part of the picture. On the sign, the name Hilton was spelled wrong!

"Jacob," said Boeltz, "how do you spell the name 'Hilton'?"

Jake's quiet eyes fixed on Boeltz. "H-I-L-T-E-N," he answered.

What in the hell, I thought to myself, *does this mean?*

By the time we left, at 8:30, Boeltz had poured a second glass of whiskey down Jake and had half a dozen pretty fair shots—four of them buildings, one a pyramid buried in tropical jungle, and one of a three-masted schooner in a storm.

Jake didn't even seem a little tight when we walked out, although he wasn't saying much. I decided he must have a thing for booze—in his generation that was apparently why most drifters became drifters, although it might have been the other way around. And Boeltz was using it as a way to keep Jake around and performing.

That's how it looked.

When we got home, I asked Jake how the evening had been for him. His answer was concise and unambiguous: "I don't like Professor Boeltz," he said. He also said he was tired, and went to get ready for bed. Maggie and I watched television until he retired, then moved together on the sofa.

* * *

There were three more sessions scattered over the next ten days, semi-public in that Boeltz invited several faculty members and Bea Lundeen to them. Bea was the owner/editor of the local paper, the *Douglas Clarion.* As chauffeur, I was welcome to sit in,

too. It was interesting as hell, although Boeltz didn't try anything
that hadn't been tried fifteen years earlier with Nick Kopac.

Under his direction, Jake found he could do things he hadn't
tried before. To start with, all he got were seemingly random shots
of buildings and ships, pretty much like Kopac had gotten—
almost nothing but buildings and statues. But Jake had a lot better
batting average—he got a picture about two times out of three,
and most of them pretty clear.

Frankly, I was surprised he did that well, because Boeltz was
really unpleasant to work for. He continued to use booze in a very
obvious way as a carrot on a stick. But I noticed that Jake never
asked for it; he didn't even say yes when Boeltz asked if he wanted
some. He just accepted it when Boeltz handed it to him.

He certainly knew what to do with it then, though.

Another thing Boeltz did was to talk to Jake as if he were
some kind of retard. "Now Jacob, I'm going to ask you to make us
a picture of a cathedral. Can you do this for us? Let's try. Do you
know what a cathedral is? Good. Very, very good." And, "Oh,
that's *good*, Jacob. You're doing very, very well tonight."

Maybe that's why Jake kept accepting the whiskey. Not
really, though, because I'd swear I saw a sort of amusement in
those pale eyes. Maybe he enjoyed seeing Boeltz unwittingly irritate everyone around him and in general make an ass of himself.

The article Bea wrote for the *Clarion* was all about Jake;
Boeltz was mentioned only once.

Then there was a lapse of a few days before the fifth session,
which was a big one, a Saturday night affair. We'd been written
up far beyond the *Clarion* by then, and interest was spreading.
More people had been invited than there was room for at Boeltz's,
and it was held in the home of Professor Tony Fournais, chairman
of the physics department. Fournais was wealthy, had a big house
outside town, was cautiously interested in the project—and made
for good positioning: physics had a lot more status than psychology.

Everyone who'd been invited was there. And relatively on
time: no one was more than twenty minutes late, even though the
streets were snow-packed and slippery and the temperature was
about ten degrees. Professor Alfred Kingsley Kenmore had flown
in from Virginia—the Kenmore of "Herz-Kenmore-Laubman
Clairvoyance Studies" fame. And Marty Martin, the award-win-
ning science writer from the *Trib*.

Maggie went with us.

It started out like a circus, or at least a drawing room comedy. Fournais announced that his assistant was going to film the whole procedure, and had a 16-mm movie camera at one side of the room, on a high tripod, to shoot down at Jake over people's heads. The film would later be examined in slow motion for any sign of hokey-pokey. Then Martin announced that he was going to match every shot of Boeltz's with his own camera and film, to provide a second, independent print. Finally, when Boeltz was ready to begin, Kenmore, who was a psychiatrist and therefore an M.D., had Jake lie down, and examined his eyes, pulling out the upper and lower lids, peering under them with a little light. I haven't the slightest what he was looking for.

Then we got started. Boeltz was on his good behavior for a change: he didn't put Jake down, and no booze was in evidence, confirming that his previous bullshit was deliberate.

He warmed Jake up by letting him do whatever he came up with. He started with an oblique aerial view of a beautiful landscaped home, with city spread out in the midground against a backdrop of mountains. Not Denver, I decided. Maybe Calgary. The next looked like Hong Kong. The third was a double row of tar-papered shacks with deep snow piled all around and forest close behind. A guy wearing what looked like a leather apron was caught in midstride between two of them. When it was shown to Jake, he identified it as the Axelson-Peltonnen logging camp in Baraga County, Michigan about 1948. He'd worked there. The guy in the apron, he said was Ole Hovde, the blacksmith. I could tell that Jake was really pleased with that one, and I got a notion that just maybe he'd gotten it deliberately.

Boeltz didn't take any of the pictures himself. Each of them was taken by a different person standing directly in front of Jake and about six feet away. The camera had been bought new by Fournais. The film packs were taken from their sealed wrappers right there in front of us.

Each shot was passed around before the next was taken. Then it was laid on a table available for further examination.

Martin was off to one side with his camera, and didn't pass his shots around. But after the third, he arranged them on the table with Boeltz's, making matched pairs.

Boeltz beamed. "Ladies and gentlemen," he announced, "we have something very interesting here: Mr. Martin's photographs.

Come and see!"

I was already there. In each instance, Martin's picture was of the same scene, but as if seen from an angle of about ninety degrees to the right, higher, and farther away.

Everyone crowded around talking, except Fournais's assistant, who stayed by his camera. A couple of them shook Jake's hand as he came over to look. The way the pictures matched up, it was as if the actual scene, the physical scene of each pair, had occupied the location of Jake's chair, in three dimensions. And it was something that hadn't come up in the work with Nick Kopac.

Boeltz was ready now to attempt something he'd tried with equivocal results the two sessions just previous. He had Bea Lundeen and me go into Fournais's library to find a picture of a building or ship—any building or ship—in the encyclopedia. Maggie went with us. Bea pulled out volume 14—KI to LE—and turned to "Kremlin." And there was the great Russian fortress looming above Red Square, the towers of its buildings showing above the massive wall. I nodded, we all looked at it, concentrating, and Bea called out, "O.K., we got one!"

Nothing more happened for about half a minute, and I got pretty fidgety, but we all kept looking at the picture. Then someone called, "Come on out. It's done."

We did. Bea took the encyclopedia to the table and laid it down open, weighting it with an ashtray. Boeltz removed his print, marked it with black grease pencil, and laid it down next to the book.

What was there made my scalp crawl. Jake had given us the Kremlin, all right, but not at all like the picture in the book. There was no broad paved parade ground. Instead, small log buildings were backed up against the fortress wall. The ground was mud, with logs laid in it as a sort of rude and partial paving. There were rows of market booths, and hundreds of people stood or walked around, some mostly naked, a few wearing long coats.

It was a photograph of the Kremlin centuries ago! A photograph of life, not of a painting!

There were some brief, quiet comments, but actually not much was said as people crowded up to look. Everyone seemed to realize the basic significance of it: Jake Savimaki could give pictures from the past, from before photography. This was not a picture of a photograph or thing he'd seen. We were in the presence of something much further beyond the limits of known science than we'd realized—a whole dimension further.

Martin crowded his way to the table and looked without comment, then silently laid his own print beside the other. Again it showed the same scene from maybe twice as far away. And here the apparent elevation was conspicuous. Boeltz's shot might have been taken from forty or fifty feet above the ground. Martin's was an oblique aerial shot, as if from a low-flying airplane. Except, of course, it wasn't.

Jake had come quietly over, and now he took a look. His eyes didn't change. People looked at him and he didn't seem to notice. It was as if he'd just dropped in and wanted to see what was going on.

My eyes found Boeltz; he was murmuring something quietly to Fournais. Fournais then called a break. In a minute or so their cook appeared with hors d'oevres, and the lid was removed from the punch bowl. Something for people to handle without getting tight. Almost everyone soon had a glass in their hand except Jake. He stood apart, watching the effects he'd caused, and caught my glance with a smile and a nod.

Fournais and Boeltz talked quietly in a corner, then Martin joined them, and Kenmore. I started over to join them too, but some out-of-towner stopped me and asked if I hadn't come in with Mr. Savimaki. By the time I was free, the four of them had left the room.

I felt a hand on my arm, and it was Maggie. "What does he do for an encore?" she asked.

"God knows," I said; *or the Devil*, I added silently. But that was unfair; if anyone around here had a devil, it was Boeltz, not Jake. Jake was as clean as anyone; we went over to him.

"*Kuinka se menee*, Mr. Savimaki?" Maggie asked him.

He grinned. "Pretty good, *tyttö*. How about you?"

"I'm impressed," she said. "Do you know how you did that?"

"Not exactly," he told her. "I just kind of—open myself up. I still don't know what a picture's going to be, but this time I decided I wanted something that would startle people."

"You want to do any more tonight?" I asked him, "or are you tired? We can go home if you'd like."

"No, I feel real good. This gets easier every session. I'd like to see what else I can do. Those last pictures look like something from the past; maybe I can get something from the future next."

I felt my gut give a little twist.

"You know what?" he went on. "I never felt this good before. In my whole life, and most of it ain't been bad." He put his full attention on me then, and called me by my first name for the first time. "Terry, I never thanked you for calling me in that night. I'd hit bottom, and you pulled me back up. I want you to know I appreciate it." He held out a hand big enough for an NFL tackle, and we shook. Then he turned to Maggie with a big grin, and she grinned back, and they shook, too.

We were interrupted; Boeltz, Fournais, Martin, and Kenmore had come back in, Boeltz practically rubbing his hands in anticipation. "Excuse me everyone, if you please," he called and conversations stopped. "We'd like to continue now."

People quieted down and shuffled themselves into a loose circle. "Do you need to warm up with something easy, Mr. Savimaki?" Boeltz asked. *Courtesy yet!* It was the first time he'd called him "Mr. Savimaki." But his eager eyes were like ice picks.

Jake shook his head and said he was ready. Fournais had his wife take over Martin's camera, and he, Boeltz, and Martin left for the library. Kenmore picked up Boeltz's camera and positioned himself in front of a slightly smiling Jake.

It was a couple of minutes before we heard a voice call, "All right, we've got one."

Jake closed his eyes. No longer was there any effortful concentration, no tightly shut lids. He looked relaxed and confident. "Now," he said. Kenmore clicked his shutter and so did Liz Fournais, and someone went to get the three from the library. Martin came in with a large book and laid it open on the table. I looked at it while Liz and Kenmore brought their prints over.

It wasn't an encyclopedia, but a book entitled *Weapons in the Sky: Military Applications of Space Technology*. The chapter it was open to was "Soviet Programs." There wasn't even a picture on the page.

Jake had outsmarted them, though. I didn't realize it at the time, but he had. Kenmore laid down his photo, and it was not of some satellite or anything like that. Instead, I saw a car, unidentifiable to me in the darkness, lying on its top in the snow. Liz's photo was the same, from another angle. In hers, I could see a body pinned underneath.

That was the end of the performance. While people donned coats and caps, I took Boeltz aside and collected. He didn't even look irritated with me—"not there" would describe him—then pulled on his gloves and left.

On the way home, nobody talked for the first mile. "Whose car do you suppose that was?" I said at last.

"I don't know," Jake answered. "I just know I didn't want to show them what they wanted, so I just decided to do a picture from the future. And that's what I got."

No one followed up on that until we got home. When we'd hung up our coats and sat down, Maggie decided she needed to know. "Jake," she asked, "could you have shown them?...What they wanted?"

His eyes were sober. "Get your camera," he told me.

The first picture was of an orbiting space station, like nothing yet built, I'm sure. It was hard to judge size and distance, with nothing familiar as a reference, but it might have been a hundred feet in diameter, bright against black space, from a viewpoint of maybe a hundred yards away. A red hammer and sickle vivid on its side.

"Holy God!" I said. A whole panorama of potential events began to shape up for me: the CIA moving in, Jake held in some secluded place doing God-knows-what kind of spying for them— and Boeltz, of course, handling Jake. Boeltz would love it; how important he'd feel!

"Take another one," Jake said. "I can see this one, too."

So he was seeing them in advance now. I aimed, he said "now," and I shot. It showed Jake strapped down on something like an operating table. He didn't even take the trouble to look at the photo. Maggie's hand found mine.

"You see why I did it," he said, and we both nodded.

* * *

The first thing I saw in the *Clarion* the next morning, right on the front page, was a picture of an overturned car. I'd seen one like it the night before. It was Bea Lundeen's. Kenmore and Martin had been with her, and Kenmore was dead.

There was nothing in either the *Clarion* or the *Trib* about the session, that day or any other. It was as if they were afraid of it, pushing it out of sight, out of mind, unable to confront what was there.

We didn't hear anything from Boeltz, either, on Sunday. Or on Monday, or for most of the week. Meanwhile, Jake got a job cooking at the Douglas Hotel. He also arranged to move into a room there, but for some reason I talked him out of it.

On Monday evening Maggie came by with her mother, Anna Lahti, who'd driven down from Minnesota to stay a week. She was a good-looking woman about fifty or fifty-five, and she and Jake hit it off right away, talking Finnish. She turned to us and laughed—said she knew he was from Savo as soon as he opened his mouth because he rolled his r's. As if she didn't; when they talked Finnish, it sounded like two chain saws.

It was Friday when Boeltz phoned. He wanted Jake again in half an hour—said I wouldn't need to bring him, that he'd come by and pick him up. I told him he'd have to talk to Jake, and put my hand over the mouthpiece, remembering the picture of Jake strapped down.

"It's Boeltz," I said. "He wants to come and get you in half an hour, for another session. He obviously doesn't want me to be there. I don't trust him; tell him to go to hell."

He smiled and took the phone. "Hello Dr. Boeltz," he said. "I'm busy tonight, but if you want to make that for tomorrow evening at eight, that will be fine...At eight, then. I'll be ready." He hung up.

"Jake!" I said, and he grinned. His eyes weren't soft anymore. They looked darker, and bright.

"It's O.K.," he said. "And what you're worried about, it's not going to happen."

"Something's fishy with him," I insisted. "He's hiding something, or I'm not Irish."

He nodded. "It's nothing to worry about, though."

"Do you *know* that?" I asked. "Do you know what he has in mind?"

"I don't know what he has in mind, but it's not dangerous. Not to me." He grinned again then. "And you told me you're only half-Irish. The other half is Dutch."

"And you're half-Swede," I said, trying to insult him. He just laughed; maybe I should have said Russian. Then Anna Lahti drove up. They had a date for supper and an evening at the ice rink.

I watched them drive away; it looked like a romance in the bud. I hoped nothing bad would happen the next evening.

* * *

The next night Boeltz was there five minutes early. After he and Jake drove away, I put on my jacket and cap, got in my car, and headed after them for Boeltz's place.

I parked half a block away, then chickened out. I couldn't think of any excuse for going up and pounding on his door, and I didn't want to get arrested for window peeking. So I got the Black Hawks pregame show on the radio and waited. At two minutes into the first period, Marcel Dionne scored on a breakaway. A couple of minutes later, Jake walked out of Boeltz's and started down the sidewalk. I rolled down the window as he approached.

"Want a ride?"

He grinned and got in.

"Care to tell me what happened?"

"Nothing much," he said. "We talked a little bit. But you don't have to worry about my going back."

"Yeah?" I said encouragingly.

"Yeah," he answered cheerfully.

I started the car and pulled away from the curb. "Yeah *what*?" I demanded.

He laughed. "He wanted me to make a picture showing some-one dead. His father. He said the old man is dying slowly of an incurable cancer, in terrible pain, and that he'd be grateful to die. He thought if I made a picture of it, it would happen.

"I asked him what his father did for a living, and he said he'd been a banker. You can see what he's after."

"So you told him to go to hell."

"No, I told him I'd see what I could do."

I almost drove up over the curb. "You *what*?"

"Then I gave him a picture of his father as he was at that moment. Playing golf." Jake laughed again. "There were palm trees in the background. Hawaii, I suppose; it's still daylight there."

"What did he say to that?"

"He got all excited, said I'd made a mistake and got some-thing from a year or two ago."

It was six minutes into the first period. Esposito stopped a Mark Hardy slapshot and fell on Dave Taylor's rebound. Charley Simmer fell on top of Esposito. Hutchinson shoved Simmer.

"Are you sure it wasn't the past?" I asked.

"Positive."

"Then what happened?"

"I told him I'd try once more." He wasn't smiling now. "Maybe I went a little bit too far then."

"What do you mean?"

"Pull over and I'll show you."

He opened his jacket while I pulled off on the shoulder, tires crunching on frozen slush, and handed me a Polaroid color print. There was Herb Boeltz, in a coffin. He didn't look a day older than he had that night at eight o'clock.

"God!" I said. "You wished him dead?"

He shook his head. "I wouldn't do a thing like that," he said soberly. "I just decided to show him a picture of himself dead. I never thought about it looking like it could be next week or something. I just wanted to see how he liked it with the shoe on his own foot. He turned white as a sheet and just kind of fell on the chair. He sat there staring at nothing and never said another thing."

"Do you think it'll come true? This picture?" I asked.

"I don't know," Jake said. "I don't think so, but I'm not sure."

I shifted back into drive again and pulled onto the pavement, half my attention on driving and the other half on the power of suggestion. Boeltz seemed susceptible. He had at least half-convinced himself that Jake could control, as well as predict, the future.

It turned out that Jake's pictures do not fix the form of the future, or even necessarily predict it closely. Though we learned later that they tended to be quite accurate.

But the picture he showed me wasn't correct, any more than Hilton has an e in it. Because the coffin was covered. About four o'clock the next morning, Herb Boeltz put a .38 pistol barrel in his mouth and pulled the trigger, and there wasn't much the mortician could do to make him presentable.

* * *

Jake got a room in the hotel, after all. He said he'd been cramping my style, but maybe I'd been cramping his. He remained as cheerful and friendly as ever. Anna Lahti went back to Duluth, put her property up for sale, and moved down, taking an apartment in the same building Maggie lived in. A couple of months later, she and Jake got married. Maggie and I took a bunch of wedding pictures, and all they showed were Jake and Anna.

I mentioned that to Jake, jokingly, and he said he wasn't doing pictures these days.

They really are a nice couple, and we went out with them fairly often, despite the age difference. Mostly to dance halls or the ice rink. I even learned to skate, though nowhere nearly as well as all three of them did.

With their example, Maggie and I decided to tie the knot, too. So Lanny was only two and a half years short of his teens; I'd been a teenager once myself. And frankly, he was more likable than I'd been. Jake took a bunch of wedding pictures; he had a brand new Polaroid 680. I couldn't help but wonder. That summer they bought a restaurant and fixed it up really nicely with a Scandinavian motif, bringing a Swede down from Duluth to round out the cuisine. I figured Anna must have had a lot of money, but Maggie said not so far as she'd ever known.

Then, one day they asked if we'd like to go to the races that weekend. I supposed they meant at Rockston Downs, only fifty miles away, but instead we flew to Maryland! And Jake bought the tickets and rented a car there!

I bet on the same horses he did, and talk about a kick in the tax bracket! We had nothing but winners. A lot of things became clear to me then.

It felt like strange money, but the bank was happy with it.

Last evening we celebrated the anniversary of Jake's and my meeting. At their place, a little farm they'd bought just outside town. They'd fixed it up really nicely.

When we got there, I noticed a big book on the table—a folio-sized book on astronomy for the informed layman. Beside it was a brand-new video camera. He told me he had an interesting project going, and asked if we'd care to take a little tour.

Out of the North a Giant

Introduction

This story lead-in will be more about writing than about the story. Specifically I'll address the advice that many writing teachers give their pupils: "Write from experience." At first listen that sounds like sage advice. But on reexamination it may sound idiotic, certainly for would-be science fiction writers. Actually it's some of both, but it's more sage than idiotic.

For now let's leave it at that. We'll come back to it in a minute.

The origins of stories are diverse. One day I sat down to my typewriter (remember typewriters?) to begin a new story, and from my fingers flowed an opening sentence: "There came out of the north a giant." I hadn't planned it, hadn't foreseen it. From there it proceeded the same way: a totally right-brain action.

But it tapped a fertile soil of experience that included readings in the history of Indiana, and a series of letters written to my mother-in-law, long rambling penciled letters from a man she would never meet—a boyhood friend of her dad. The first letter was dated 1906, when she was a child, the last in 1942, when the writer was a very old man. Letters that, along with much else, told what life was like, and how land was cleared, in the years following the Civil War. And before. All secondhand experience for me, but it fitted my own experience in "deadening timber"—in my case cull trees—in the 1950s. Also, by the time I wrote this story, I'd come to know, first hand and at length, the nature of wild and semi-wild land, including mountain terrain and mountain winters in Colorado.

Even so, the heart of this story is far from anything I've experienced. It is sheer imagination. But experience direct and at second hand provided a setting, and details, that help make the story real to the reader. While experience with people, experience both live and second hand, help make it poignant.

And taking it further, in writing, particularly in writing science fiction, "second-hand experience" plays an important role. I'm referring to the experience of reading. It's not surprising that almost all professional science fiction writers have read a lot, including a lot of science fiction, and typically quite a lot of science.

* * *

There come out of the north a giant. Teeth he had like knives, claws like more of em, and the breath from his mouth was like carrion in the sun. And he walked on his hind legs like a man.

That's what Vance and Purdy said. Me—I wondered. For if they'd been near enough to smell that breath, how'd they lived to tell it? For another part of their tale was, it moved as fast as a great round boulder bounding down the mountain.

I didn't year em tell it myself, or there's questions I'd of asked. Sure they must of seen something, and it weren't likely a coney nor yet a hare, nor even a bear brute; folks know a bear brute when they see one. And tigers be noisy enough with their thrumming that we know when one's about, and *what's* about.

Anyway, a giant wasted their camp and killed the other three men and all their horses, which was hobbled at the time. Vance and Purdy run off. And why none of the five killed it weren't part of the tale.

I weren't about to leave my claim on its account. Nor was my neighbors—Egolfs and Glum Flynn. It be agin principle to give up the farms we was making—give land back to the wilderness. Besides, it'd been fifty kilometers off north, way t'other side of Bad River and the tule glades.

A farther off neighbor had left though—Gentle Tom, who I've seen pull a stump with his arms, with only the side roots chopped off. Was Tom to rassle a bear brute, my brass would be on Tom. (No, not really. I just be making a point: Tom be moughty stout.) But his woman were frighty. Shouldn't of married her in the first place, she's that frail. Likely to die on him first time he blows her up. A throwback to the oldy times, to those among the firstfolk what died carrying child, or birthing it, or swelled up in the legs and went bad. Or got gurgly lung and coughed theirself to death.

Must of been bad days back then, even though they still had the machines they'd brought with them from old Earth, where folk was skinny in the limbs, and things was said to weigh lighter'n on Hardy's World, strange as that mought sound.

Anyways, Egolfs and Flynn and me held to our claims, but kept our guns by us in the field, and all stayed in my cabin by night, my stead being the center of the three, and my dog Brutus, the biggest and most fierce.

I set aside my axe to take a drink from my skin, for though it were fall, and cold at night, the leaves was down and the sun were bright, and I was starting a sweat. My field were too thick to see far, the tree trunks being close together for so big. I weren't like some, to take land easy to clear. I wanted the best of land, the kind that grows a thick stand of big stout hardwood trees.

I'd already ringed seven hecters, beating a girdle round each tree with my axe so's it'd die and let the sun through and the corn grow. Three more hecters and I could make good my stead claim and be wife-eligible. Then I'd go south and get wed. To Mary Lou, Bill's daughter, with legs and arms like tree trunks, a belly as big and hard as a brass still, and axe-handle wide across the hips.

Cause there'd be a lot of snags to fell over the years, and stumps to grub. Even dead trees throw too much shade for proper crops, and shelter for pounce cats looking for a lamb or a chicken. And there'd be younguns to birth and raise and learn to do.

Anyhow, I'd just hooked the water skin back on my belt and were reaching for my axe when Brutus, who'd been snoozing with one ear up, jerked up his head. I caught it out the corner of my een and turned to my rifle while grabbing up my axe. It could of been a squirrel he'd yeared, but I doubted.

For a blink or two of time he listened, then got up and trotted off like he were going somewheres. I trotted after with old "Straight Shot," my moccasins rustling soft on last moon's fallen leaves.

Up ahead, Brutus started to bark, sounding like he'd cornered a bear brute, his voice raging, and I wondered if I were about to learn the truth about the giant from the north. But then I yeared a man-voice, and knew it were some stranger what Brutus knowed not, and the feeling with it were both relief and disappointment. For a man likes a bit of excitement and adventure, even though he wants not to be laid waste by some wild beast.

Nor the stranger neither, for I yeared him holler: "For God's sake call off your hound, before I have to shoot him!"

Well that quickened my feet, and I were there in a thrice.

When I'd thought, "It's a stranger," I hadn't realized *how* strange; a stranger stranger never I'd seen. Looking back now, I should've known. For on Hardy's World, those what believes in God don't so use his name, while those what believe not, why, why would we use it at all?

Anyway there he was, backed between two big buttresses of a

rope-bark tree, where Brutus could come at him only from the front. And he had no gun—that were a feint, purpose to speed my feet. He had not even a knife, only a club drawed up ready to strike, and not much of a club at that.

Before I thought to call, or had time, Brutus went for him, bounced back as the club come down, and then back in agin. I'd never seen him go for a man afore. The man poked at his face and Brutus closed jaws on the club, jaws that'd daunt a bear brute, and had, and he pulled. He pulled so quick, the stranger was jerked out by him and let go.

"Brutus!" I yelled. "Back!" I put all my intention in it, leaving room for neither disregard nor one last grab. Step by step he backed off, a parlous growl bubbling in his throat, till three meters lay tween them. The hair twixt Brutus's shoulders and up his neck stood in a bristly ridge. He were a sight! Weighed more'n seventy kilos, out of Big Maud, by Bull Killer, and the pick of the litter.

The stranger sagged like his bones'd went to mud, and he leaned back agin the tree. His clothes was all of one piece, from neck to ankle, and his hair was cut close like a bear dog's fur, instead of a proper bob. And he was a *tall* one, the tallest ever I'd seen, a meter'n three-quarters, I judged, and terrible thin, mought of been 110 kilos.

"Gentle Jesus!" the man said, "I thought I was a goner." That's the way he talked. "That your dog?"

"Right," I said. "You be lucky I were about. That be Brutus, no less, out of Bull Killer. He and his daddy pulled down a bear brute by theirself last year. Weren't hardly worth shooting when we cotched up."

"Don't tell me about it," he said, and give a shudder. He put his little hand to his forehead when he said it, and the growl out of Brutus took new life at the move. I spoke sharp, and the beast flattened on his belly, embarrassed.

"Who be ye?" I asked, "and what's yer business?" saying it bresk, there being that about him I didn't trust.

"I came to warn you," he said. "There are a dozen yorash north of here, a dozen crazy yorash that hijacked my ship. If nothing's done about..."

I frowned and raised my hand, and his gob shut in mid-word, cause it were the hand what held the axe, and it afeared him.

"Wait," I said. "First your name, like a right man."

"Fermin the ver...ah, Fermin Jones," he said. A man with

summat to hide, I thought, but his eyes wasn't evil, just shifty.

"Fermin Jones, I be Big Jack the wrestler, Sean's son."

"Big Jack," he said after me. I seen the name surprised him, I being near a head shorter than him. But he made no sneer, for without Brutus, gun, or axe, I still had twenty or more kilos on him, and doubt not I could squash his head with one hand.

"Next," I said, "what's a yorash?"

"A yorash stands about this tall," he said, reaching an arm's length overhead to show me, then froze like that, for Brutus's growled swelled up in his throat agin. I had to go to the brute and raise my hand to him, which shut him off. Then I put down my axe, patted his head, and scratched round his ears, and slightly his tail-end tapped the leaves. But his een left not the stranger.

"So they be tall—two meters or better," I said. "What else?"

"Closer to three meters," he answered, "teeth twice as big as Brutus's, and a claw like a cargo hook in each wrist. And totally carnivorous. Meat-eaters, that is. And sapient—intelligent, more or less—not dumb animals. They build huts, form clans and tribes, and make war. What it comes down to is, they do three things: they hunt, have lots of young, and kill each other.

"They're so bad, their planet is quarantined—off limits. No one's supposed to go there. If the yorash get established here, you people are in deep trouble. There are females in this bunch. They'll be dropping pups, by the litter, and they grow to maturity in two years. Instead of a dozen, you people could have half a hundred ravenous monsters in your backyard in a few years. And with humans to fight, they probably won't fight one another much, especially since these are all from one clan.

"How come they here?" I asked.

"Um. Well—first of all, uh, I'm an undercover agent for the galactic patrol. And I..."

"What be that?" I asked. "An undercover something for something."

"A constable. You understand constable? Marshal?" He seen I didn't. "A lawman," he said. I nodded. "And I went to Threllkild's World because—it's a terrible thing to even think about, but the story was that someone had been capturing yorash and taking them off planet to exhibit in zoos on some out-league planets!

"So I went there to look around and ask questions. And the next thing I knew, a dozen yorash had grabbed me and taken over my ship. And made me bring them to the nearest world where they could live and that was fairly wild. They planned to kill me, once they got here, but I tricked them and escaped. I'd seen farms over this way before I landed, so I hurried south to warn you."

I understood not all he said, but enough to get the gist of it. Likely it weren't all true anyway, but I knew now what the giant were, and that there was a dozen of em up there. I tried to catch those slippery een but they slid away.

"What smell have they?" I asked.

"Ugh!" said he. "Like a straddle trench on Sorrel's World. Bad. They've got musk glands."

"And hunt as a pack, these yorash?"

"Pretty much. But when they're looking for herds, they scatter or send out scouts."

"Well then, I yeared of em. One of em jumped some trappers over north."

"Um. Did they kill him?"

I shook my head. "The opposite; he killed three of them, and their horse beasts. Two got away and brought the tale."

"You mean—*one* of them attacked five of *you*? Killed three and ran off the other two?" He looked shook by that. "Did they have dogs? Your people?"

"Nay. They was fur trappers. They'd not have dogs with them."

"Hm-m. Dogs would be helpful, dogs like yours." He pursed his lips. "And the yorash know there are humans here. They're likely to move on you. When was it they killed your people?"

"Three days past. No, four. Vance and Purdy, that got away, come through the next day—hit some farmsteads over south and spread the tale. Then Gentle Tom, what lives there, come by and told us what he'd yeared."

Then a thought come to me. "When were it you run off from them?"

His eyes drifted off and he began to tally on his little fingers. "Five days," he said.

"What took you so long?"

"I traveled mostly by night; it was too cold to sleep except after the sun was up. And I moved slowly; in your gravity I must weigh a hundred and twenty kilos." He seen I understood not. "My body weighs about half again as much here as I'm used to. Slows me down and tires me out.

"And without the sun to guide me, I followed creeks, assuming they led south more or less. I knew the mountains were to the north. But the creeks curved around a lot, and I had to detour around sloughs and marshes."

Then his voice went doleful. "You got something I can eat?"

I should of realized. The man had no weapon and no skill; he'd not of eaten on the trail, except happen some berries or such. I called Brutus to heel and we went to my cabin, where I fed the man.

Not all to once. First some dried apples, their blue skins all puckered but the flesh sweet. And after a little bit, spuds. Later yon some sardo bread with syrup, and later still a cold roast dove.

Atween, we talked. He'd crossed Bad River the night afore, and near perished with cold. Lucky he were that the season been dry and river low. Then the sun come up, and he'd kept walking to dry off and get warm, until he yeared my axe.

After he ate the dove, he dozed, and I let him be awhile. At length I roused him, which were not easy, called Brutus to me, and we started off for Glum Flynn's field. In a few words I told the tale to Flynn. Then we found Egolfs and went off south to round up more men. It weren't likely to be no frolic getting rid of them yorash.

'twere a glad surprise to find Gentle Tom back, a giant of a man only half a head shorter than Fermin, and surely a hundred and eighty kilos. He'd gave his wife back to her daddy as not fitty for a border farm.

He said he'd come along, grabbed his gun and whistled in Bull Killer. Then, with Fermin gnawing on a heel of sardo, we went about and gathered up eight of Tom's neighbors, this tract being well settled and not just outliers like Egolfs and Flynn and me. They even had cattle now.

Fermin told about the yorash agin, giants indeed, tween two and half, three meters. Lank, said he, but fierce strong, could tear a man in pieces.

Maybe you, I thought, but I weren't so sure about me.

And they had short fur, but their land ben't never cold, only maybe a little chilled sometimes when it rained. They hadn't no weapons but clubs, what they throwed with dead aim. What they used best was their fangs, and two big wrist claws to pull things in close where they could fang em.

After that we all set and parleyed over whether to go on south and gather more men. That's what Fermin counseled, but after he'd ate some more he fell to sleep, and when he woke up it were already decided. Next morning early, Buster, Marty's son, would take the women on the horse beasts and drive the cattle over the Piney Hills trail to Sweet Grass Valley. We'd send the dogs with em, all but Bull Killer and Brutus, to protect em, case of varmints or maybe some scout of the giants were about.

Once over to the Valley, Buster were to gather whatever men were willing and able, and leave within a day or two. They could follow our trace.

I were the leader, that being my nature. And I deemed we'd do better, us twelve, than a mob, in killing yorash. There'd be less mixup. But if the yorash was to scatter, we'd need more men to trail em; the trackers ought to be by threes, naught less, which could take a slew of men. Fermin weren't too happy bout this plan. One yorash had beat five men and killed three of em, and we was going out about even. But the giant took em unawares; they hadn't knowed what it was or how bad. And they hadn't no dogs. All that was different now.

So bout daybreak, eleven good men, plus Fermin, Bull Killer and Brutus, set off on a nice easy trot, traveling light, each man carrying a sleeping robe of water hare pelts, a belt pouch of dried meat, one of dried berries, and another of cartridges. Plus a belt axe and skinning knife.

Not to despise Fermin, but he were no man for Hardy's World. We even took a horse beast for him so he wouldn't slow us. Even though it mought well be the death of a good beast, from what we yeared of the yorash.

First thing we had to do was *find* the giants. And Fermin couldn't show us the way cause he didn't know how, even was they still there. So what we'd do was follow the trace of Vance and Purdy's folk, which was less than a quarter-moon old, about eight, nine days. That weren't likely to be hard, cause they'd no doubt followed the old trail through the glades, it hadn't rained since, and they'd had horse beasts, shod at that, which left plain tracks.

We waded the Bad River at Sandy Ford, the water colder'n a fur trader's heart, holding our gear up overhead, then warmed ourself agin by running on the trail.

We kept trotting and sweating, chewing a little dried meat now and then, and happen a few berries. Fermin got saddle sore.

He complained not, but I could tell by the way he sat and the pained look on his face. Weren't made for Hardy's World, all right. Watching him, I better understood what the firstfolk had borne with, especially after he told me he were pretty husky and strong for an Earthman.

After a while we got into the tule glades, where the scape be half open with marshes and wet meadows and laced through with slow little creeks. Sloughs be here and there, and little ponds and pools, with timber atween and on islands humped out of the marshes. The fur trail was blazed and easy followed, winding about to keep to drier ground as much as mought be.

It be known as fine fur country, with hundreds of colonies of water hare and beaver, their reed mounds standing on the edges of the deeper creeks and pools, and many water cat and otter to hunt em. Vance and Purdy's folk would have made their camp just t'north of the glades, where the land starts sloping up to the Icy Mountains. From there they could range along the whole length of the glades without miring their horse beasts, then drop the reins and go into the wetlands afoot to set and tend traps. It be a nice way to spend the trapper's moon—that season when the nights be frosty and critters' coats thick and prime but the country ben't froze up hard yet.

"Fermin," I said, "you told 'tweren't never cold where the yorash come from. Know they to make fire?"

"I don't think so. It would say so in our compu—we'd know about it if they did. And it does say they eat their meat raw. Really they're animals, not men. But they can reason—figure things out."

"How come they to take over your spaceship?"

"Uh, well," he said, "they, uh, they knew about spaceships— knew they came from other planets, that is. I'm not sure who told them; maybe it was an oral tradition—word of mouth passed down from the time of the old study team. Anyway, I was questioning some of them when they jumped me and told me to take them to another planet."

I could smell that he lied. "So you know their language then," I said.

"Uh, yeah. Well, not a whole lot, but I can get by with it. More or less. There's different dialects."

"Good," I said, "you can talk to em for us."

I'd just finished saying it when there were the boom of a rifle, and Bobby, Bass's son, fell backward in the trail. It took us total by surprise. There weren't no cover where we was, so we all hit the dirt. Fermin was off his horse so quick! I hadn't thought he were so nimble. The shot hadn't come from far—a patch of trees some sixty meters off.

"Spread out!" I snapped. "Al, Barney, you and me'll watch careful up ahead and shoot anything what moves. The rest of you keep low and move out to the sides."

"Who do you think it is?" asked Tom.

"It's got to be a giant," I said. "No *man* around here'd do that. Must of got a gun from Fermin's ship."

I saw a movement then, a gun barl and part of an arm from behind a tree, and two of us shot the same time. Splinters tore from the side of the trunk and there was a yowl. Brutus started for it then; I called him to heel, and Tom heeled Bull Killer, not to waste them.

Guns ready, we hadn't no more than got up when there was another shot, from heavy timber across a pool to the west, and Fermin grunted and went down. None of us seen the gunner, but we all shot in that direction to put him to cover.

"Flynn," I yelled, "you and Egolfs with me! Barney and Al, look to the wounded. T'others get the one what shot last." Then I run toward the first ambusher, reloading as I went, Brutus trotting alongside. "Flank the giant," I said to Egolfs and Flynn, and they angled off. When I was close, it stepped out from back of the tree, its gun raised, and Brutus charged. I went to snap off a shot, and for the first time ever, old Straight Shot misfired. The giant shot an instant afore Egolfs, and Brutus went down.

Egolfs's bullet knocked it back a step, which is all the reason Flynn missed. I dropped Straight Shot and drew my axe as the critter charged me, its good arm cocked to strike with its hook-claw. I went for it, and the arm started its blow. My belt axe took it just below the elbow, and we crashed together and went down. I had just time to get a forearm under its jaw to hold them big yeller teeth away while I tried for my knife with t'other hand. I felt and yeared the thud as Egolfs clubbed its head with his rifle barl, and the big body went slack.

"You all right?" Egolfs asked.

"I think so," I said. The critter stunk, all right. I crawled out from under and looked off to the west, where the other giant had been. I yeared a shot, and then another, but I couldn't see naught.

"Fermin never said they had guns," Flynn complained.

I went to Brutus and knelt, but the life was gone out of him. I give his ears one last rub. There were another shot then, but still I couldn't see naught, so went back to Bobby and Fermin.

Bobby laid dead where he'd fell, took through the heart by the first shot. I didn't know whether the giant were a natural good marksman or just lucky.

Fermin were lungshot, the air breathing in and out through the blue hole in his chest. His skin had a blueness too. Barney come up with two pads of moss he'd rinsed the dirt off of, and laid them on the bullet hole, front and back. Then, while he held them in place, I cut a strip offen Bobby's shirt and tied them on.

We yeared two more shots farther off in the woods, and I got fidgety, wondering. We'd lost one good man and one of our two dogs already.

Plus Fermin wounded bad. But he were wide awake and seemed in no pain. He was talking calm, though not very loud.

"I don't suppose you've got a cigarette," he said.

"Cigarette?"

"Never mind. I've got some confessions to get off my mind before I die, Jack."

I nodded.

"First, I'm no lawman; I'm a poacher and smuggler. A poacher is someone who goes around to different worlds and takes animals he's not supposed to, and takes them somewhere where he can sell them for good money.

"I went to a place called Threllkild's World and captured twelve yorash. They didn't hijack me and I can't talk to them. I just landed, ran up my commast, turned on the force shield, and waited for a pack of yorash to show up and investigate."

I followed only part of what he were telling me—there was words new to me—but I interrupted not. He were too bad hurt, and I wanted to let him get it all out. I'd ask questions later, if there was a later.

"The commast stood up above the shield," he said, "and when, after awhile, a pack appeared, I let go with a sound bomb that knocked them out. I went out and shot them all with knock-out shots, and used the cargo handler—a machine—to load them into a cargo module that was modified to haul animals."

He were sagging some now, his voice weaker.

"Then I took off, but before I'd gotten far—maybe ten or

twelve parsecs—I developed abnormal feedback in my drive and knew I had to set down somewhere fairly soon. I checked the computer for the nearest system with human inhabitants—here—and came out of hyperdrive.

"I didn't dare use landing mode—I couldn't trust the drive for that—and just came in on a flat angle into a marsh at about a hundred kilometers an hour.

"When the water and mud had run off the glass and I'd gotten my breath back from restrainer shock, I didn't have power of any sort, not even electric. I made a quick check, and it wasn't any of the simple-to-fix things, and I'm no engineer. But I did know that the locks on the cargo modules were electric and would have deactivated. All that was keeping them closed was residual magnetism in the seals. Which wouldn't last long. In maybe a day or an hour, a heavy push or kick would open them, and there'd be a pack of mad yorash running loose."

He chuckled a little then, but not like 'twere funny.

"Now, I told you some lies before, but not all lies. Threllkild's World is quarantined, and the reason is that the yorash are considered a pathologically dangerous combination of intelligence and sheer murderousness. So the next thing I needed was a laser rifle and sidearms. But would you believe! The goddamn lock on the weapons locker opens with a command from the console! And it was dead! No electricity!

"Can you imagine? The next ship I buy won't have a crazy damn lock like that, I'll guarantee you."

He seen then the unlikeliness of any next ship for him, and begin laughing, which started him to cough. I thought the coughing mought finish him right then, but if his body were weak, *he* weren't. When he'd quit coughing and spitting blood, he smiled weak at me, his face sweaty now. His voice weren't hardly a whisper when he started talking again.

"You guys are good people," he said. "I'm sorry I brought down trouble on you. But I brought you more than trouble. I brought four dinotheres from Prinz's World, a heavy-gravity water-oxygen planet like this one. Big animals, furry, with a nose like a long arm or a thick snake. Bought them legal, too! They're tame—domestic. Used for...carrying and pulling. Yours. I give them to you."

He began to cough again, strangling, and when it passed, he just laid there with his eyes shut, saying naught. I felt bad about him; I finally found out I liked him. After a minute he coughed some more, and I took his hand and give it a little squeeze. He went to choking and strangling, and turned on his side to throw up, but died afore he hardly got started.

I stood up and saw Whitey and Al coming with a stretcher. They was shirtless; their shirts was part of the stretcher. Two others was walking with em: Flatnose Mike with his rifle slung and one arm tied agin his body, and Gentle Tom with his gun ready and another across his back, watching behind em looking grim. I seen naught of Bull Killer, and from Tom's face, I wouldn't.

It was Kootch in the stretcher. "Where's Charley?" I asked.

"Dead," said Tom. "We'll have to go back for him."

"And the giant?"

He shook his head, his face even grimmer. So the giant had got away, with his rifle. I knowed now where the giants had got em. The rifle we'd took from the killed yorash was engraved "Wilfred Sykes," the make we all carried. So they'd got the weapons of the three killed trappers, and was lucky enough and smart enough to find out what they done and how to use em.

Al and Whitey'd put down the stretcher and I knelt by it. Kootch's eyes was shut and there weren't no pulse. He was shot in the chest. I lifted an eyelid.

"Dead," I said. Tom nodded.

So we'd lost three fighting men plus Fermin, and another out of action. And the giants lost but one, unless the one what run off was bad wounded. Them having guns and us not knowing it had made the difference.

"You're one gun short," I said to Tom. "Where be t'other one?"

"Charley's? Out there with him."

"Get it!" I said. "We don't want the giants to get it. They got two now."

He nodded and started off. "Barney, Al," I said, "take the stretcher and go with him. Whitey, go with em and give em cover."

Now we knew; they'd not surprise us like that agin. But what was next for us to do? We could wait for more men. But if twenty or thirty more showed up, the yorash might run off and we'd have naught but trouble finding them all. And they had only two guns we knowed of, while every one of us was armed.

While we waited, I had a good look at the dead giant. It were a he-brute, maybe two and a half meters tall, with arms as long as my whole body. Hands was shaped like a man's, but long for their width. On each wrist were a big claw shaped like a hook but summat sharp on the inside. The teeth was like a bear brute's, except the corner teeth was longer.

And they was armed, and man-smart, and mean. Naught we wanted for neighbors.

When we was all together agin I had our dead put in half a meter of water and weighed em down with a waterlogged length of tree trunk. They'd keep till we come back for em, cold as it were.

Then we went on ahead, alert, ready to start shooting or hit the ground. We'd not need to find the yorash, I thought; they'd come to us. Mought be they'd lay in ambush and rush us from close quarters, so we kept knives and axes unstrapped in their sheaths—we'd each fire once and draw blades.

Were Fermin right, they'd started with twelve, and ought to be eleven now while we was eight. Seven able-bodied. But we was seven riflemen while they was two. I hoped.

But naught of us questioned should we be doing this, for these be deadly savage critters, to be cleaned out afore they multiplied.

As much as we could, we kept to the open. Tom rode the horse beast now—'twere his—and from its height he could better spy anything laying in wait in the dead and brittle grass ahead. Course, he were also the best target up there. It were only a short time afore we seen two platforms made of saplings and branches, lashed in trees ahead, well up towards the tops, and it seemed like they must of been built by yorash. I never yeared of people doing ought like that.

The two trees was opengrown and branchy; easy to climb. So we went to em, and with a boost from Tom, I started up one of em. Several croakers—carrion birds—flapped their brown wings and flew up from the platform.

There were carrion there, I knowed by the smell. But what I found were a surprise for sure—a dead giant. A she giant, bloated some but still too firm for the croakers to open up yet. I could easy tell what it were killed her, for the claw and teeth marks were of bear brute.

I looked over to Whitey, who were climbing t'other tree twenty meters off, and waited till he got to the platform. He waved his hand in front of him as if trying to fan stink away, and made a terrible face.

"What be it?" I called.

"A dead giant," he answered. "Gutshot. I reckon he be the one what killed the trappers, and one of em got him afore it were over."

So there was nine of em instead of eleven.

"This one here's killed by a bear brute," I said. "She's laid out with hands over her chest. Happen the giants be religious and put their dead in treetops for their gods to find."

"This'n be the same," said Whitey. "I bet they'd not like our being up here like this."

That, I thought, they wouldn't, and clumb down. Now they seemed more to me like deadly enemy men instead of savage beasts, but I could see no other end except to kill em all. I wished Fermin had let em be on their own world.

But here they was, and just now I needed to get their attention. So on the ground agin, I struck flint on steel with my fire striker, catching the sparks in a wad of dry grass, and lit off the grass at the base of my tree, while Whitey done the same by his. It begin to burn slow, the breeze pushing it north. We all backed off south some thirty meters and lit a whole line of em across the tongue of dry ground from the marsh on one side to that on t'other. White smoke rose up; the yorash was sure to see it.

The fire were burning the dead grass off the whole width of the tongue.

As soon as we could, Whitey and me went back through the thin ashes to the trees. With rifles slung, we clumb agin into the bare branches, where we could see and be seen a good distance.

'tweren't long afore we could see yorash coming on a good trot, out of the timber some two hundred meters north. Nine of em, all right. There were shallow standing water twixt us and them, where the fire would stop and burn itself out, maybe a hundred meters ahead. They come on, stopping far enough back that they was out of the heavy smoke. One raised his rifle, and I thought, here's where we learn how well they really shoot. Till then their shooting had been at fifty, sixty meters range; at a hundred fifty it'd be harder. They wasn't experienced, and probably didn't even know to allow for range and trajectory.

I yeared a bullet click against branches, followed by the boom of the rifle what sent it. There were another boom. I yeared naught of the second bullet; it were probably aimed at Whitey.

"Don't shoot back," I called to him. "Let em come closer. Wait till I shoot."

The fire had reached the little stretch of water and was burning itself out now. After a minute or two the yorash come on toward us, two with guns, the rest with axes or clubs. At a hundred meters they stopped at the water. The two with guns aimed agin, and I got as much behind the trunk as I could, although it weren't very big around up where I were.

Whitey looked at me, but I called "not yet." It were risky, but I wanted em closer, where we could really waste em. They fired and naught happened. Then I started chopping at the vines what held the platform, and Whitey seen and did the same.

They shot agin, and bout that time the platform partly fell away and dumped the giant body off. It fell, sliding and bumping off lower branches to the ground.

We could year em yell then, and like a small mob, all nine come running at us, splashing through the shallow water and then the ashes. We drew up, and at about sixty yards let fly. I shot one of their riflemen down and Whitey the other. The others come on, and from the grass behind us come a whole little volley, and four more went down. Of the six down, four got up agin and all turned tail.

I'd already thumbed in another cartridge, and fired agin at a rifleman what'd got back up. This time he stayed down. Others was shooting agin too, and my but them big critters run fast! Took a lot of killing, too, but even so, only four of em made it into the timber.

Five of their people lay out there on the ground, but I were disgusted to see that both rifles got carried off. Near as I could tell, of the four what got away, at least two was wounded.

And none of us had got touched this time. So we'd won this battle, and I couldn't see how they could win the war after this one. Unless we just quit and let em go off somewhere and breed.

We went around then and made sure the ones laying out there was dead.

Still, I weren't feeling all as good as I mought. Dumping that body out of the tree was what set em off and let us kill that many, but it weren't the kind of thing that sets well with me. 'twere like messing with somebody's grave.

It were late afternoon now. We went on to the timber and in

amongst the trees, carrying our rifles ready, hammers back. Spite of all, we were took by surprise. Not by gunfire this time; two giants jumped out at us from back of a big windfall, right in close. Over its fallen trunk they come, and one went down at once with two balls in her chest and one in her face. T'other swung his war club, though shot in the neck, and down went Whitey. I give him another shot that went in under the arm, but he swung agin and down went Al. There was a couple of more booms and down went the giant, dead as can be.

Both of em had dried blood on em; they'd been wounded earlier.

And that left just two. The most dangerous of the pack, cause they was the survivor type and had guns as well. I wondered were one of em female. A mated pair or a pregnant female was most dangerous. If they lost theirself in the far outback....

Whitey were dead, his skull crushed like a bird's egg. Al's arm were broke and so was some ribs on that side. I knowed now why the body in the tree weren't mauled and tore up worse than it were by the bear brute. These were powerful critters and hard to kill. I be willing to bet that there be a dead bear out there somewheres, killed by a yorash; a she-yorash at that.

And now we was just seven left, out of twelve, two of us stove up. It were time to council again. And not there in the timber; get to talking and we mought get slipped up on and jumped. So I give the word and we went back to the opening, picking up dry wood along the way, and built us a fire back far enough, we couldn't smell the yorash what we dumped off the platforms.

The sun were low now, and the air taking a chill to it. The sky were clear—no threat to rain—so we decided to make camp right there in the open. We gathered more wood, to keep fire up, and then more still cause I decided to make point fires a little ways out, to light things up for the watchguards. We worked at a trot, so we'd be out of the woods afore dusk.

It'd been a long day. We'd started at dawn, covered bout fifty kilometers, lost five dead and two busted up, and killed eight giants. Wouldn't none of us be the same agin.

The two giants left would do one of two things: come after us when it were dark, or run off. If they was both he-brutes, or shes what weren't pregnant, they'd probably attack; there weren't no more hope for em on Hardy's World, with no chance for young-uns. But if they was a mated pair or one was pregnant, seemed to

me they'd run off—try to start a new tribe, far from any humans.
We all agreed on that.

"Tell you what I think," said Tom. "If'n they don't come at us tonight, I say we waits till more folk come, with dogs. Then we tracks down the last two giants and kills em, and that's that."

I didn't like it, but afore I could speak, Hard Egolfs, who usually says little, spoke his mind and mine. "Too dangerous to wait," he said. "Could be three or four days afore more folk comes up. The giants could be clear out of the territory by then, into the wild back. And it could rain and wash out their spoor so no dog could track em. It could even come an early snow. I say we goes after em, come day light."

But Tom stood his ground. "There's two of em, each with a rifle. They could shoot and run, shoot and run, keeping always to cover. I say we waits for more folk and for dogs."

"All right," says Egolfs, "then let all what's too frighty stay behind, and all what's got guts go after the giants come sunup."

I didn't want my two best men in a fight that might leave one or both out of action, so I stepped in with an edge to my voice.

"Ben't no question of frighty," I said to Egolfs. "No man here showed yeller today." Then I turned to Tom. "Egolfs is right about the danger of waiting. But we can't go hunting giants with two cripples along. So Tom, I wants you to start back with the wounded—you and Flynn and Barney—first thing in the morning. Or stay here if anyone gets hurting too bad to travel. The wounded ride the horse beast. Egolfs and me will track the giants."

"Too dangerous," said Tom. "They can jump you. And then, with you dead, they can follow and waylay us somewhere. We all got to stay."

"You're part right," I told him. "They *could* ambush us. We'll all stay long enough to build you a couple of lean-tos here in the open, or get em started anyway. Then you can stay here and wait, while the able-bodied takes turn about, watching. We'll stack up a good pile of firewood for night fires. But that's as far as I'll put off following the giants.

"Egolfs and me will stay on their spoor and leave a good trace ourself—blaze trees, break twigs. When help comes up, they can easy follow us, rain or no.

"Send along half a dozen good men and dogs. That's all it'll take. Two or three ought to be enough, but half a dozen makes it sure."

Flat-nosed Mike grunted something like a laugh. "That's if the giants don't come busting in here tonight. It's getting dark."

"Right," I said. "Mike, you hurting too much to sleep?"

"I'll probably sleep afore morning."

"All right, you take first night watch with Tom. One watch off north and east; you, Mike. Tom watches south and west. You'll have the watch till the Fish stands on his tail in the south sky, then wake up Flynn and Barney. The moon be in the last quarter, so Egolfs and me takes the watch when it rises."

There weren't no more argument. We lit the fires, chewed more dried meat and fruit, and rolled up in our sleeping robes. Regardless of any danger, I doubt any but the hurt had trouble sleeping. Like I said, it were a long day.

* * *

On our watch, long toward morning, a tiger thrummed maybe two, two and a half kilometers off north at the edge of yearing. A little bit later we yeared a far off shot from the same direction. They was on their way out of the territory, all right. Well, we'd catch em. Most critters could outrun a man easy on the short run. But weren't hardly nothing could keep our pace on the long run—sixty, eighty, a hundred kilometers.

Meanwhile, what were going through their minds out there? Were they frighty, big and fierce as they were? One thing I were sure of: they wanted to live, and they wanted their kind to live, same as us.

* * *

Not long after, the dawnlight come. The dark kind of thinned a little over east, then silvered behind the treetops off across the marsh. Pale yellow come behind it, and by then the night had paled to the top of the sky. In the west, most of the stars was shining yet, but in the east only the bigger ones, like silver specks. I seen Egolfs stand up, stiff and silent in the cold dawn. He weren't an easy man to know; we'd been neighbors and strangers for near two years. But now I felt a tie with him, a likeness of feeling, a friendship, and I knowed he felt the same. Even though he weren't like to say anything bout it.

I stood up too, and paced the chill out of my legs, putting a stick or two fresh on each point fire. Not that the point fires was needed now, for already I could see five times farther than an hour afore.

On the center fire I laid several more stout pieces, for 'twere the coldest hour, and them sleeping lay like wheel spokes, "with their feet to the heat," as the saying goes.

When the last stars were fading in the west, I waked up Tom to come along and cover us, and Mike to watch camp. I told em of the gunshot Egolfs and me'd yeared, but beyond that it were no time of day to talk much.

Egolfs and me took belt axes, leaving rifles in camp, and trotted off for the timber. The grass was crisp and white with frost, and where water stood shallow, 'twere skinned with ice. We cut a slew of saplings and young poles for building lean-tos. When these was dragged up, we felled a few dry snags of shingle ash, long and slim, crowded to death by stouter kin, and dragged em in for firewood.

I wondered if, far off in Sweet Grass Valley, men was gathering now to start off with dogs and guns. A two-day march 'twould be for them, and the sooner begun, the better.

The sun weren't far up when Egolfs and me rolled up our sleeping robes, filled our provision pouches from them of the dead, took rifles in hand, and said goodbye to our trail mates.

Trailing went slow at first, though helped by having yeared the gunshot and knowing they went north. From tracks in soft ground, one of the giants was considerable smaller than t'other—a she or a youngun, and I was willing to bet a she. After an hour or so we seen where they scraped up lots of dead leaves and stuffed em in the hole under a root-tipped bur-nut tree, to sleep warm. Weren't thirty meters from it we found the dead tiger, laying yellow and spotted like dappled sunshine. Shot in the face, from so close it were powder burned. A haunch were hacked off, so they had a belt axe with em, or maybe two.

Not long after, tracking got easier, cause they'd hit a pretty good river, some fifteen meters wide and too deep to see bottom. Seemed like they wanted not to cross it; water too cold I guessed. So we picked up our pace to a trot, taking turns, one watching for sign, t'other for the giants theirself and leaving sign of our own. Snap a brush here, blaze a tree there. Sign weren't hard to find, cause the ground were soft in lots of places. And we didn't worry too quick if we saw none, cause they just followed the river anyway.

Finally we come to a grassy valley at the foot of the first foothill ridge of the Big Icy Mountains. Here we come to where two branches had joined to make our river, the righthand branch the smallest, and the giants had crossed. It looked shallow enough, so I crossed too, holding my gear overhead, with Egolfs ready to cover me with rifle fire.

On t'other side, the stones was dry where the giants come out, though shaded by a bush, so they was probably an hour or more ahead.

Their spoor led up the ridge, through woods, and tracking went good cause there was good leaf cover, leaving scuff marks from their feet. They'd went right over the top and down t'other side, where there were a ribbon of grassy meadow in the draw. I walked out of the timber just in time to meet a she bear coming out across from me. If it weren't for the cub with her, we mought of bypassed each other. She raised up to peer at me—maybe never seen a man before—and I stood still as could be till she dropped down and charged. I fired point blank, and from behind me Egolfs's rifle banged in my ear. She went down skidding, stopping bout five meters short.

I just stood there then, scowling at the dead sow while the cub run off. The giants likely yeared the gunfire; they'd know we was following em.

Anyway we rallied and went on. The tracks went up the little dry creek there; the meadow ended and we was in timber agin. We kept our een open to not be took by surprise, but I really thought they'd not try to waylay us. Their best hope was to escape, to lose us, and they knew not—I hoped they knew not—that there be just two of us. And they was longlegged and wild-living; they ought to feel sure of their ability to travel far and fast.

It mought come down to who give out first. I was sure it'd never be Egolfs and me. And if they played out, *then* they mought try for us.

We kept going all day, breaking a little every hour or two to lay on a high point while we chewed dried meat and dried berries. Once we got into the worst ravine I ever thought to see, full of down timber. I hated like poison to go in there. Good thinking by the giants it were; they could step over trunks we had to belly over, and belly over trunks we had to either pick our way around or find a place to crawl under. When we come out of there without being ambushed, I were pretty sure they was only trying to get away.

I wished we could let em, but it'd never do. Were it just one, and a known male, we mought of let be, but it weren't.

By midday we'd got much higher, up into pine woods, and by sundown was above the pure pine, to where larch and spruce was mixed with it. I'd never seen larch nor spruce afore, but I'd yeared of em enough to know when I seen em. The larch was bare now, their slim needles a fiery red carpet round their feet.

We camped cold and dry that evening on a poor stony ridge top and a hundred meters off their trail, where they couldn't hardly find us in the dark if they come looking. Unless they could follow a scent. And I wouldn't hardly expect something with its face two and a half meters from the ground to have that good a sniffer. Even so we each took a turn watching for the first few hours, which was the likeliest time for them to come hunting us. After that we just laid there, with no fire, the cold wind blowing through the skimpy trees, and both slept the best we could. We needed the rest.

Water hare robes be the warmest you're like to find, short of something bulky and heavy, but that night were well below freezing. Part of the night I laid awake from cold, and part of it asleep, and it seemed a lot of the time I were about half and half. I remember wondering how the giants was faring, having naught but short fuzzy fur, and them from a place where 'twere always summer. And up here in the high ridges there weren't even lots of leaves to rake up for bedding.

Come light enough to track by and we was on our way. The yorash probably started an hour earlier, or maybe more, to gain time on us, which were exasperating, but we made good speed a lot of the time, trotting, cause on slopes, needles slide underfoot and leave clear marks.

I got to worrying about meat, ours getting low. Covering ground like we was, we kept eating away on it. So when we come out in a meadow and seen a doe deer, I up and shot her, the sound of the gun echoing through the ridges round about. This surprised Egolfs, but I told him to shoot too, so he shot into the air. By that time I'd reloaded and did the same, and he took the meaning of it and quick shot agin, and me right after.

That made five shots in the space of a few breaths. Now we

not only had fresh meat, but if the giants were in yearing, which I doubted not, we sounded like a whole party after em. They'd be less likely to ambush us now, or so I figured, and I'd a lot rather come on em from behind.

We quick carved plenty of good red meat into strips and draped em over our belts, enough to last three, four days. The whole thing took less than five minutes, and we was on our way agin.

That were the only thing happened all day, till late. They kept going higher and higher, like they wanted to put the Big Icies tween them and where they'd been. As if they knowed there be no men on the north side at all. In places, now, the tracking were slow, where the ground were gravelly and not much needles, or the cover mostly short bunch grass. Up and down we went, more up than down, till the only trees left were spruce, and them getting shorter and less close together. We tired easier and walked slower, and hardly run at all. The air were not just colder; it were hard to breathe. Like it were thinner.

We could look off up the big ravines and see where they come out of great coves above. The coves was like stone bowls, hundreds of meters deep and open on the downslope side, with patches and even fields of snow on their shadowed walls. But mostly they was dark gray rock, and patches of rusty red where something growed, with little white streams like far-off ribbons running and falling out of em.

They looked beautiful, and cruel, and deadly cold. I begin to feel like the chase weren't far from over. For the giants was naked and without fire, and from everlasting summer.

Finally we was following along a ridgetop where the ravine below clumb steep to the cove above. Much of the ground were open, and where there were timber, the spruces was stubby and stout. I almost missed where their tracks took off angling toward the creek that clattered below down rock stairs.

We passed through a belt of trees on the lower slope, but the bottom were meadow, with here and there an old spruce or two, bout half of em dead and bleached silvery gray. I went to cross the creek on a blowdown when there come a shot from the timber on the ridge in front of us. I felt it the same time I yeared the sound. I'd just bent to steady myself when the bullet hit the rolled up sleeping robe slung over my back. I jumped back and off just when another bullet smacked into the log.

Egolfs had already took cover behind another blowdown, and I hopped over it beside him. We looked up into the timber but saw naught but trees.

"Egolfs," I said, "they ben't just sniping. One of em be up there trying to hold us down while t'other's somewheres about looking to flank us. They been watching for us and know we be just two."

He nodded.

"So let's break for the timber behind us. Then they'll have to cross the creek theirself to get at us."

"All right."

"Both to once," I said, "you that way and me this. Go!"

We broke for it, running crouched. There was one boom and right quick another, and then we was in the cover of the timber on our side of the ravine, puffing. As I knelt behind a fat spruce, ready to fire at any sight of em, I yeared a giant call in a strange hollowy voice different from the yells we'd yeared afore. And they was words he called, strange words.

But they never give us a glimpse, and after we knelt there awhile it started to get dark. We couldn't tell if they was still in the timber opposite or if they'd clumb out of the timber and on up the mountain.

Anyway, tracking were done for the day, and when it'd got summat darker, we crept back a way in the shadowy dusk and slipped off through the trees, angling upslope towards the cove above. After a little the timber petered out, and we was in the lower end of the cove itself. The only cover there was patches of scrub on the bottom and lower slopes.

Stars was starting to show as we snuck to the downslope side of the nearest scrub patch. It were matted and thick, so thick 'twould be dusk beneath it at high noon, and no wind would ever get through. Already it were freezing cold, the night wind like ice from above. Egolfs crawled right in a hole in the scrub, sheltered above and on three sides. I rolled up in my robe just outside the edge, still out of the breeze but feeling less closed in.

We lay there chewing on fresh venison, and raw though it were, it were a welcome change from dry. We was about out of dried berries, and finished what we had.

After a bit I could year the slow breathing of Egolfs asleep, back in his dark sprucey cave a couple of meters from me. I looked up at the sky. Even in my robe and out of the breeze I shivered; it weren't going to be the best I'd ever slept.

Soon it were full dark, and the night so clear 'twere beyond belief, with twice the stars I were used to. From somewheres out there the firstfolk come; somewhere out there were Earth. And Fermin had flew about out there and visited lots of em, lots of worlds, and I knowed I wanted to do that too. Took me by surprise, but I wanted it more than any farmstead or anything. Fermin left me that, too.

And somewhere out there were Threllkild's World. I wondered if the yorash knowed that—if maybe they was huddled somewhere looking at those same stars and feeling desperate homesick.

I waked a few times from cold, and then waked up agin and it had gone cloudy. Snowflakes was drifting down. I crawled out of my robe and moved back in the sprucey cave with Egolfs.

*   *   *

Toward morning I slept hard, and it were bright sunshine when at last I woke feeling stiff from cold, and tired. I peered out; there were half a meter of snow, but we was dry in our hidey hole. I poked Egolfs and he muttered something, and neither of us much wanted to go out in it, yorash or not. But we couldn't spend the winter there, so I got out of my robe and rolled it up, and Egolfs likewise.

We didn't know if the giants was one kilometer away or half a dozen, but suspected they'd stayed the night in timber. We went downstream to the first blowdown what bridged the creek, ready to take cover quick, and crossed moughty careful not to slip.

Then we skirted round the timber to the uphill side and run onto the tracks of the yorash in the snow, striking off up the mountain. It'd still been snowing when they'd come through, cause considerable snow had fell in their tracks. Seemed like they mought be quite a piece ahead, but somehow I knowed 'twould be over by midday, one way or another.

We waded up the steep open ridge, following in their path. Our legs being lots shorter than theirs, it was good to have the trail broke for us. Sun or not, it were hard cold, but we was warm and to spare when we reached the top. From there we could see south over many kilometers of snowy mountains and far off foothills, to flatlands at the edge of seeing, and it were all white.

'twere going to be a hard trail back, but we'd be able to have fire. I was moughty glad I'd shot that doe deer, too.

Close by on the north was high peaks, our ridge crest climbing up to meet em, giant tracks marking the way.

We followed, our rifles slung cross our backs with our bedrolls, our hands in our pockets for warmth. The ridge became a rim tween great coves to east and west, then curved round tween one of them and a greater cove to the north. We seen there what looked to be a great tilted wall of ice beneath the snow, cause they was big open cracks in it that went down to who knows where. Below it in the bottom of the cove were a big lake with a great thick crescent of white ice sticking out of the lake ice. I never seen nor dreamed then of anyplace what looked so savage and cruel as that mountain, nor so beautiful.

But the accident we come on was in one of the littler coves, big though it were, that faced southeast. By the look, one of the giants had fell, and rolled and slid down the steep slope a long ways, and over an edge. The other looked then to of set down and followed, sliding on his seat. I looked and Egolfs looked, and then we looked at each other. I give a shrug and set down and followed, and Egolfs likewise. I didn't see any other way.

The edge, when we got there, weren't near as bad as I'd feared it mought be, just a rim with the slope steeper below than above, and over it we went. It got a little wild then, but the snow being deep and loose, it weren't deadly, and when the slope finally tailed out below, we just sort of slowed down and stopped.

We hadn't more than got up when there were a shot from not far off, and we both flattened back into the snow. But the shot sounded strange, and there were a terrible howl right after.

Of cover we had none, except snow. I looked at my rifle. It were okay to shoot; somehow there weren't no snow in the muzzle. Then I peered about to see where the giants mought be. The tracks led to the foot of a low rock face bout eighty meters off, where there were a big patch of matted spruce twice as high as me, like we'd camped in night afore.

Even naked to bullets, it were time to close and finish it. I jumped up, run a few meters, and dived down in the snow. Then Egolfs come up by me, and we took turns. Whichever of us were down, he laid ready to shoot at any sign of movement ahead. We did this a few times until there were only twenty-five meters left, and hadn't naught happened. So we just both got up and walked ahead, cold-clumsy fingers ready on the triggers. If I'd of shot, 'twould of took me a minute or more to reload, my fingers was that cold.

The tracks went into a gap in the scrub, one to two meters wide. I could see into it, back bout ten or twelve meters to a shallow cave-like hollow in the cliff. I didn't much want to go in there. If I could of, I'd of lit off the scrub and smoked em out, but there were too much snow on it to carry fire, and I'd of had to warm my hands anyway to strike one.

Then I seen something laying part covered with snow at the opening of the gap, went to it and raised it with a foot. A rifle with the barl split and curled back; the poor devil fired it plugged with snow.

I told Egolfs to stay back. If anything jumped at me, I'd drop down and he were to shoot over me. 'twas the only thing we could think of to do. Then I started in.

It were a *long* ten meters—finger on the trigger, not hardly breathing—and finally I come to the end. And that's what it were, the end, the end of the chase. To one side of the shallow cave, the bigger giant sat crosslegged with the head of the littler on his lap. He were stroking it. She weren't even moaning. Her face were shredded by the explosion, and surely blind.

I just stood there, staring, seeing every bit of it. Him stroking, his red-brown een steady on me, waiting. The feet of both of em was swelled and split, and I knowed they was froze. Thaw em and they'd rot off with gangrene. I yeared Egolfs come in behind me; his breath kind of hissed in at the sight.

I pointed my rifle. The big one just kept looking and stroking. "I'm sorry," I told him. "Awful awful sorry." Then I pulled the trigger; the he-giant fell backward with the top of his head gone. "I really truly am," I said, and shot the poor blind she-giant.

I hoped they knowed.

The yorash weren't all what had broke out of Fermin's spaceship. The dinotheres was loose too, the four of em browsing on brush and just general enjoying theirself. Shaggy they was, and big—the biggest stood tall as the tallest yorash. We never did get em weighed, though there were talk of it, but I wager they'd of gone six, seven ton.

And tame, like Fermin said. Took a little rounding up—they wasn't all that eager to be penned—but after we got a stockade built, we baited em in with hay we hauled on sleds all the way from Sweet Grass Valley. The whole countryside were in on it. Then we learned to get on em and steer em about, and finally drove em to Tom's settlement.

You ought to of seen em the next spring. We could get em to wrap that long nose round a stump, and up it would come, roots popping and dirt flying!

I never did marry Mary Lou, for 'twere that summer the space trader landed in Grass Valley, the first ever on Hardy's World, and I talked em into hiring me on for bread and board to do whatever needed done. Mostly cleaning and cargo handling.

And learned to write and figure, and more after that.

On Peng's Station I joined the Survey Bureau as a surface crew security guard, seen a lot of interesting worlds—some of em more interesting than I liked—and made sergeant first class.

Then, here at Przbylski's Station I yeared bout you fixing to go to Threllkild's World to learn more bout the yorash and see if they's any prospect of civilizing em.

Well, maybe you can see why I want to go long. I'll admit I got my own opinion. I've felt for years now that I killed a kind of man and woman in that cave back home. Deadly dangerous they was, and savage—they'd proved that afore ever they left their world—and they was goners anyway, but I'd like to be along in case anything can be done for their kinfolk.

After all, us humans started out pretty savage too—can be yet sometimes—and *we've* come a long way. Mought be they can too.

The Railroad

Introduction

Jerry Pournelle has a Ph.D. in physics, among other things. And back in the 1980s, brainstorming with some other knowledgeable and imaginative people, he created an imaginary but plausible star system. It was centered on a white dwarf, one of whose planets was a brown dwarf circled by a large habitable moon. The geophysical complexities of that system resulted in very peculiar living conditions for the life forms that evolved there, and the humans who migrated there. Conditions that include several variations of night and day, variations in both intensity and length, resulting in extreme weather fluctuations. Fun to play with in writing, but I wouldn't care to live there.

Next, Jerry and friends gave the colonists a history, rooted in an earlier series of stories by Pournelle and Niven. A history no kinder to the immigrants than the planet was. After writing it all up, they sent it to some science-fiction authors, inviting them to write stories set on that world, for a series of shared-world anthologies: *War World One* through at least *Five*.

When you set up a shared universe like that, you leave enough slack for your authors to postulate conditions of their own within the broader context, and this creates potentials for embarrassment. Thus in the first volume, one story included, peripherally, a Finnish colony named "Novy Finlandia." The story was a dandy, but the name of the colony? *Novy* is Russian, and *Finlandia* is latinized Swedish. And the Finns are language proud, and Russia is their traditional enemy. Historically the Finns have borrowed words from German (during the Middle Ages), the Swedes (through much of their history), Latin (via the medieval church), and most recently English. But *not* Russian. The name "Novy Finlandia" was going to irritate just about any Finn, or Finnish-American, who read it.

I mentioned this to the editor, and he told me if they got another manuscript dealing with "Novy Finlandia," he'd let me see it during the editing process.

So guess what. There was one volume the editing of which was turned over to someone else. And it included a story in which the focus was "Finns" from "Novy Finlandia"—New Finland. I won't enumerate the flubs; the author batted zero, starting with his Finns having Russian names and speaking their "Finnish dialect of Russian." In fact, the story would have been fine—if he'd simply called his characters Russian, and his colony, say, Novy Oksko. The author was, in fact, a skilled story spinner with a good sense of people. But he was new to the print media; his previous credits were as a screenplay writer.

So when the original editor invited me to write a story for volume 4, I said sure, providing I could set it in "Uusi Suomi" (Finnish for "New Finland"). I also wanted to ignore the geographic location implied in the offending story. If those were permissible, I told him, I could get the earlier boo-boos to make sense. And the editor, bless his heart, said "great; go ahead."

So here's what I came up with. I hope you like it.

* * *

Fedor Demidov sat with a book open in his lap, watching out the window as the railroad coach rocked and swayed its slow way up a grade. The terrain and forest outside could have been approximated in numerous places in his native Novy Rossiya: high hills that by some would be called mountains, and forest largely of the common Haven "pine." To his practiced eye, the area they were crossing had been clearcut about, oh, eighty Terran years previously, and the replacement stand thinned at about age fifty, for pulpwood and fuel. In states like Novy Finlandia— *Uusi Suomi*; he'd have to watch himself on that. In states like Uusi Suomi, where forest was plentiful, forest thinnings, logging debris and sawmill waste were the usual fuel in rural villages. In fact, they were much used in towns as well. Electricity was cheap enough, but electric cookstoves were very expensive.

There was a patter of quiet Finnish conversations in the car, which was mostly empty. Uusi Suomi's Foreign Ministry had reserved it for two small groups of technical people: the one Demidov was with, and one made up of mining engineers, including a consultant from New Nevada. From the far end of the car, the consultant was holding forth loudly. Demidov allowed it to annoy him; the man was arrogant and offensive, as well as loud.

They were in the second of the two passenger cars. Demidov had the impression that the other was empty, except for the con-

ductor who apparently had an office compartment in it. The rest
of the train was of log cars; he could see them out the window,
rounding a curve his own car had rounded moments earlier.
They'd picked them up from different sidings along the line, and
would leave them at the next sawmill they came to. On iron-poor
Haven where forest too was not abundant, lumber was valuable,
and the management of forests quite technical and organized.

A voice began to speak from the loudspeaker at one end of
the car, but he paid it little heed. It was in Finnish, a language in
which he knew only a few polite phrases learned especially for
this trip. Its rapid, tonal staccato and grammatical inflections hid
even the scattered technical words it had in common with Russian
and Americ.

Demidov glanced at Anna Vuorinen, the young interpreter in
the seat facing his, and her stricken expression jerked his attention. She stared toward the loudspeaker behind him, and he
turned as if looking might enlighten him. Virtually every other
person in the coach was looking that way too, he realized now,
and the conversations had died.

He turned back to the young woman as the speaker went
silent. "What was it, Anna?" he asked in quiet Russian.

"Pirates," she said. "Extra-atmospheric fighter craft have
been reported from several locations, and have engaged military
aircraft near Fort Kursk."

Engaged! That meant destroyed; extra-atmospheric fighters
would be infinitely superior to anything any state of Haven could
put in the air. For a moment, resentment flared in Demidov. Not
at the pirates, but at the Imperium that had left the planet unde-
fended. Pirates were an aberration, but there had always been
such predators, among humans. And the Imperium knew it. Yet
some wretched bureaucrats in—what? The Ministry of State? Of
War? Some faceless imperial bureaucrats had decided that the
forty or so million citizens on Haven were not worth a squadron
to protect them.

He overlooked that he was a bureaucrat himself. A bureaucrat was always the other person, usually someone you didn't
know.

And Anna Vuorinen's husband was an officer in the Finnish
air force. She'd mentioned that while they were getting
acquainted at the Ministry of Forests the day before. So it was
hardly surprising that the news had shaken her. But the border of

Uusi Suomi was two thousand kilometers from Fort Kursk, and there were various places in the vast Shangri-La Valley that offered better looting.

He was thinking of pointing that out, when the conductor entered the car, a blocky man, gray of hair and mustache. He walked past the seated Demidov and his interpreter, stopping close ahead to talk to Veikko Ikola, Demidov's guide and principal host on this trip. Ikola lacked a doctorate, but as a silviculturist, an ecological engineer specializing in the management of forests, his reputation was international. He was said to look through the innumerable apparencies and recognize the key relevancies, then formulate working solutions more surely than anyone else in the profession. Which was why Demidov was there— to visit representative sites on the ground, ask questions, and hopefully learn.

Ikola's conversation with the conductor was in Finnish of course, but he glanced at the Russian while they spoke. Then the conductor went on to talk to the man in charge of the group around the mining consultant from New Nevada.

Ikola stepped over and sat down next to Anna Vuorinen, across from Demidov. Although the Finn read technical papers in Americ well enough, in general conversation he used it clumsily, having particular difficulty following it when spoken. Thus the interpreter.

"Perhaps," Ikola said through her, "you would prefer to return to Hautaharju. Considering the pirate raid." On a world like Haven, with little or no high-tech military capacity, a mere raid by space pirates could be far more devastating than an earnest war between local states. "Our train will lay over at Tammipuro, where we will eat while it recharges its storage batteries. There will he a southbound train there. We can go back on it."

"Do you consider that there is danger to your country?" Demidov asked. "Or to mine?"

Ikola shrugged and answered, this time in Americ. "Probably not. It is hard to know."

Demidov nodded. "I prefer to continue. I traveled 620 kilometers by rail, plus whatever we have come today. I would not care to return with nothing accomplished."

Ikola nodded, and returned to his seat across the aisle, where Demidov's two other hosts sat, the tall and massive Reino Dufva, and the similarly tall but rangy Kaarlo Lytikäinen.

By now the conductor had finished what he'd had to say to the other group. The mining engineer, Migruder was his name, Carney Migruder, was laughing, a loud braying laugh that grated Demidov's nerves like fingernails on chalkboard. The laugh ended with a long string of "huh huh huhs," releasing the Russian, and he glanced again at Anna Vuorinen. An attractive young woman, though not actually pretty.

More interesting to him was her background. Her Finnish name had come with marriage. Her background was as Russian as his own, though very different. Her spoken Russian was soft, the effect of having begun life among the peasant sectarians of "Pikku Venäjä." They were descendants of Russian religious deportees forcibly relocated on Haven more than five hundred years earlier. Entirely enclosed within the borders of Uusi Suomi, the sectarians remained calmly unabsorbed, culturally and linguistically. There was constant attrition, of course, of young people in reaction to the rigid rules of the sect. They went to the towns or to Russian-speaking states, and were assimilated. Anna's parents had broken away late, she'd said; they'd been nearly thirty, with three living children.

But the community remained closed, impenetrable from the outside, and the Finns had never tried to Finnicize them. The *Pikku Venäläiset* were hard working and productive, and used their land well. That was good enough for the Finns.

Demidov had asked her to speak the dialect for him, and had understood only a little of it. It was quaint to an extreme. According to her it was not greatly changed from the mother tongue, at least in vocabulary and grammar. They still read the ancient bible—in cyrillic!—chanted prayers and hymns from ancient books, and recited a catechism centuries old. Apparently even pronunciations had not changed much; according to Anna, speech still largely fitted the ancient spellings.

Knowing it, though, had made it easy for her to learn the modern speech of Novy Rossiya, she'd told him. Certainly she spoke modern Russki fluently, despite her light accent.

* * *

Veikko Ikola watched the village of Tammipuro appear through the trees. Actually, the first he saw of it was the railroad siding with its loaded and unloaded strings of log cars. The village itself was almost like forest, its gravel streets lined with trees. Though not pines. Its trademark was its steelwood trees, the *tammi* in Tammipuro. He knew the place well enough, and a number of others more or less like it.

The morning was far enough along that they left their overcoats in the luggage rack when they got off the train. The local tavern doubled as the dining room for the railroad, and for whatever locals chose to eat out. At this particular hour there were no other dining guests. As was customary, the passengers would sit at a long trestle table set up for them. Nor was there a charge; meals were covered in their fare.

There was no menu. They simply needed to wait till the food was ready. Some of the men went to the taproom, but Ikola sat down at the long trestle table and waited. He preferred to do his drinking in more intimate situations, with one or two friends in private conversation, or with Toini, his wife, at supper. Dufva and Lytikäinen too abstained, Lytikäinen because his temper, never the best, was inversely correlated with his blood alcohol. That was how Lytikäinen himself put it. Ikola thought the problem was psychological; the forest supervisor could get disagreeable just drawing the stopper.

Minutes later the mining experts returned with a large pitcher of beer and a liter of whiskey, "bourbon" imported from New Nevada. The loud consultant had bought it. Migruder was his name, Ikola recalled, Carney Migruder, a rather large burly man looking not quite solid but not flabby either.

As usual the tavernkeeper had the radio on. The station played peasant music almost continually, energetic music you could dance to. There was room to dance in the dining room. Sawmill workers would dance there, and the forest workers when they were in town, with their wives and girlfriends, or with each other if they had none there. But just now the railroad passengers had the place to themselves. During trueday the forest workers were away in the woods, working shift and shift, six hours on and six off through four cycles, spending their off time collapsed on their bunks. Busses brought them to town for dim-day and true night, when woods work was unsafe or impossible. Ikola knew their life first hand; he'd lived it. Had grown up in a village much like Tammipuro, as had Dufva and Lytikäinen. You needed the practical experience to be accepted into the forestry curricula at the university.

Migruder stood up, cleared his throat to draw their attention, then held his glass high. "Here's to Novy Finlandia!" he said loudly in Americ. "Long may she—do whatever it is she does!" He laughed then like a jackass, loudly and without humor.

Except for Migruder's laughter, the people there were silent as stone. Ikola had seen Lytikäinen stiffen, and had put a hand on his arm. The Nevadan was an official guest, invited by the Minerals Ministry to help evaluate some iron ore deposits in the upper foothills. Small concentrated deposits, typical of those developed volcanically, and potentially very valuable on iron-poor Haven.

The men from Minerals who accompanied the Nevadan raised their glasses stony faced. Migruder's mining expertise, Ikola told himself, must be very good indeed for them to put up with him. It was hard to believe that someone who found such pleasure in mindfuck, could do good work. He wondered if the man was married, and if so, what kind of husband he was, what kind of father.

* * *

Novy Finlandia! That was deliberate, thought Demidov. Migruder was either pathologically vicious or had a death wish. Or both.

Demidov knew more history than most Haveners. He was an avid reader, an accumulator of knowledge. Back on Terra, the Finns had had a long record of resistance, more or less successful resistance, to Russian dominance. Something that some Terran Russians—intellectuals and ruling circles—had found exasperating, and resented.

After the CoDominium was established, no Terran state was independent. So in Finland, the original Finland, a corporation was founded that sold shares in a new colony. In the worldwide depression of the time, however, even 7,000 shareholders were limited in what they could pay for. Thus the Finns settled for a place in Haven. Had chosen a place with much forest—hardly surprising, considering Finnish skills and traditions—and nearly six centuries ago had emigrated, moving families, livestock, and equipment.

They'd named their corporation *Uusi Suomi Yhtiö*—"New Finland, Limited." But some CoDominium bureaucrat, no doubt a Russian, had quietly entered it into the records as *Novy Finlan-*

dia, the first word Russian, the second latinized Swedish. And once in the CoDominium computers that way, it was not only official. From there it got into all official and commercial computers and onto all map updates for Haven. Which was as close to being graven in stone on Mount Sinai as you could get. Of course, when the CoDominium collapsed, all that became null, and the Empire, when it arrived, accepted the name *Uusi Suomi* as official. But old habits die hard, and among other Haveners, "Novy Finlandia" was still common, if offehsive usage.

The Finns, one of the most language-proud peoples, had resented it intensely at first, and still were sensitive about it. It would no doubt have been more acceptable had it been in Americ: "New Finland." But in Russian!

Another part of the original contract was that Uusi Suomi's territorial integrity was legally protected. But as with most of their contracts, the CoDominium ignored this one too. After BuReloc, the Bureau of Relocation, was established and forced deportations began, dissident Russians of various stripes were deported to Haven. Most went to mining districts, to work and die as forced laborers. Others were unloaded on the two established Russian colonies to accommodate as best they could; Demidov's ancestry included such deportees. But a shipload of religious dissidents had been unloaded in "Novy Finlandia."

It seemed doubtful that CoDo officialdom planned it that way. Aside from "trivial" matters—matters not coming before high-level officials—it seemed doubtful to Demidov that the CoDominium had gone out of its way to do vicious things, things not substantially profitable to one of its power factions. More probably some mid-level *apparatchik* had arranged it with the ship's captain out of spite. Tradition had it that shiploads of deportees had been put down nowhere near the site officially specified, for nothing more than a case of good whiskey, from someone who wanted slave labor and didn't have pull with BuReloc.

To make it worse, the newcomers had arrived in early winter with nothing to live on and little to make a living with. While the Finns themselves were still struggling to survive. At once there'd been a schism of sorts among the Finns, between those who wanted to leave the 2,800 newcomers to die, and those who refused to. The colony's council had voted to help them—indeed such help had already begun, unofficially—but the vote had been close. And the decision had held a proviso: aid to the Russians would come from a special fund of provisions: those who didn't wish to, need not give.

Fortunately the newcomers were mostly farmers, people with knowledge and skills, even with some tools. They could contribute effective muscle and work, though nothing of food, medicines, or initial shelter. At the end of the first years-long winter, nearly 1,200 still lived. But among those Finns who'd helped, the winter's death toll, not to mention other suffering, had been notably worse than among those who hadn't. The rift it had opened between the *halukkait*, "the willing," and the *sydämettömiä*, "the heartless," had taken several generations and the blurring of gradual intermarriage to close.

The fact that both the name Novy Finlandia and the burden of unwanted dependents were Russian, tied the two together in the psyche of the Finns. Migruder, Demidov told himself, was prodding a very sore spot.

The music was interrupted in mid-line by a voice in dry staccato Finnish, and it seemed to him it was something he should know about. He turned to Anna Vuorinen, questioningly. Her words in Russian, were soft, almost murmured, her eyes unfocused. "They say a Finnish squadron, the seventh Air Reconnaissance Squadron, has been attacked by the pirates, and most of it destroyed."

There'd been much more to the report than that. Apparently the information about the Finnish Squadron had preempted her attention. He didn't know if that was her husband's unit or not, but thought it must be. Judging from her face, her eyes. She excused herself then and left the table, which seemed to answer his unasked question.

He had another, and turned to Ikola with it. "Have the pirates visited Uusi Suomi, then?"

The Finn shook his head. "That squadron was on"—he groped for the Americ words—"it had our duty for the Council, at Sabbad."

Demidov nodded. Detached service in the south. The new Council of States had instituted an air patrol to discourage the corsairs that occasionally pillaged towns along the southern coast. The biplanes and triplanes they put in the air would mean little to space pirates though.

"And her husband was with the destroyed squadron?"

The Finn pursed his lips. "I think. From the way Anna

react."

* * *

The food had been brought to their table more in the manner of a boarding house than a restaurant. It was plain but good, the sort of meal a solid working-class family might eat at home. Eating, Ikola told himself, served the additional function here of keeping Migruder's mouth occupied. Afterward the cook himself brought out individual bowls of a sweet but spicy dessert, and served each person himself.

When they'd finished, they reboarded the train. Both Demidov and Migruder had wanted to continue to their original destination, the town of Rajakuilu in the northeast corner of the country.

There were more than enough seats on the car. No one needed to sit beside anyone, or even across from anyone if they wanted to be alone. And indeed, most did sit alone. Why, Ikola asked himself, isn't everyone talking about the pirates? The place should be a-buzz. Yet he felt no urge himself to talk about it. Perhaps because so little was known—the skimpiest of information and no rumors at all.

One man was talking though. At the far end of the car, Migruder sat wearying his interpreter with his usual loud Americ. His monolog was rich in idiom and slang, well beyond Ikola's ability to follow, even had he been in the mood. It seemed to be something derogatory about someone.

One of the men from the Minerals Ministry passed on his way to the restroom. On his return, Ikola reached and touched his arm. "Sit," he invited, gesturing toward the seat opposite. The man hesitated, then sat.

"What do you know about Migruder?" Ikola asked.

The man shrugged, his face a grimace. "He is famous for his ability. As well as his character or lack of it. The Ministry studied the records of all the experts on Haven, and Migruder seems to be the best of them. We'll just have to put up with him for a few days."

"It's surprising someone hasn't killed him."

The man nodded. "His father is Baron Migruder of New Reno, very rich and influential. They fight like two land gators over a dead goat. The old man has disinherited him, or that's the report we have, but protects him nonetheless." The Ministry man shrugged and started to stand.

Just then Migruder hurried past him, headed for the restrooms at the end of the car.

* * *

Demidov still sat across from Anna Vuorinen, across the aisle from Ikola. And guessed it was Migruder that Ikola talked about with the Minerals official. What else? He looked at the young woman. "What did they say?" he asked.

She looked at him woodenly, and he realized she didn't know, hadn't listened. She must have been thinking about her husband, wondering if he was dead or alive. "Excuse me," he said. "I didn't mean to intrude on your thoughts. My question was idle curiosity."

She nodded slightly, then seemed to blank him out, her focus turning inward.

They rolled past a recent clearcutting, thick with seedlings knee high to a man, and lovely to Demidov's eyes. Haven pine produced two crops of tiny winged seeds in the long summer, the first remaining in the tough leathery pods. If a summer fire killed the stand, the pods, chemically changed by the heat, opened and released the seed onto the ash, where it germinated to produce a virtual carpet of seedlings. The later seed crop was born in pods much more fragile, which opened in winter storms. The spring thaw worked the seeds down into the needle litter. If fire then burned through before the early crop matured, the crowns might burn and the trees be killed, but of the needle litter, only the top centimeter or two were dry enough to burn. Last year's late crop, stimulated by the heat, germinated quickly then; at least what was left of it did.

In which case the new stand was often patchy and more or less thin and limby, but nature cared little about form factor or coarse knots, only presence and energy gradients. The trick in management was to use such general knowledge, along with the specifics of local conditions, to harvest the mature stand and obtain a new one without fire. The Finns, Ikola in particular, were masters at it, which was why Demidov had come.

The loudspeaker sounded again. This time it wasn't the conductor's voice. He'd been sitting in his compartment listening to the radio, apparently, and switched on the speaker so the passengers could hear. It began in mid-sentence. Demidov watched as the woman listened. Her face paled almost to chalk, then the color returned to it as the report ended. Tears began to run down her face.

"Excuse me," she whispered and getting up, hurried toward the restrooms. Ikola had been watching; he came over and sat where she had. "Radio gave names of dead flyers," he said. "One was *Luutnantti* Eino Vuorinen. I think her husband."

Demidov felt his own throat constrict, and his eyes burned. For an embarrassed moment he thought he might weep. That would never do! He didn't know the woman well enough for that. What would Ikola think?

* * *

Through the long slow hours of early morning, most of the passengers dozed intermittently. The car rocked and swayed, the seemingly endless forest slid slowly past, and reading led easily to drowsiness. There were occasional short stops to pick up and drop off strings of log cars.

Migruder was the exception; he spent much of the next several hours in one or the other of the car's two restrooms, emerging more and more haggard. It seemed to Ikola that the tavernkeeper or cook in Tammipuro must have overheard the man's insulting toast, and prepared a dessert portion especially for him. That would explain the personal service.

Toward midmorning, some of them adjusted their seats into beds, took their pillows from the overhead, and lay down to sleep. Even Migruder lay down between trips to the restroom.

The next news bulletin was switched into the speaker almost from the first word: The intruders had nuked Hell's-A-Comin' and Castell City! The mushroom cloud at Hell's-A-Comin' could be seen from Nothing Ventured, 215 kilometers away. Unofficial reports were that the intruders were not pirates! Supposedly, satellite transmissions had shown the ship to be a Sauron heavy cruiser!

Saurons! A chill rucked Ikola's skin. Talk of Saurons on Haven drove the report of nukings into the background. If Saurons had come...If Saurons had come, the Empire had lost, and they faced a new empire, a Sauron empire, that would make their old troubles seem trivial.

On the other hand—for unofficial report, read "rumor." Of course, rumors could be true; that was eighty percent of their fascination, but more often than not—

* * *

Drowsing was over with; no one was sleepy anymore. Nor likely to become so, Demidov thought. The conductor let the radio play continuously now. At least it wasn't dance music; under the circumstances it wouldn't have been appropriate. This was old music in the classical vein, played on an orchestral synthesizer. Dark music. He didn't recognize it; perhaps it was Finnish. Men adjusted their beds back into seats. Still nothing much was said for a few minutes. People began to draw together, talking sporadically in undertones. Lytikäinen and Dufva drifted over to sit again by Ikola.

Demidov looked openly at Anna Vuorinen. Her eyes occupied dark depressions in a pale face. He thought to start a conversation with her; it might draw her out of herself and her shock. But be could think of nothing. Partly it seemed too little was known, and the Saurons—the Saurons might be only a rumor. And partly—if it was true, it was too big and too new to confront all at once.

Even so, he found himself speaking. "Mrs. Vuorinen, do you know what music that is?" *Inane!* he told himself. *You're being inane!*

"It is 'Lemminkäinen in Tuonela.'"

"Thank you." He hesitated. "Was lieutenant Eino Vuorinen...?"

"My husband."

"I am terribly sorry."

"Thank you. Feel sorry for yourself." She said it almost bitterly, as if she held him somehow accountable. Then spoke further, contrite and clarifying: "It is kind of you to say so. But I feel—" She shrugged, a shrug that was half shudder. "I think our troubles are just beginning."

He turned inward, wondering if they were. There was no proof, only the rumors. He'd demoted the reports of nukings to rumors now, too, along with the Saurons.

But only for a moment, because the music was interrupted by

another report from Hautaharju. The interpreter listened without changing expression. As if nothing more could affect her now. When it was done, she translated for Demidov without his asking. "Falkenberg has been destroyed by a nuclear explosion. Other places have been attacked by powerful weapons, believed to be orbital weapons. There has been a massive explosion at the power plant near Lermontovgrad, not nuclear, but a fire is said to be raging there, sending a smoke plume toward the east. It is thought to be radioactive." Her mouth twisted as if in cynicism. "People are warned to get out of its way."

As if they could, most of them, Demidov thought.

* * *

He tried to read then, but repeatedly found himself without a clue as to what his eyes had just passed over. He had to look again at the cover: *Physiological characteristics of the roots of pine seedlings in the Atlas foothills of...*He set it aside. It seemed to belong to a time past. Not long past, but past and now irrelevant. It seemed to him the days of managing forests for the export market were gone. They'd been there when the train had left Hautaharju, twelve hours earlier, but now they were finished. At any rate they were if the Saurons had come.

The conductor entered the car and walked along the aisle, speaking directly instead of through the speaker. He stopped by Demidov's seat and repeated in halting Americ: "We come to Sahakylä soon. We stop there. Eat and charge batteries."

Demidov wondered if Migruder was well enough to eat now. Or if he'd eat if he was well enough. It seemed doubtful he'd offer his foolish toast again. He looked backward out the window. Rounding one of the innumerable curves was the long string of log cars they'd gathered. And would no doubt leave at the place they were coming to.

"What is the town again?" he asked Anna Vuorinen.

"Sahakylä," she said. Then surprising him added, "Saha means sawmill, and kylä is village, Sahakylä." As if knowing, he might better remember. Or as if, with the world coming apart, he'd never leave this country, and had best start learning the language.

The thought triggered chills almost too intense to bear. Was that it? he thought, and it seemed to him the answer was yes.

* * *

When they left the railway car at Sahakylä, Migruder looked pale but generally recovered. In the dining hall, however, though he bought another bottle, he drank quietly, moodily. To Ikola it felt that what the man had on his mind was not the bombings nor the rumor of Saurons, but what had been done to him at Tammi-puro. His mood seemed not one of worry or shock, but of smolder-ing resentment. Ikola was glad the man wasn't his responsibility.

He sat down across from Demidov. The Russian had impressed him at first as someone who perhaps thought of himself as more refined than other people. His hands were small for his size, and rather slender. But he'd comported himself courteously and thoughtfully at all times.

"What you think of news today?" Ikola asked quietly in Americ.

"I think—" Demidov began slowly, "I think it may be the end of things as we've known them. The end of civilized life for humans on Haven."

The Finn raised an eyebrow. "On Haven were terrible times before. After wars destroyed CoDominium, and Haven left by itself. Our ancestors fell to—" He groped. "Primitive. We have come back long way. Come back again if need."

The Russian shook his head. "If the Saurons have come, it will mean worse than primitivism. It will mean slavery!"

The Finn's eyes were calm but intent. "What will you do then, if Saurons are here?"

Demidov sighed and shook his head. "What can one do? Expend one's life as best one can."

"Expend?"

Demidov looked to Anna Vuorinen and spoke in Russian. "If the Saurons have indeed come, they will make slaves of people. And if they've come here, it means they've defeated the Empire. That is hard to believe, but perhaps they have done it. Then one can either be their slave, or one can expend his life with honor, and die fighting."

The interpreter didn't begin translating till after Demidov had finished, as if she was looking at the situation for the first time. When she'd repeated it in Finnish, Ikola peered at the Russian curiously.

"Only those two alternatives, you think?"

Anna passed his words on. "What else?" the Russian asked.

"Seventeen standard years ago when the Marines were pulled off Haven," Ikola replied, "the Empire was still very powerful. There were wars of secession, but the Navy was large—immense—and loyal."

His Finnish was flowing more slowly than it might have, and Anna kept pace not many words behind.

"Sauron was also powerful," he went on, "but not nearly so large. And if the Empire was beset by wars of secession, the Sauron slave worlds were less than loyal to their masters. They might, perhaps, fear to revolt, but surely they would do such sabotage as they could. Do you really believe the Saurons could have defeated the Empire?"

"Obviously the Saurons believed they could. And if they are here—" The Russian's shrug was different than the Finn's had been, more expressive. "They must have."

"You asked for another alternative," Ikola countered. "I think there is one. A second explanation for the Saurons being here, if they are, and a third alternative for us. Seventeen standard years is not so long. Would it be long enough for the Saurons to defeat the Imperial Fleet, and the Imperial Marines? I think of the young Finns who joined the 77th. They were roughnecks, most of them, and adventurous. And mostly they were not the big-mouths, while those who were, were more as well. They were the youths who liked brawls, and who more often than not won their fights. I think the same was true in other states, and probably on other worlds.

"And when, after training, they came home on leave, they had changed. They were still tough, but proud with a different pride than before. Pride in their regiment, their division. And they walked differently, moved differently. They even spoke politely to their parents! They knew discipline. In a tavern they might not show it, but they knew discipline where it counted."

He paused to let the interpreter catch up, for as he'd warmed to his subject, he'd spoken faster. Now he changed tack.

"Suppose the Navy beat the Saurons. What do you suppose would happen then?"

Demidov frowned, pursed his lips. "If they defeated them, really defeated them—They would surely destroy Sauron, their home world. And everyone on it. But to do that, they'd have to destroy the Sauron fleet, first."

Ikola nodded, saying nothing, leaving Demidov to carry his thoughts further.

The Russian shrugged again. "I suppose the Saurons, what were left of them, would scatter. And the Fleet would pursue them, try to eradicate them to the last ship, the last man. And woman." He frowned. "What you want me to say is that the Saurons who've come here, if they have come here, are a ship of refugees."

Ikola nodded. "It seems more probable. The alternative, if the Saurons are really here—the alternative is that in just seventeen years they have destroyed the Imperial Fleet. And in those same seventeen years have spread through the entire Empire, occupying every world to the last. And this world would be the very last, or one of them.

"I do not think all that could happen in seventeen years."

The two men hadn't realized that the rest of the table had fallen silent and was listening, the Finns to Ikola and to Anna's translation of the Russian, Migruder to his own interpreter.

It was Migruder who interrupted, his laugh half bark, half sneer. "Shit!" he said. "Saurons! No Saurons would waste their time with a crummy back-water world like this! Some pansy saw something and panicked. Over the radio. Some other pansies heard him squawk, and they panicked. Now you sad sacks of shit are flapping around ready to suicide."

Lytikäinen was sitting on the same side of the table as Migruder. He stood abruptly, his chair clattering backward onto the pine floor, and with two quick strides had the Nevadan by the hair, even as the man turned in his seat. Lytikäinen jerked him backward, and Migruder's chair went over, Migruder in it. The man scrambled to his feet ready to fight, but the massive Dufva was between the two, keeping them apart. Lytikäinen he'd shoved sharply backward, sending him staggering. Migruder's shirt he'd gripped with a massive left hand, twisted, and jerked him close. The Nevadan looked paralyzed.

"We will be polite here," he said in ponderous Americ. With a grin, his face in Migruder's. Demidov, himself startled breathless, realized he'd misread the quiet, smiling logging engineer. The man was not placid, simply amiable. He'd probably smile at you even while throwing you through the wall. Seemingly Migruder realized this too, realized something at any rate, realized that this man could gobble up both Lytikäinen and himself with little effort. He snarled non-verbally as Dufva freed him, and straightened his shirt. His interpreter had retrieved Migruder's chair and stood it up again.

The man from Minerals was on his feet too, tightlipped. Demidov suspected the man would like to have done what Lytikäinen had, but still he was responsible for Migruder's mission here. Now it would be a miracle if the man didn't head back for Hautaharju; this could even result in a break in diplomatic relations. On the other hand there was no point in anyone's raising hell with Lytikäinen; the damage was already done. Demidov was glad he wasn't involved.

That's when the music was interrupted with another report. Morgan, Migruder's interpreter, gave the outlanders a running translation into Americ. "This is Radio Metsäjoki. We have just received a report from Weather Service radio on Iron Hill, broadcasting on emergency backup power. Severe explosions have erupted in the power plant at Kivikuilu. There is fire there, and heavy smoke, presumably radioactive, is drifting down the canyon toward the capital. Extra-atmospheric fighter craft have attacked both the city and the military base south of it. Great explosions have occurred over the government district and the military base. The very air appeared to explode; the center of the city has been flattened. Of the government district and the apartment blocks around it, hardly a wall is standing. There is no sign of anyone left alive.

"Immediately after we received the preceding report, the Weather Service personnel reported that a fighter craft was circling their installation. Transmission then cut off.

"We will try to keep you informed of anything further that happens. Meanwhile we return you to our music program."

Someone—the cook or the tavernkeeper—turned the volume well down then, and for a long moment the room was silent. Demidov looked around at the Finns. None were moving, though he could hear someone's labored breathing above the muted music. It was as if they'd been turned to stone. Then Migruder began to chuckle, the sound escalating, becoming a laugh, at first harsh and bitter, then loud, uncontrolled, as if driven by some psychotic mirth.

Demidov stared. He expected someone to strike the man, but no one moved. When Migruder had choked back his laughter, he spoke: "You Finns! You goddamm ridiculous people! Now you see how weak you are! You're fucked now, fucked good!"

He looked around leering. Then Demidov was surprised to find himself speaking, his voice loud in the stillness. "Migruder, you are a fool!"

Migruder's head jerked to stare at him.

"Think man!" Demidov went on. "Where have you been all day? Haven't you been listening? Do you believe the Saurons make war only on people you don't like? They've already destroyed the planet's major military bases. Now they destroy the minor ones. They're also destroying the power-generating plants of the planet, and the governing capacity. What do you think is left of your father's barony? Of the government district at New Reno? Of New Reno itself?

"Your father can't protect you from this. He can't buy you out of it. You're in a foreign land a thousand kilometers from home, except now you don't have a home. You're alone here in the midst of a people you've insulted repeatedly."

Migruder's eyes bulged, not with rage, but seemingly in shock. The man is insane, Demidov realized. *Truly* insane. He's been walking around with insanity seething just below the surface, for god knows how long.

The Nevadan turned abruptly and strode toward the door. No one tried to stop him.

* * *

The rest waited for dinner. The cook continued cooking and when the food was ready, the tavernkeeper served them. The only things unusual about it were the quiet, and that two of the Finnish passengers went to the kitchen and helped bring out the food.

The food, it seemed to Demidov, was as good as it would otherwise have been. He even enjoyed it in a detached sort of way: ate detachedly, tasted detachedly, and watched those around him detachedly. He didn't wonder about his father in Novy Petrograd, or his brothers or sisters; he knew. Knew all he needed to.

A question did occur to him though, and when he'd finished his main course, he turned to Anna Vuorinen. "I have a question for *Herra* Ikola." He looked at the Finn. "If the nuclear plant has been destroyed, how are the locomotive's storage batteries being recharged?"

"Beginning here at Sahakylä, the railroad's power comes

from the dam at Rajakuilu. The power for the whole northeastern part of the country does." Ikola raised his voice then, enough to get everyone's attention. "Who here wishes to return south?" He didn't say south to Hautaharju; just south.

Three of the four men from Minerals raised their hands. Probably they felt compelled to seek their families. Demidov didn't know whether to be surprised or not when Anna Vuorinen didn't raise her hand. He was definitely surprised when Migruder's interpreter didn't; he'd been sure the man was from New Nevada, and south was the direction of home for him. Perhaps, Demidov thought, he intended to wait and see what Migruder wished to do.

Ikola's home was south too, in Hautaharju, but he hadn't raised his hand. Demidov thought he knew why: Ikola had mentioned that his wife worked in the Agriculture Ministry, and that they lived in an apartment almost across the street from it. At home or at work, she'd have died. Of course, there might be children...

"There is a reserve armory at Metsäjoki," the Finn went on. "There will be infantry weapons there, including mortars and rockets, along with officers and noncoms. And field rations for two months. Field radios too, for as long as their batteries last. It will take about fifteen hours to get there by train. Or perhaps only eight or ten, if the conductor decides we need not stop for log cars." He turned to the conductor. "Personally, I think it would be futile to haul logs. Perhaps later, if it should turn out that the Saurons are just a rumor."

The conductor said nothing. Shortly the engineer came in to say that the batteries were recharged. Walking to the train, Demidov spoke again to Ikola through Anna Vuorinen: "You never told me your alternative to slavery or dying in combat."

"Ah," said the Finn. "The other is to survive free. Survive and wait." His eyes were hard. "I've read considerable history, of both Haven and Earth. The Russian people, like the Finns, are good at surviving, at outlasting oppression."

Demidov said nothing more as they walked. He was digesting Ikola's answer.

* * 8

Migruder stayed on the northbound train, drinking. Demidov suspected that Morgan hadn't said anything to him about going south. Meanwhile the conductor had decided to follow standard practice; they stopped several times to drop off empties and take on cars of logs.

It seemed to Demidov that what had happened at Hautaharju had caught up with Ikola. Early on, the Finn had gone to the restrooom and not reappeared for quite a while. When he did, his eyelids were swollen and spongy looking, his face pasty pale. Now he sat as if dead, his features slack, and he did not talk at all. Even Lytikäinen and Dufva left him to himself.

Vuorinen gave Demidov his first Finnish lesson: "*olen*, I am; *olet*, you are; *hän on*, he or she is..." The language, Vuorinen told him, was so conservative, a modern Finn could read the ancient books. It came, she said, from the tradition of learning ancient verse verbatim, and from pronouncing everything the way it was spelled. *Perhaps*, thought Demidov. *But at a deeper level it came from valuing the old, even while adapting to and living with the new.*

Six hours after they'd left Sahakylä, the conductor announced they were approaching the village of Susilähde, where they would eat again. About time, Demidov thought; his stomach had been grumbling. "Susilähde." *Susi*, Anna told him, was Finnish for stobor, although on Earth it had meant a different pack-hunting animal. *Lähde* meant a spring of water. He sat repeating the name to himself, to the measure of the wheels clicking over the expansion joints in the rails.

* * *

It was near noon when they arrived, noon in a forty-hour day, and it was warm, nearly hot. Walking down the graveled street in the rays of Byers' Sun, Demidov sweated. Migruder hadn't gotten off the train with them; hadn't eaten since Tammipuro, and presumably had puked up that. Or had it been nothing more than diarrhea? As he walked, Demidov drilled the verb to be: *olen, olet, hän on, se on; olemme, olette...*

Inside the tavern was half dark. No light burned. The place seemed deserted. Demidov looked in past Ikola, who'd led off from the train and stood just inside the doorway. The Finn called a halloo in Finnish, and the tavernkeeper came in from a back room. Then they all entered. "We cannot cook," the tavernkeeper said simply. "There is no electricity."

"No electricity?" Ikola sounded more vexed than surprised. "Those Sauron bastards! There won't be any at the railroad either then. The engineer won't be able to recharge the batteries."

Anna interpreted for Demidov while the others cursed or stood silent.

"How did it happen?" Demidov asked, and Anna passed his question on.

"It's damned obvious!" Ikola said angrily. "The Sauron sons of bitches have bombed the dam at Rajakuilu! They can't leave anything alone! They want to send us back to the stone age!"

He turned to the tavernkeeper. "When did this happen?"

"Less than an hour ago."

"Can you feed us cold food?"

"*Limppu* and butter, cold boiled eggs, some cold meat...I might as well use the meat up; there's no refrigeration now. Uno and Arvo are digging a cold hole on the shady side of the tavern, like in the old days. When they're done, I can keep things in it. But not frozen; not in summer."

They went to the table and sat down in the half-dark. There were only seven of them now, the three Finnish forestry people plus one from the Minerals Ministry, along with Anna Vuorinen, Demidov, and Migruder's interpreter, Morgan. The tavernkeeper, who'd sent his cook home, went into the kitchen and clattered around. Meanwhile there was no radio—no music, no news bulletins.

The conductor came stamping in. "There is no power!" he said. "I cannot recharge the batteries!"

"Tell us something we don't know," growled Lytikäinen, and gestured at the wooden chandelier, lightless overhead.

"How far can we go on the charge left in the batteries?" Ikola asked.

The conductor shook his head. "I don't know. Not all the way to Metsäjoki though, I think. The engineer should he here soon. He'll at least have some idea."

They ate in a silence broken only once, by the tavernkeeper. "You really think they've blown up the dam?" he asked Ikola.

"I don't know it," Ikola answered, "but I feel sure of it. I've never heard of the power failing in Koillinen Province before. Not along the railroad, anyway."

The cook stared thoughtfully at an upper corner of the room, then brightened. "When I was a boy, there was a big wood range in the kitchen here, and a tall, wood-burning oven. My father made me split wood for them each day. I think they may be in Pesonen's old barn. I could move them back in here." He paused. "But it wouldn't be worthwhile if the trains don't run. I wonder if they cut up the old wood-burning engines for scrap?"

Perhaps, Demidov thought, *the dam wasn't blown up. Perhaps somehow the power line was broken. True it was underground, but there might have been a landslide somewhere along the line, or a torrent.* He shook his head. *No. The dam is blown up.*

The engineer came in then, swearing. "*Saatana!*" Those bastards have really done it to us! Now I can't recharge the batteries!"

"How close to Metsäjoki can we get without a recharge?" Ikola asked.

"What's the point of going to Metsäjoki?" the engineer countered. "There won't be any electricity there either. Take my word for it."

"The point is the reserve armory there."

The engineer said nothing for a long half minute. "You think the Saurons will come even here? To Koillinen Province?"

"Maybe, maybe not; we need to be prepared." Ikola repeated his question then, "How far can we get?"

"I'm not sure. We might get halfway."

"That's a lot closer than this," Lytikäinen said.

"Shit." The engineer looked dejected. "I'm only two standard years short of my pension. And now this! And Erkki"—he indicated the conductor—"is almost as close."

"Four and a half," the conductor said. He looked as if he hadn't considered that aspect of it before. "Those rotten bastards!"

The room was quiet then, except for the sounds of tableware and eating. When they were done, they left, but not until Lytikäinen and the conductor had each bought a liter of whiskey. Demidov wondered if the tavernkeeper would be paid for their meals, now that the trains had stopped. He also wondered if it would make any difference. Would the economy continue in some sort of clumsy fashion, adjusting as it went?

The sun shone as if nothing had happened. The radio had said the radioactive plume from the power plant was drifting south. At least they didn't have that to worry about. At least not yet.

Partway to the train they met Migruder coming down the street. He was drunk and looked truculent. The rest went on while Ikola, Dufva, and Morgan tried to talk the Nevadan into turning around and going back to the train. Anna Vuorinen waited nearby in the shade of a steelwood tree. When Migruder insisted on eating first, Dufva and Morgan started with him to the tavern. They'd grab something he could eat on the train, Dufva said. Ikola and Demidov, with Vuorinen, began sauntering back toward the railroad.

* * *

They were eighty meters from the train when Ikola heard the howl of a fighter's heavy engines. Instinctively, without ever having heard the sound before, he sprinted for the cover of a cluster of trees near the street, the others a jump behind. A series of explosions stunned them, and the locomotive and passenger cars split apart where they stood, pieces of debris raining down for ten seconds or more.

Ikola was up and running again. After their heads cleared, Demidov and Vuorinen dashed after him.

Indeed the stone age! They were even destroying the railroad rolling stock.

They didn't find actual bodies, only what was left of them: the engineer's in the wreckage of the locomotive cab, the conductor's in the first car, Lytikäinen's and the man from Minerals in the second. By that time Dufva and Morgan had run up too, and within minutes there were some hundred townspeople as well. And Migruder. The Nevadan looked sober now, Ikola thought, sober and full of anger. Somehow Ikola's own anger had receded. *Migruder! I should tell him he saved our lives*, Ikola told himself. *He'd really he mad then.*

Susilähde had a reserve rifle platoon, with its own small armory that held nothing heavier than rifles. One of its radiomen called battalion headquarters at Metsäjoki. The armory there was intact; presumably the Saurons hadn't recognized it.

Within the hour, Ikola, a captain in the reserves, had signed out several surplus packsacks, canteens and sleeping bags from the supply sergeant, along with five assault rifles, magazine belts, and an automatic pistol. All of them, including Vuorinen, had worn heavy woods boots when they'd left Hautaharju. The tavernkeeper provided them with potatoes and turnips and a large block of cheese. It was 130 kilometers to Metsäjoki, with no guarantee what they'd find there, but there were two small villages along the way, and some logging camps. With luck they wouldn't have to sleep out in the chill of dimday or the hard cold of true night.

Ikola had given one of the packs to Migruder and one to Morgan. Migruder was grimly determined to walk the thousand or so kilometers to New Reno. Like the others, he had a small stock of groceries, but supplemented with two liters of whiskey. He'd had a revolver in his luggage all along, and had salvaged it from the wreckage. Now it rode in its holster at his waist.

Finally they started for the railroad again: Ikola, Dufva, Demidov, and Anna Vuorinen. And Morgan; Morgan was going with the Finns. His mother had been Finnish—it was she who'd taught him the language—and he'd had a bellyful of Migruder.

They didn't know what the world situation would be when they arrived at Metsäjoki.

Migruder too walked to the railroad, but apart from the others and somewhat behind them. When they reached the right-of-way, Ikolo told the others to go on, he'd catch up with them. Then he waited till Migruder arrived.

"Migruder," he said.

The Nevadan didn't answer, merely stopped and scowled.

"Good luck," Ikola said in Americ, and held out his hand.

Migruder stared for a moment, first at the hand, then into Ikola's face and his hostility seemed to fade. Nonetheless he turned without answering or meeting Ikola's proffered hand. He simply showed his broad back and started south along the right-of-way past the string of log cars on the siding. Ikola watched him go, then turning, strode north past the wreckage.

The others had gone only a little way, glancing back. Now they stopped to wait. Ikola caught up with them, and together they hiked north along the tracks, past the railyard and into the forest.

The Stoor's Map

Introduction

One evening in 1990, Brian Thomsen, a senior editor at Warner Books, called and said that he and Baird Searles were planning a theme anthology to be titled *Halflings, Hobbits, Warrows & Wee-folk*. He had a great piece of cover art for it—a Hildebrandt!—and wondered if I'd write a story to go with the cover.

I said I'd have to see the picture first. When I saw it, I loved it. "The Stoor's Map" is the story that grew out of it.

* * *

Rory Hoy heaved on the stout oak pry pole with all the hard strength of his forty-four pounds, and felt the stone pallet's edge lift a bit. Liam Maqsween got a deeper purchase with his own then, and in a moment the granite block slid off both pallet and cart, thudding heavily to the ground. Liam straightened and wiped sweat from his forehead with the big red kerchief that normally hung like a flag from his pocket. Then both men hopped down from the low cart.

"Well, lad," said Liam, "that's it for the day. Come in and I'll pay you." They went into the low shed, one end of which served as his office, and from a chest beside his writing table he took a purse, loosening the drawstring and peering inside. Plucking out a silver half crown, he pressed it into the younger man's thick hand.

"Thank thee, sir."

Liam nodded. "Thank you for the help," he said, completing the formula. Then added, "I've got odds and ends to tend to in the smithy in the morning—small tasks that won't need help. Meet me at the quarry after lunch."

"Noon at the quarry. I'll be there, Mr. Maqsween."

Rory stuffed the half crown in his pocket and left the office.

That last block had taken a while to cut and drag. Then add the loading and hauling...And his mother didn't stand for coming late to the table; he'd best take his supper at the inn. That was an advantage in being the innkeeper's son; he could eat there without charge, since he paid full board at home.

The graveled road, the only road, wound through Meadowvale, curling around low stone houses that had been built not in rows but wherever the builders had built them, starting four hundred years earlier when Meadowvale was newly settled. The inn was near the village center, at one end of the common, where spreading elms awaited picnickers, and where, on fall evenings, young tomtaihn, kin to hobbits, stood in the dusk, rakes in hand around burning leaf piles, talking in the fragrant smoke.

Hoy's Inn was more a tavern than an inn, for Meadowvale, being well within the Great Forest, was small, and saw few travelers. In olden times, the founders of Meadowvale had lived in or around the town of Oak Hill, thirty leagues away. Until, some four hundred years back, the big people arrived, and said the land belonged now to King Gnaup of Saxmark.

Around Oak Hill, the countryside was rolling farmland, with woods mainly on the steeper slopes and along the streams. And Oak Hill itself had been—no doubt still was—a town, not a village. A sizable stream, the Abhainn Hobb, flowed past it from the south, and a highway passed through from southwest to northeast, with a bridge over the Hobb. There'd been both barge traffic and wagon traffic, and folk traveling through on ponyback. Thus there'd been a need in Oak Hill for a sizable inn, with rooms and beds large enough for stoors. (The rare big people who'd come by, however, had slept in the stable, in the hay; the rooms hadn't been *that* big.) The Oak Hill innkeepers, the Hoy family, had been both well-to-do and influential; Hoys had been sheriff, even mayor.

Here in Meadowvale though, they were no more than most other families. Which grated on the Hoys, even after four hundred years.

Just now, Rory Hoy wasn't thinking about that, though. He was thinking about roast beef, parsnips, and buttered beets, or maybe sweet yellow peas, with wheat bread and butter, a wedge of good Mirrorudh cheese, and perhaps a mug of his father's ale, if the old tomteen wasn't watching closely. (Nob Hoy didn't approve of youngsters drinking, especially on the house, and the tomtaihn regarded twenty-five-year-olds as youngsters.)

Rory went in through the kitchen—the front way was for pay-ing guests—though he'd eat in the pot room, the common room, with the customers.

"Rory!"

The sharp voice was his father's. "Yessir?"

"Doney's off on an errand for me, and there's a customer waiting to be served; a stoor. See to it!"

"Yessir." It wasn't fair, Rory thought; he'd worked hard all day. But he put a good face on, and went into the pot room.

The stoor was hulking and angular, ill-fitted to the bench and table. Meadowvale could go months without seeing one, and the villagers had mixed feelings about them. Stoors were wanderers, not settled reliable folk, though surely they had homes some-where, with mothers and fathers. Mostly they traveled singly, which in itself made them strange to the social, even gregarious tomtaihn. They traded, bought, and sold. Bargains could be had from them, or what seemed like bargains—things you couldn't otherwise get, at a price you were content with, or at least willing to pay. But people had been fleeced by them, too, and it was rumored that some were spies for King Hreolf.

"Sir," Rory said, "may I serve you?"

The stoor's black eyes were level with Rory's own, though the stoor was seated and the bench low. He was far smaller than big people, but he'd probably stand an ell in height, Rory thought, about half again his own thirty-one inches. The face was lean and knobby—checkbones, brows, and jaw—flagged with great flaring eyebrows like wings, and topped by a thatch of stiff, curly hair. The hands were knobby too, with tufts of wiry hair on the fingers.

The stoor looked the tomteen over and spoke in a thick stoor brogue. "Tha's weerin' a smith's leather apron," he said, ignoring the young tomteen's question.

"Yessir. A quarryman's apron, actually. May I serve you?"

"Tha's just koom fra work, then?"

"Yessir. To eat my supper. My father's the host here, and the potboy is off on errands, so he told me to serve you. What would you like?" He recited the fare to the man, then, and the stoor ordered, seeming not to consider cost, though his clothes were rough and worn. When Rory brought his food, the stoor motioned to the bench across from him.

"Tha hasn't eaten. Happen tha'd sup wi' me."

The temptation was strong. Rory had never talked with a

stoor before, had scarcely seen one close up. In fact, he hadn't talked to a stranger of any sort more than three or four times in his life, and those had been tomtaihn from other villages. And if the stoor *was* a spy for King Hreolf, surely there was nothing he could tell him that would harm Meadowvale.

So though his father might well berate him for it afterward, he brought his own meal to the table, and they talked. The stoor, instead of pumping Rory, told him of places the young tomteen had never heard of. He favored the Great Forest and the districts adjacent though, he said. For the stoors, like the other halfling folk, had the protection of the Forest Soul. Otherwise he'd not travel here, where trolls, it was said, could be met with.

When he'd finished eating, he took his purse from his pack and shook out some coins, to sort the cost with knobby fingers. Several of the coins seemed to be gold! The young tomteen's eyes widened. "Sir," he said, almost in a whisper, "are those—gold pieces?"

The winglike eyebrows rose while the stoor's voice lowered. "Aye. Would tha keer to be toochin' one of 'em?"

"If I might. I've never seen one before." Rory picked one up. The currency used in Meadowvale was mostly old and worn smooth, minted long ago at Oak Hill in the days of tomtaidh dominion there, though other coins, mostly Saxi, were also seen, having entered the Meadowvale economy through trade with the occasional traveler. This one looked—not fresh minted perhaps, but not worn. Though the marks on it, he thought, might be dwarf runes. "Do you know where it came from?" he asked.

The stoor looked around before answering, as if to be sure that no one else heard. "Oh, aye! Tha mought say, in a manner of speakin'. Near enough ah'd gaw for more, if ah—Though 'tis a dangerous place, s'truth. 'Twere a long time agaw, an ah'd plenty of time, ah tawd maself. But theer were always another place to see, an' ah were never one to set great store on wealth. Long as ah'm eatin'." He gestured as if pointing out his own worn clothes, then shrugged. "An naw that ah'm so near the place, ah dawn't be yoong an' venturesome naw more."

The stoor didn't look so old to Rory, maybe fifty. Stoor bodies must wear out more quickly than tomtaidh bodies, he decided. "There's more gold then?" he asked. "Near here?"

"Hoo! More? A whole cask more!" He motioned with his hands as if to indicate size, a chest more than two feet long, and half as wide and high. "Thaw not all gold; some o' it's jewels—rubies and emeralds and pearls. Ah only tewk a handful. Ah were afoot—hadn't naw pony—an'...'Twas near the Dank Land, tha sees, wi' trawlls an' bears abawt, an' wargs an' worse. An' the Forest Soul dawn't tooch there." The stoor's brow knitted, as if in troubled thought. "The Dank Land's got its awn soul, dark..." He shrugged. "Though naw doot a bold lad with a good pony, if he didn't linger..." Another shrug. "But ah'm nae yoong naw. Mah awd knays dawn't let me climb brants naw more, nor clamber through rocks and windfalls.

As for bein' near—It's naw farther, or not mooch, than a long day's pony ride. Even given that the way's through trackless forest and rough hills." He waved toward the west, then suddenly thrust his face at the young tomteen, his voice a whisper. "Why? Were tha thinkin' of gawin' theer?"

Rory didn't flinch. "If you'd draw me a map," he murmured. "I'd pay."

The black eyes examined him thoughtfully. "Can I troost thee?"

Rory nodded vigorously, though unsure where trust entered in, or where it might lead.

"What would tha pay for sooch a map?"

Rory knew exactly how much money he had, including the half crown in his pocket, and being a Hoy, named a sum that left room for dickering. "Twenty-five crowns."

The stoor shook his head. "'Tis worth far more than that."

"Thirty then."

The stoor examined him thoughtfully. "Ah'd take naw less than a hoondred."

Rory felt his hopes fall like the granite block had when pried from the cart.

"Ah'll tell thee what. Tha'rt an honest-lewkin' lad, an' ah have little doot tha's a man o' thy word. So ah'll take the risk. Besides, ah'm gettin' naw yoonger. An' if a hoondred crowns is more than tha has naw—why later, with the treasure cask in thy cellar, payin' a hoondred will seem like nawthin' to thee." The stoor looked around again, then murmured: "Fifty crowns naw, an' a hoondred more when ah next koom through Meadowvale. Which ah'll make a point of doin' within the year."

"Thirty-eight," the young tomteen said desperately. "It's all I have." Then he remembered the coin in his pocket. "Thirty-eight

and a half. And the other hundred for sure, when I've got the treasure."

The stoor seemed to brood on it a long minute. Then, "Bring
me a paper," he said. "Naw, a parchment. Paper's naw good for
sunthin' 'portant as this."

*Parchment? Where could he lay hands on a parch-
ment?...*"Wait here a minute, sir," said Rory, "I'll be right back."
He left the room then, deliberately not hurrying. Once outside
though, he speeded to a trot. His home was less than forty yards
away, and as he walked through the front door, no one was in the
living room. He could hear his mother in the kitchen, rattling
pans. What he sought was on the wall, a parchment perhaps a
dozen inches on a side, with a motto inked on it:

HE WHO WOULD HAVE
MUST FIRST LABOR
THEN HOLD

and coins in watercolors. A great-grandmother had made it. With
a tough thumbnail, the young tomteen pried the tacks from the
corners, then went quietly to his room, where he kept his money,
and left with it.

It could be days before anyone missed the parchment, he told
himself. It had been there forever; people rarely looked at it anymore. And by the time it was missed, he'd be rich. Then no one
would mind, not even his mother.

* * *

Sween Maqsween, his missus Aleen, and Megh, their only
daughter, were in the sitting room. The supper things had been
put away, and Megh, like her mother, sat embroidering. Megh
was good at needlework, as at most things she did.

The figure her needle was shaping was a young tomteen, well
formed and with the rare, coppery red hair that made all the lasses
of Meadowvale cluck and coo at the sight of Rory Hoy, the hand-
somest lad in the valley.

There was a knock at the door, and as the only offspring
present, Megh got to her feet and answered. At twenty-six inches
in height and twenty-eight pounds, to get off a chair was no effort
at all, surely not for someone just nineteen years old.

It was Rory Hoy she opened to. Pleased, she asked him in.

Among the tomtaihn, a young person, child or grown, doesn't enter the home of a peer and begin a conversation until respects have been paid to any parent present. Thus when he stepped in, Rory bowed deeply.

"Good evening, Mister Maqsween, Missus Maqsween. I trust the Forest Soul is being good to you."

"Come in, young Hoy," the old tomteen grunted. "The Forest Soul is as good to us as we deserve, no more, no less." The formula complete, he raised an eyebrow. "I suppose it's Megh you've come too see."

"Begging your pardon, sir, ma'am, it is indeed."

"Well, then," the old man said, and gestured to two chairs in a corner by the family bookshelf.

"Begging your pardon, sir, but I'd hoped to speak in greater privacy than this."

Both eyebrows rose this time. "Did you now? Are you thinking we'd eavesdrop, the missus and me?"

"Sir," Rory answered, "I have no doubt you'd never strain to listen, but the room is small, and it would be hard not to hear."

"Hmh!" Rory could feel the old tomteen's eyes sharpen. "And what might it be you'd not want us to hear?"

He dug in his heels. Politely. "Sir, ma'am, you were young and unwed once. What was it you said to one another then?"

Aleen Maqsween hid a smile, while old Sween's eyebrows, instead of rising again, drew down in a knot. "You're overbold, young Hoy."

"Yessir. I'm sorry, sir."

"And you Meghwan, do you wish to step outside with this young scoundrel?"

She blushed. "Yes, Father."

The frown relaxed and died. "So." He reached to his smoking stand, then turned to his daughter while he packed his pipe with pipeweed. "Meghwan, you may go out and sit with this young man in the arbor for the time it takes me to smoke two bowls. But by the time I knock the dottle from my pipe, you're to be back inside."

She brightened. "Thank you, Da. We'll be perfectly nice."

"Hmh!" Old Sween watched them move to the door. "And Meghwan!"

"Yes, Da?"

"*No kissing!*"

Megh Maqsween blushed. "Da! Of course not!" The young people stepped outside then, closing the door behind them.

Aleen Maqsween laughed quietly, gently, when they'd gone, and mimicked her daughter. "'Da! Of course not!'" She laughed again. "You're hard on the lad, Maqsween."

"Indeed. He'd not know what to think if I wasn't. And after all, he's only twenty-five. He's five more years, or four and a half, before he's of marrying age." Maqsween grunted again. "It's too bad he got interested in the girl so young." He reached, and squeezed his wife's hand gently. "It's not easy, being in love with the prettiest girl in the valley, and having to wait. I know. But it's my duty to see that he does."

* * *

Megh let Rory hold her hand while they walked to the arbor. A humpbacked moon rode high, the moonlight shining on her straw-blond hair. There'd not been a tomteen with hair like hers, in Meadowvale, since Maev the Lovely, some hundred years since, and Maev lacked the sweet disposition of Megh Maqsween. Also Megh was lovelier, Rory was sure, a fairy child grown to womanhood. He longed to cup her face and kiss it tenderly. He had once, and it had troubled her.

Now, at the arbor, she sat down on the single seat, leaving him to sit alone on the double seat opposite. "What was it thou came to tell me, Rory?" she asked.

And her eyes were blue, in Meadowvale a rarity almost as great as her blond hair, though her grandmother had blue eyes before her.

"Rory?"

"Oh! Yes. I—I'm going to be rich, Megheen."

"Rich?"

He reached inside his shirt, took out the parchment, and held it so the moonlight shone on it for her. "Look!"

She peered, straining. "He who would have..." she began.

"Oh! Sorry," he said, and turned it over. "This side."

"It...Is it a map?"

"A treasure map."

"Treasure map? Where did you get it?"

"From a stoor, at the inn. He sold it to me."

"And it's real? How do you know?"

The question jarred Rory, jarred words out of him. "He was wealthy. Oh, not that he dressed wealthy, but his purse...I waited on him, and when it was time to pay, he opened his purse and poured part of it out on the table. So full of gold pieces it was, he had to sort through them to find coppers to pay with! Old coins, with dwarf runes on them! And pearls, emeralds, rubies! My eyes were out to here!" He gestured.

"And he sold you the map?"

"He did!"

"For how much?"

"All the money I had—thirty-eight crowns. Thirty-eight and a half, but he left me the half crown. Plus another hundred I'm to pay him when he next comes by. He trusts me. And a hundred crowns will seem like nothing to me then, I'll be so wealthy."

"But—Why would he sell you the map? He could go there himself and get the treasure."

"You'd have to see him to understand. He's old, old and lame. And the treasure's hard to get to, in a cave in the Cliffy Mountains. On the side toward the Dank Land!"

Her eyes were large in the moonlight, large and shadowed dark.

"Oh, Megheen!" he whispered, "my love, you're so beautiful! And I love you so much! I can't stand to wait another four years. With the treasure, I'll be rich enough, no one will complain if we marry young. We'll give a wedding party they'll talk about forever!"

He looked longingly at her.

"And I love you, Rory Hoy. Enough that, wait or not, rich or not, you're the one I'll marry."

He slid off the seat onto his knees before her. Her hands had been folded in her lap, and he took them in his own, kissing them passionately. Gently she removed them. "Da will be smoking that second pipe by now."

Rory Hoy got slowly to his feet. Surely not the second pipe already. But she was right: it wouldn't do to stay out here kissing her like that in the night. It would tear him up inside.

She stood too, and hand in hand they walked back to the house, saying nothing.

When he left the Maqsweens', despondency settled on Rory Hoy, and a feeling of unworthiness. He saw himself now as gull-

ible, a fool, and he'd lied to Megh—been less than truthful. Even
the night was darker; clouds covered the moon now. It would rain
tonight, he guessed. He hoped it would be over by morning.

* * *

It was pitch-dark when he awoke, as he'd intended when he'd
laid down. He went to his window and, looking out, saw stars.
Which meant dawn was near, for the moon was down, and it was
late in the second quarter.

It was time.

He'd packed everything he needed, before ever he'd snuffed
his candle. Now he had only to pull on his clothes, buckle his belt,
grab his pack, and leave. He'd left his window open to the night;
even mosquitoes don't bite halflings where the Forest Soul rules.
Now he climbed out and trotted softly to the pony barn.

Not only the grass was wet, but the dirt as well. It had rained
while he slept, as he'd thought it would.

In the barn he'd prepared too. The pack saddle and straps
he'd set on the floor, just inside the door. He went to Blacky, the
pony he'd chosen, led him outside and strapped the pack saddle to
his back. The pony nickered softly, and Rory hushed him. His
mother was a light sleeper (though not as light as he thought), and
it wouldn't do to waken her.

As he led it toward the road, he saw a rider approaching, a
large, dark figure on a large, dark pony, with a pack pony trailing.
The stoor, he thought, and held back, not wanting to meet him.
An emptiness filled him as he watched the stoor ride by. It seemed
to him the man had tricked him, that there was no treasure, that
he'd given his life savings for—a piece of sky.

He pushed the thought away. It was done now. The stoor had
cheated him or he hadn't. If he hadn't, there was a treasure out
there, waiting. A treasure that could make the Hoys rich again,
important again, that would make his father respect him at last. A
treasure that would let him marry Megh Maqsween without waiting all those years.

The stoor and his animals passed on down the road, and Rory
Hoy started off, jaw set. He stopped at the inn, tying his pony to a
pear tree in back. Lantern light shone through the rear windows;
his cousin Doney would be inside, firing up the big cookstove,
and the ovens for the morning's baking.

Doney was surprised to see him, and even more to see the short sword at his side. As Rory packed food for three days, he explained to Doney that he had business to attend to. Doney, who was seventeen, stared wide-eyed; it sounded very mysterious.

The first hint of dawnlight was showing in the east when Rory left. He paused at the Maqsween smithy, and on the anvil left a note to Liam, prepared the evening before, weighting it with a chisel.

Visibility was improving notably when he reached the upper end of the meadow from which Meadowvale took its name. According to the rough map the stoor had drawn for him, he needed to follow the Mirrorudh west to its source in the Cliffy Mountains. There'd be a pass above the headwaters, of course, and on the other side, the headwaters of another stream, one that flowed into the Dank Land. Where that stream flowed out of the mountains, the map showed a talus slide at the foot of a steep, a "brant" the stoor had called it, and near the talus slide, a cave. The cave. According to the map.

The young tomteen ground his teeth. The treasure he'd believed in without questioning, the evening before, he greatly doubted now. Disbelieved. And was sure that Megh had disbelieved when he'd told her. But he'd carry through with his plan; it was the only way he could truly and finally know.

* * *

At age thirty, a young man was sent out of his father's home, unless of course the old man was dead or disabled and he the inheriting son. And while old Sween Maqsween had had a foot crushed by a granite block that slipped from a sling, he could hobble well enough to take care of a man's duties about the house and garden.

Thus Liam Maqsween lived in a bachelor house at the upper end of the valley, against the very edge of the forest, not a furlong from where Rory Hoy had passed in the first faint light of dawn. At Oak Hill, their ancestors had followed the old custom of living in hillside burrows, and this bachelor house, with its thick rock walls, was dug into the side of a low hummock, looking like a stony extension of it. On the hummock stood a huge golden birch with curling yellow bark that seemed almost to grow from the mossy, sod-covered slate roof.

An old widow came in each evening to cook a proper meal; the others were each bachelor's own responsibility. The sun was up, and Liam Maqsween had eaten bacon and eggs, with bread toasted in the oven and spread with butter and marmalade. Now he sat outside in the sunshine, which felt good in the morning cool, smoking his pipe and drinking a cup of shade-mint tea before going to the smithy. It had rained in the night, laying the dust and sweetening the air.

While he drank, his young cousin Tom came trotting up. "Liam," said the lad, "I've just come from your da's. Megh's gone! Disappeared!" Tom's job it was to climb the ladder into Sween Maqsween's hayloft each morning and throw down hay for the cow and ponies. While he was doing it, old Sween had stumped out to the barn and told him, asking him to bring the message. The old man was upset, as well he might be.

Liam thanked him, quickly finished his tea, and hurried off to his parents' house. Megh had left on her pony before they'd wakened, they told him, taking only her cloak and raincape, a loaf of bread, and some cheese.

"And have you no idea where she might have gone?" Liam asked.

"I've a suspicion," his father answered. "Rory Hoy was here last evening and asked to speak to her alone. I agreed, and they went to the arbor to talk. She was back sooner than I could smoke a pipe, but long enough to set some plan in motion, something they'd thought out beforehand. I think they've run off," he finished glumly.

Liam went out and saddled a pony, thinking as he did. He didn't believe she'd do that, or that Rory would ask her to. But then, he didn't know what else to think. He'd ride by the Hoys and ask for Rory, then decide what next to do.

Margo Hoy was no help to him. She didn't know where her son was, she said. He'd gone before breakfast. If Liam found him, he was to tell him his mother was upset with him. It scarcely needed telling; Margo Hoy was usually upset with someone, most often her son. Liam promised and left.

So. Rory and Megh had both disappeared. It seemed his father suspected rightly. But where would they have gone? Five leagues north was Troutrudh, the largest of the three tomtaidh villages in the forest. Four leagues south was Mulberry, smaller than Meadowvale. If a lad was to run off, he'd need to find work, and

Troutrudh was the likeliest for that. But...Liam shook his head. It didn't add up. Rory had at least some idea what it cost to keep a home and wife. What would there be for him in Troutrudh, or anywhere else? His whole family lived in Meadowvale, and all his friends.

Muttering a coarse word beneath his mustache, Liam touched the pony's ribs with his heels and rode home. If he was going to ride to Troutrudh, he'd want his raincape, and happen his cloak to sleep in, if it came to that.

On his way, he stopped at the smithy. He'd forged an ax head for a customer, earlier that week. He'd lay it out on the bench, with a note, so the purchaser could pick it up, should he stop by. On the anvil he found the note that Rory had left him. "Dear Mister Maqsween—I'm sorry I won't be able to meet you at the quarry after lunch. Something has come up. I hope to be back in a few days. I'll tell you about it then. Respectfully, Rory Hoy."

Somehow it made the hair bristle on Liam's neck. He stared hard at the note, as if to see what lay behind it, but saw nothing that wasn't written. On an impulse he went outside and scanned the moist ground for tracks. And found hoofprints, shod, left since last night's rain. They had to be Rory's.

He jogged his pony home, where he got not only his raincape and cloak, but his short sword and bow. Then he took the sporting arrows from his quiver and replaced them with the broad-headed arrows that each male tomteen kept to defend the village, should it ever be necessary. As he did, he wondered why. He'd never shoot Rory, or strike him with the sword.

He took them anyway, then rode back to the smithy and followed the tracks. Near the forest's edge they came to the Mirrorudh, where he found a second set, of a smaller pony. Megh's, he had no doubt. So they'd connived. He shook his head.

They'd ridden into the forest, along the stream. Her pony followed; here and there it's hoof marks lay atop the larger. In the forest though, in places, the tracks separated, as if Megh was picking a different way around the occasional patches of blowdown. Then they'd rejoin. Almost as if they hadn't ridden together—as if they were going to the same place separately, with the Mirrorudh their guide.

None of it made sense. There was nothing for them in the forest—no way to live, to shelter and feed themselves. Yet if they were looking for privacy—if that was all—they needn't have gone more than a furlong into the woods. Nor would they have run off in a way to make themselves missed, and invite pursuit.

Liam shook his head as if to shake off confusion. He thought of simply following the stream himself—it would be faster than watching for hoofprints—but if he did and they left it, he'd lose them. Best keep on as he was. They'd surely stop to rest along the way; he'd catch them then.

* * *

As a boy with other boys, Rory had explored up the Mirrorudh as much as a mile, a long distance for short tomtaidh legs, particularly in pathless wilderness. Now he'd gone well beyond that, dismounting at times to lead his pony through sapling patches or awkward terrain. For the low rolling hills of home had given way to higher, rougher hills, and pack saddles weren't made for comfortable riding.

Here the Mirrorudh had cut a ravine, and he'd had to leave it, riding and walking along a bordering ridge, sometimes on the crest, sometimes picking his way along the side. It was noon, give or take a bit, and broken ground had shunted him into a notch, shaggy with firs. Now, close before his pony, a rivulet rattled over a pebbled bed toward the Mirrorudh, itself audible a distance to his right.

He paused to wipe sweat, and wondered if these were the Cliffy Mountains yet, or if there was worse to come.

Meanwhile it seemed a good place to eat. He led the pony to the rivulet, then on hands and knees, lowered his face to the water, just upcurrent of his thirsty mount. Thirst slaked, he refilled his leather flask, and moved to take his rucksack from the pack saddle.

A jay began to shriek on the slope behind him, the same jay, he guessed, that had called alarms at his own passing, minutes earlier. *What's roused it now?* he wondered. *Bear? Wolf? Troll?* The possibilities interested but didn't worry him. The Forest Soul had laid her protection over halflings. Within her domain, only creatures with souls of their own—men and other halflings—could harm him. Even his pony was immune when he was with it.

He stood with a hand on the reins, hoping to spy something interesting. In his whole life, all he'd ever seen of wolf and bear was tracks and dung, though once he'd thought he'd seen a troll at twilight, peering from the forest's edge.

The jay continued for a noisy minute, and having done its duty, stilled. Then Rory heard shod hooves clatter on rock outcrop, and curiosity became concern. Quickly he led the pony behind a thicket of sapling firs, and peered out. Shortly he saw movement, glimpsed first a dun hide, then a bobbing pony head. Then the entire pony came into view, with its rider.

Rory stared. "Megh!" he called softly, and led his own pony out where she could see.

"Rory!" Her expression was of relief, gladness.

He met her at the rivulet, took her hand and helped her down. "What are you doing here?"

"I—It seemed to me that—you might not come back. If you were disappointed. If the stoor had lied to you. But if I was with you, you would." She paused, then spoke more softly. "And I don't want to lose you."

"Ah, Megheen!" He longed to take her in his arms, but held back. It would be risky, and unfair to both of them.

Her eyes met his, soberly. "Have you eaten yet?" she asked.

He shook his head.

"Neither have I."

"Well then—"

They ate by the rivulet, side by side on a rock, while their ponies, one dun, one black, grazed a patch of clover on the bank. When they'd finished, they looked again at the map. With her there, somehow hope took root in Rory's heart. Maybe there was a treasure; maybe they'd return rich to Meadowvale.

Then they got on their ponies again and rode west.

*   *   *

In midafternoon they reached a bowl-like cove, the birthplace of the Mirrorudh, the spring that gave it being. The climb to the divide above, though not rough or long, was steep; the two tomtaihn hiked it to spare their ponies. The crest was mostly stone, its trees sparse. From it they looked back over miles of high hills that diminished eastward. Westward they dropped more sharply, to the Dank Lands that stretched flat to the horizon, partly wooded, partly open fen, bathed in sunlight but somehow murky.

The two young tomtaihn stood for a minute. "Best we go on,"

Rory said at last and, meshing his fingers for a step, boosted Megh atop her pony. Then he climbed onto his own, and they set off downhill. The creek below, according to his map, would take them to the cave and wealth. Or not, as the case might be.

They'd gone scarcely a furlong when a fly bit Rory's temple. He'd never been bitten before.

* * *

The troll had little tolerance for daylight, and in summer, when nights were short, he grew restless toward sundown.

On this particular day he'd sheltered in a hole where a pine had been uprooted by wind, and hung up in the tops of others. Between the uptilted root disk and the lip of the hole, there'd been just room for him to crawl in. He'd slept there most of the day. Then hunger had wakened him, strong hunger; he hadn't eaten for two days, and trolls are notorious for their appetites.

Now he lay peering out, eyes squinted nearly shut against what to him was blinding glare, though the late sunlight was soft, mellow. A movement caught his eyes, and through the blur he saw two animals moving down the creek, each big enough to feed him for a day. They'd pass him seventy or eighty yards away. Their scent on the breeze was complex and unfamiliar, though perhaps long ago...His mouth began to water, and he strained to see more clearly. One of them had two necks, one at the front where it belonged, the second rising from the middle of its back. The other—The other seemed to be following something that walked upright.

He shook his shaggy head. Before long the sun would set. When the dusk was thick enough, he'd come out and follow them, follow and kill them, for he trailed by scent.

They were passing in front of him when the spider came, one of the great spiders that even he took care to avoid.

* * *

Rory saw it before Megh did, saw it charge from ambush across the foot of a talus slope, charge so fast, so shockingly fast, he had no time to draw his sword. He didn't see Megh's dun rear back, didn't see her fall, and her scream didn't register. Then the spider was on him, clawed front limbs grasping, palps clutching, and in a moment beyond horror he saw the two great jaws gape, each with its curved fang, then mercifully passed out. The fangs sank into his shoulders, and from them venom flowed.

Because he'd gone limp, the fangs withdrew more quickly than they might have. Then the spinnerets secreted thread almost as thick as wrapping cord, and sticky, the spider wrapping them 'round and 'round him till the tomteen was nearly mummified. But the mummy was porous. It was no part of the spider's intention that he suffocate.

When he was wrapped, it went to Megh Maqsween, who lay in an unconscious heap where she'd landed. It bit her briefly and wrapped her too. Then, with its palps, it picked Rory up and carried him to its lair. When he was deposited, it returned for Megh.

It crushed neither of them against its hard sharp shoulder plates. It didn't intend to eat them itself.

* * *

Liam Maqsween had traveled without a break, eating in the saddle and walking from time to time to rest his pony. He too had been bitten by flies and mosquitoes after crossing the divide; he'd left the domain of the Forest Soul.

He knew he wasn't far behind the others now. Twice, where they'd crossed the small creek, the water that had dripped from their horses hadn't entirely dried yet on the rocks.

Here and there along the creek were narrow stretches of meadow, and as he entered one of them from a stand of pines, he saw two ponies plodding uphill toward him. He recognized the dun at once, his sister's. The other wore a pack saddle, like a sawbuck on its back. They slowed down when they saw him, then stopped, waiting. He kicked his own pony to a trot, hurrying to them, and they stayed for him. He stopped when he reached them, examining.

Nothing all day had made much sense: his sister's departure, Rory's note, the nature of their early trail, or their coming to this country of fearful reputation. Now here were their ponies, riderless, with lathered sweat drying on them. Megh's still wore saddlebags.

And the sun was low; in an hour, dusk would begin. Liam Maqsween shivered. Sliding from his saddle, he gathered their reins and remounted. At first the other ponies were reluctant to follow, but he was firm, and after a moment they fell in behind him.

In a quarter hour he came out of forest into open grassy meadow, flanked on one side by thick pines and on the other by a talus slope, a fan of loose rocks, with boulders heaped and jumbled in places at its foot. The hair bristled on his neck; it seemed to him he was watched. Rory and Megh had been thrown from their ponies. Must have been. And being no expert rider—no one in Meadowvale was—he stopped. He transferred his quiver to his back, unholstered his bow and slung it from his right shoulder, then dismounted, to lead the animals by the reins, gripping his short sword with his left hand. The way led downward, the slope tapering, easing. A hundred yards more brought him to Megh's cloak, lying on the ground. She'd have removed it in the heat of day, perhaps laying it loose across the pony's withers. This must be where she'd been thrown.

Again his neck hairs crawled, and he stopped to scan about him. He saw nothing, but felt danger, and detoured to his left, to put more distance between himself and the forest edge. He'd passed the foot of the talus slope before he saw the two cave mouths, the smaller nearby. Tunnel mouths more likely, for they were square.

Then he saw movement in the larger. Something extended from it, and he dropped the reins. Behind him the ponies stamped, snorting nervously; Liam edged upslope toward the smaller opening.

The spider came out then, looked at him, and for just a moment Liam froze. Behind him the ponies stampeded; he didn't notice; his attention was riveted on the spider. Even at eighty yards it looked huge, taller than the ponies, and the spread of its legs was several times its height. Then it charged, and the spell was broken. Running faster than he'd have thought possible, Liam sprinted toward the smaller hole, and when it seemed he'd be too late, stopped abruptly. Bristly legs swept to clutch him, and he swung his sword with all the strength of his rock-hard body. It struck, severing a leg at a joint, and at the same instant he ducked low. The other leg missed, and somehow Liam found himself in the tunnel entrance, scrabbling for safety on all fours. Two spans inside he stopped, panting, eyes stinging with sweat. Half a minute earlier there'd been none.

He was aware of a dry, high-pitched chittering close outside, and a bristly limb reached in, groping. There was no room to swing freely—there was little more than room to stand—but with his short sword he struck at it as best he could, and cut it deeply behind the claws. The limb jerked back, and the chittering shrilled almost beyond Liam's frequency perception, setting his teeth on edge. Then it stopped, and silken threads the size of stout string began to lash the opening. Liam took quick steps backward, afraid of being snared. After a moment though, he realized that the spider was simply closing the opening with a tough silken mesh.

He sat back onto the floor and examined his surroundings by the thin light that shone through the newly woven door. The tunnel had been roughly squared, its walls and ceiling showing chisel marks. The floor had been spread with sand, and now was littered with small bones; some predator had denned there, might still den there, might be behind him now. He rolled to his knees and peered back into the dimness, seeing nothing. Who, he wondered, had carved it, and when?

Crouching, sword in hand, he began to explore. Gradually the tunnel curved, darkening, and in some seventy or eighty yards met a larger tunnel, high enough for a big person to walk upright. He stood at the junction, evaluating. Was it big enough for the spider? In height perhaps, but clearly not in width, which he judged at four arm spans. To his left, deeper in the mountain, he thought he heard water splashing on stone. To his right he could see the daylit square of the large entrance, distant enough that where he stood, the tunnel was almost as dark as night. Slowly, softly, sword tightly gripped, Liam moved toward the light.

He'd gone most of the way when he heard a sound, faint and dry, as if something had scuffed against rock. Holding his breath, he stopped. The sound did not repeat. There was more light here, but he saw nothing to account for the sound, and moved forward again, even more cautiously, hardly breathing. Suddenly the spider was in front of him, blocking the light, its row of eyes, like big black beads, staring at him from scant ells away. Its bristly palps groped, and with a cry he jumped back.

He crouched panting, heart thudding. The groping palps couldn't reach him, and striding forward, he struck at one with all his strength, felt the sword bite. The spider jumped back, chittering wildly, the move jerking the sword from Liam's hand. The tomteen pounced after it, snatched it up, and scampered well back in the tunnel.

The spider had jumped to his right, out of view. Clearly there was a larger room, an entryway of some sort, between him and the entrance. Its lair, he decided, the place it took its victims, its food. Megh and Rory might well be there, or their bodies, what was left of them.

Liam knew more about spiders than was comfortable just then. The forest tomtaihn, normally unthreatened by other life forms, and being small themselves, close to nature, and typically unhurried, tended to watch things like spiders and insects—study them if you will. Especially during childhood and adolescence. He knew, for example, that spiders, after biting their prey, commonly crush them before sucking the juices from them. Sometimes though, the crushing and feeding are postponed, while at least sometimes the prey still lived after being bitten.

Megh and Rory might be alive in the entryway, though no doubt well wrapped with silk.

So despite the frenzied, high-pitched chittering, Liam edged toward the room again, keeping close to the right wall, his short sword in his left hand. From just short of the tunnel mouth, he could see much of the entryway's left half. It was square, about twelve yards long and twelve wide, and perhaps twice as high as the tunnel he was in. High enough for the dwarves or orcs of old, or big men if it came to that, to stand with long spears upright, ready to sally forth. There was even a ledge along the wall, for them to sit on while waiting.

On the sand-covered floor, among bones and other debris, were six silk-wrapped objects. Five were oblong, of various sizes. The other was larger and round, its diameter possibly twice Liam's height; an egg sac, he decided, and felt hope. The silk-wrapped food might well be alive, alive and fresh, awaiting the hatch.

Then the mother would crush the bundled victims as food for her hatchlings. He'd have to act before then.

The chittering had died. Quietly Liam moved back down the tunnel to the smaller branch he'd come from, and up it to its entrance. Cautiously he touched the silk that covered it. It was less sticky than he'd feared. Seemingly the stickiness dried in time, and was lost. With his sword he cut till the door covering was free, then pulled it inside and folded it against a wall. Warily he looked out. The sun had nearly set, and daylight had begun to dim, the beginning of dusk. He stepped outside, picked up a stone the size of his fist, and threw it as far downhill as he could. It struck audibly on bare rock and bounced, and as he'd hoped, the spider came half out the other entrance, looking not toward him, but in the direction of the sound.

Slowly he stepped back into the opening, watching. The spider moved farther, a step at a time, then rushed downhill a few steps and paused. A thought occurred to Liam, a plan. He backed inside, then hurried down the narrow tunnel as fast as he dared in the darkness, into the larger tunnel, and up it to the entryway.

The spider was still outside. Quickly he went to the bundle he suspected was Megh, and dragged it into the tunnel, then returned for the one he hoped was Rory. One at a time he dragged them to the side tunnel, and up it to near its opening.

It was time to learn the worst. He started with the smallest bundle, using his pocket knife to saw the tough threads, not sticky at all now, only tacky. Once cut, the casing peeled off readily. Inside was Megh, her face slack, her limbs limp. Liam wet his cheek, held it to her open mouth, and felt faint cooling. She breathed, barely.

Then he freed Rory. The lad's short sword was still in its scabbard, and his rucksack on his back. Liam removed them and laid them aside.

For a few minutes he massaged and pummeled first Megh, then Rory, hoping to stimulate circulation, but his mind was on other things. Assuming he could revive them, how could they escape? Was the spider active at night? Many small ones were. He'd injured it twice, but not seriously. Could he somehow cripple or kill it?

He stopped his massaging to peer out the entrance. He couldn't see the spider. Was it hunting? Had it returned to her lair? *Or was it crouching in ambush on the steep slope just above his door?* A typical spider could cling to a wall or cross a ceiling, but not one weighing hundreds of pounds, even with eight feet to grip with...It would be a matter of steepness and surface.

His eyes found a pebble just outside the opening. He snatched it up and jumped back, then hurried again through the tunnels. The entryway was darker than before. He threw the pebble in, against the wall. There was no response, so sword ready, he followed it.

One of the other food bundles was small enough for him to drag readily. He pulled it from the room, and through the tunnels

to where Megh and Rory lay. There he freed it, a wildcat as large
as Megh, or larger; so far, so good.

Again he looked out, then jumped out and back. Nothing had
pounced. Grabbing the wildcat by the tail, he pulled it just outside
the opening and arranged it in a pose of natural sleep. The sun
was down now. Would the spider see it? Would she be fooled?

He went back inside, laid his unsheathed sword on a piece of
casing, and massaged the comatose tomtaihn, first one, then the
other, positioning himself so he could see the wildcat as he
worked. Shortly Rory responded, muttering incoherently for a
moment. When he stilled again, his breathing was more nearly the
normal breathing of sleep, and Liam gave his full attention to
Megh.

It was full twilight when suddenly the spider was there. Liam
saw her crouch over the wildcat, grasp it awkwardly with
wounded palps, and thrust her two fangs into the body. Moving
quickly but smoothly, Liam took his sword and was at the opening, striking hard at the spider's head. He felt the blade bite
through thick chiton armor. The creature didn't try at once to grab
him. Instead she jumped backward a dozen feet, chittering wildly,
gathering herself as Liam scurried back inside.

Had he damaged it critically? Enough that it might die, or...?
Again it began weaving threads of silk across the opening, this
time not stopping so soon, and his shelter grew almost pitch-dark.
He crouched in the blackness, massaging his sister till at last she
too muttered something briefly and lapsed into sleep.

That accomplished, Liam took a swallow of water from the
leather flask on his belt, lay down beside his sword, and slept himself.

But only briefly. He awoke, galvanized by a snuffling outside
the tunnel, and rolled to a crouch. His hand found his sword.
Something pushed on the door mesh, then abruptly it burst inward
as a hand thrust through, huge and hairy. With a spasm of energy,
Liam hacked at it. Its hardness startled him; the blade cut, but not
as deeply as he'd hoped.

The hand jerked back, accompanied by a roar of pain and
rage, and Liam grabbed first Megh, then Rory, pulling them farther into the tunnel. The huge hand thrust in again, six feet or
more, groped and withdrew empty. Liam shook like an aspen leaf.
A troll, he thought. *It's a troll.*

There was silence for a long three or four minutes, then he

heard something grunting, coming nearer, until it was just out-side. Abruptly there was a loud thud, and the moonlight was gone, except for a little that came in at one side. The troll had brought a boulder, and blocked the opening with it.

Liam felt chagrin; he'd lost an option, his exit. On the other hand it had been a dangerous option, with a troll snooping around. He lay back down, but this time sleep failed to come. He thought of the egg sac. When would it hatch? And what? A hun-dred young the size of his head? Likelier, he thought, a dozen the size of Megh. And in his experience, the young were simply small copies of the mother. Suppose they hatched tonight? Would they come down the tunnel hunting?

He sat up, found the door mesh where he'd set it aside, and with his pocket knife cut off a fistful of strands. Then he groped for Rory's rucksack; perhaps there'd be a match pot. There was, and striking a match, he held its yellow flame to the strands, which lit, burning more strongly than he'd hoped, too rapidly for good torches. It lasted long enough, though, for him to cut several more, should they be needed.

That done, he lay down again, and this time slept.

* * *

He awoke to Rory's hand on his shoulder. His first thought, as he shook off an evil dream and sat up, was that the Dank Land had its own vile soul.

Enough light got in past the boulder to see by, dimly; day had come. The younger tomteen's face was drawn as if he had a bad case of grippe. He spoke in a near whisper.

"Liam! What happened?"

Despite Rory's whispering, Liam touched finger to lips, then answered as quietly. "What do you remember?"

The young man's eyes went out of focus. "A—spider. Huge! Taller than the ponies! It was on me almost before I knew it."

Liam gestured at the intact shells that had been Rory's cocoon. "It stung you and wrapped you up in that. Then took you to its lair. Both of you; you and Megh."

There was accusation in his voice. Then Rory told him what had happened: the stoor, the map, everything. "How did you res-cue us?" he finished.

It was Liam's turn to recite, all of it including the troll, the boulder, and the egg sac. "And now," he finished, "it's time to do away with her. And her eggs. Then we can go home."

While Liam described his plan, he took the lid from the match pot and handed matches to Rory, who put one in each pocket. Then, by the thin light, he tied patches of silk to several of his broad-headed arrows. Meanwhile Megh awoke, and Rory talked to her briefly in an undertone. "All right," Liam murmured when he'd finished his work, "let's do it."

"Right," said Rory. He'd already buckled on his scabbard, and had his short sword in hand. Liam looked at Megh, who nodded, and the two male tomtaihn moved off quietly down the tunnel. At the junction, Liam took two arrows from his quiver and held them, with his bow, in his right hand. Then they moved up the larger tunnel even more quietly. Liam didn't know if spiders slept, but if they could catch her sleeping, they might drive several arrows into her before she could leave.

She was awake. Almost unbreathing, they peered at her. She was palpating the egg sac, and Liam could see it move. It reminded him of kittens playing in a bag. The arrow he nocked had a swatch of silk tied below the head. His left hand held the arrow at his ear; the right held the bow, slightly bent. "Now!" he hissed. Rory struck a match against the rock wall, once, then again before it flared. The spider had turned, the row of beady eyes fixed on them. Rory touched flame to silk; it caught, and in the manner of his people, Liam straightened his how arm, thrusting the bow forward, and let go the arrow. It drove into the egg sac, the swatch of burning silk sticking to the outside, and instantly it began to burn.

Almost as quickly the spider rushed at them, her already damaged forelimbs reaching futilely. Liam nocked and loosed the other arrow, driving it almost to the feathers between breastplate and head. She rose tall and curved her abdomen, pointing her spinnerets forward between her legs, and began to spew silk wildly, loops of it snaking into the tunnel, sending the two tomtaihn stumbling backward out of the way. Before Liam could shoot again, the opening was half-obscured, but he sent another arrow through it, and another, hearing them sock into flesh. His head hurt fiercely, and he realized it was from the chittering, which had risen above hearing. Together they turned and ran, missing the side tunnel the first time. Before they got back to Megh, both of them had stopped to retch, their already empty stomachs spasming.

* * *

They dozed briefly, then returned to the junction of the two tunnels. The chittering still went on, dropping to audibility, then rising above it, so they retreated again. Next they tried to move the boulder, to no avail. *Of all the times not to have hammer and chisel*, Liam thought. Surely, though, the spider couldn't keep it up indefinitely. Either she'd die or go out to hunt, perhaps after laying more eggs if she was able.

After a bit they slept again, again with evil dreams, and awoke to hunger. The younger tomtaihn were hungriest, and weak from the venom. Liam and Rory went to the junction, this time with all the torch material they could carry, then deeper down the large tunnel, lighting their short-lived torches one by one. They found the water Liam had heard the first day, drank and filled their leather flasks. The last quick torch burned out, and they walked back in darkness.

The curtain the spider had woven was thick enough that little light glowed through. Gathering his resolve, Liam struck it with his sword, and at once the chittering began again. Once more they fled. Back in their side tunnel they paused.

"She didn't sound as strong as before," Rory said.

Liam considered. "I think you're right," he said. "She must be weakening. Maybe tomorrow she'll be dead, or the day after. We've got water, and we can do without food a few days."

So they went back to Megh, and all three lay about dozing. Liam woke again to Rory's touch. "Liam! I've been back down the tunnel, to the entryway. I tried the curtain and heard nothing, so I cut a hole to see through. She's down, Liam, she's down! I saw a leg move, but it was weak!"

Liam rolled to his feet, reaching for belt and sword, then slung his quiver and strung his bow. Together they went down the tunnel, this time with Megh following.

At the silk curtain, Liam peered through the hole. It was as Rory'd said. Together they began to chop on the thick mesh, clearing the way entirely, dragging the segments aside. There was a smell of charred protein, the young in the egg sac. Meanwhile the spider didn't move. When the doorway was clear, Liam stepped forward and drove a broad-headed arrow into the thorax, just in front of the waist. It drove through the chiton and disappeared, feathers and all. He sent another, and another, and they became aware of a different smell, vile gases issuing from the arrow holes.

"She's dead," Liam said. "She must be." But still he didn't move to strike her with his sword; there might be a final spasm of life left in her. Turning, he looked at the egg sac. Rory was already staring, but not at the charred remains of spiders half his size. On the ledge behind them was a casket, half an ell long, a foot wide, and higher than its width. He kicked dead spiders aside and opened it; when he spoke, it was with awe.

"Liam! It's real!"

Liam strode to it. It was nearly full of gold and jewels. "Well!" he said. He could think of nothing more. Megh had come in, and stood peering between them without enthusiasm, saying nothing at all.

"We'll need the ponies," Liam said. Before they left, though, he went to the spider after all and drew the arrow from between her head and breastplate, putting it in his quiver. While he did this, Rory put a handful of coins into each front pocket. They hurried out then, into the sunshine, hunger forgotten. Fingers in their mouths, they whistled, loud and shrill, then stood waiting, intent for the sound of hooves.

"They could be halfway home by now," Rory said.

"Let's see if we can find tracks," Liam replied. "My Tam would hang around if he could. If the troll didn't take him."

The troll. Rory looked about, despite the sunshine. They went to the creek and started up it, going half a mile or more, then stopped. Ahead three ravens were flapping up, and the tomtaihn went to see what had drawn them. The bones of a pony lay strewn about, with patches of hide and black hair. The pack saddle lay smashed.

"I can make another saddle," Rory said. He picked up the pack saddle straps, folded them, and stuffed them in his rucksack. "I'll use saplings and spider cord."

Liam nodded. "If we can find a pony to wear it."

He'd hardly said it before they heard hooves. Megh's little dun came galloping out of the woods ahead, slowed when it saw them, and trotted the rest of the way, stopping beside its mistress.

"Well then, Megh," Liam said, "are you willing that she carry the chest?" He turned to Rory. "We'll have to dump part of it out. It's too heavy as it is."

"Liam." It was Megh who spoke. "I'm not sure I am. Willing, that is."

Her brother stared, brows raised, but it was Rory Hoy she looked at now. "What would you do with it?" she said. "The treasure, I mean."

Rory stammered, confused. "Why—I'd—I'd take some of it to—to Abhaihnseth, and hire a builder to build a grand home for us beside the rudh. And you could buy the furnishings. And some of it..." He stopped. "Between the two of us, we'd find things to use it for. Buy old Connorleigh's farm; he's getting old for all that work and has no children. The money would keep him well the rest of his life."

"You'd make the village famous then? For its wealth?"

He stared, beginning to see her point.

"What's kept Meadowvale safe these years?" she asked. "Since our grandsires settled it, four hundred years ago. And what would happen when it became known there was wealth there?"

Rory looked at Liam for help. The rock cutter looked back thoughtfully. "How much gold could you carry in your pockets, Rory?" he asked.

"I suppose—a hundred pounds' worth in each, or a hundred fifty. Five hundred pounds, more or less."

"More than I'll ever own," Liam said.

Rory shook his head. "Not so! I'll share! Without your help I'd be spider food right now."

Liam shook his head. "For a bit there, the sight of all that treasure went to my head. But Megh's right: for us, wealth is dangerous. Even deadly. And I live well, Rory, without riches. I'll live even better when Caithlain A'Duill comes of age, three months hence."

Rory stared sullenly at his furry feet. "My family was wealthy once," he said, then turned defiantly to Liam. "Wealthy and important."

"A different time, Rory, a different world. Before the big folk came. And old Connorleigh would sell for two hundred pounds, or so I've heard."

"And a hundred crowns for the stoor, when he comes," Megh put in. "That comes to twelve pounds more." She frowned. "Even four hundred pounds would cause talk, if people knew."

Liam took it from there. "You can say the stoor told you about a map to a pot of coins he'd heard of. Hidden in a hollow

tree on the South Fork of the Mirror, near where it crosses the
Mulberry Road. He less than half believed in it, so he sold it to
you. You told Megh of it, and she told me, and the three of us
went to look. Found it, too, we did, though it took us a while. The
map was rough, and there are lots of hollow trees. It was a clay
pot, with two hundred twelve pounds all told. Enough to buy old
Connorleigh out. You can give me ten, to help make the story
convincing. Anything more than two hundred twelve you can
hide, and use later."

Rory Hoy looked first at Liam, then Megh, seeing not friends
now but antagonists. The treasure was his to decide on. They'd
played their part, to be sure, but he'd led them. Paid his life savings for the map. And wealth would buy more than a mansion and
goods, it would buy the respect of his father, his...

Howling broke his thoughts and galvanized all three of the
tomtaihn. They turned downstream to see. A pack of wolves was
running toward them. Beside the tomtaihn stood a pine, not large,
its dead lower branches within reach. "Climb!" roared Liam, and
grabbing Megh, boosted her, then he and Rory followed, using
branch stubs like ladder rungs, breaking some of them in the
scramble. They didn't stop till they were among green branches, a
safe height up.

The wolves stopped in a ring around the base, seven of them.
The leader was bigger than any wolf ought to be, Liam thought.
"Who are you, and what do you want?" he called down.

The leader grinned, tongue lolling. "You killed one of my
master's sentries here, and the other cannot abide the daylight. So
we were sent."

Each of the tomtaihn heard the unspoken words. "Well
then," said Liam, who sat lowest. He took the bow from his shoulder, nocked an arrow, and shot at him. An awkward shot, from a
branch, but not awkward enough to explain the result. The shot
seemed straight, then turned aside. The other wolves moved about
restlessly now, but the leader still grinned.

"Your arrows cannot harm me, halfling. I have my master's
essence."

"Well then!" Liam drew again, but this time sent the arrow at
the nearest other wolf. It struck between ribs, and with a yelp the
animal went down. The others scattered, all but the leader, to circle at a little distance.

Now the grin was gone. "No loss, halfling, no loss."

"Maybe not. But you cannot reach us, any more than my arrows can reach you."

"I need not. At dusk the other sentry will come, and pluck you like cherries, or shake you out, or break off the tree if he'd rather."

Liam glowered, then spoke, not to the wolf. "Rory, take the bow," he said, "and the quiver. The soul of the Dank Land didn't send seven of them by accident, and now they're only six. And I'm left-handed."

Staring, Rory took bow and quiver as Liam had ordered. Seven was the perfect number; there was power in it. And stories had it that the left hand had strength against magic. "What are you going to do?" he asked.

"It's one thing for sorcery to stop a flying arrow. It's something else to stop a blow delivered by a living arm. Be ready to shoot any of the others that try to enter in." With that, the tomtaidh rock cutter drew his short sword and jumped from the tree.

The move was so unexpected, the lead wolf jumped back, and Liam set upon him, hacking. The first stroke took an ear off, and a cheek, and dug into a shoulder, but the next missed as the animal jumped aside. The others moved in then, but warily, and from his perch, Rory downed another. They drew back.

"You took me by surprise, halfling." The leader's thoughts seemed to hiss like a snake. "You will not surprise me again." Then it drove at Liam. His blade seemed to land, as if the creature lacked the power to stop it, but this time did not cut, striking like a cudgel. Again the others drew in, again one took an arrow deeply, and again the survivors retreated, far enough that from his branch, Rory had no shot at them.

Now the leader circled the sturdy tomteen. No trace of a sneer remained on its damaged face. Its right eye was swelling where the last blow had struck.

"Hold the bow," Rory told Megh. She took it, and he clambered quickly to a lower branch, then took the bow back. The lead wolf moved in again, slashing, shed a blow off its shoulder and tore Liam's sleeve half off before he beat it back. Another wolf rushed. An arrow took it in the neck, and after spinning, snapping at the shaft, it fled. But bright blood ran from Liam's right arm now, dripping on the ground.

Again the leader circled, and again drove in. This time

though, instead of slashing, it held on, and with a terrible snarling swung the tomteen like a doll and dashed him to the ground. Another darted in, and Rory's arrow missed. It grabbed Liam by a leg before a second arrow took it in the flank. It yelped, grabbed again, and again Rory shot, felling it.

"The bow! Take it!" he shouted, then moved the quiver from his shoulder to a branch stub and jumped even before he drew his short sword. The sixth wolf had also moved in; now it sidled away, and Rory attacked the leader from behind, taking it by surprise as it shook Liam, his blade slamming its hindquarters—but not biting!

It dropped the mauled, unmoving tomteen and turned. "You are dead, halfling," it thought to Rory. The other wolf, paler than the rest, circled to get behind him.

As a girl, Megh Maqsween had often shot with her brother at the archery butts. Sisters sometimes did. Now she nocked the last arrow, not heeding its corroded head. From where she sat she had no shot at the pale wolf, so she drew down on the leader and let fly.

The arrow struck, but not deeply. It hit the shoulder, then sliced along ribs and flank, leaving an ugly bloody streak, but no major wound. The leader started, stared upward a long moment in surprise, then staggered, fell, got half up and fell again. The final wolf, the pale one, turned away and trotted off.

Rory stared up at Megh, then in amazement at the park leader. Then he moved to Liam and dropped to his knees. "Liam! Liam! Oh, Liam!" The rock cutter's arm and shoulder were deeply lacerated, and blood soaked his torn breeches. Quickly, Rory pulled the breeches off him. The leg bites too were deep, but the flesh was not greatly torn.

"Megh!" Rory cried. "He'll live! Get the dun, if you can. We'll tie him on. Quickly, lass, before something else comes!"

She tossed down the bow and empty quiver and climbed down. While she whistled for her pony, Rory gathered arrows and put them in the quiver, noting the corrosion on one. *The one from the spider,* he thought, *and poisonous.* Then he gave bow and quiver to his sweetheart, hoisted the thick-bodied Liam onto his back, and started hiking up the pass, Megh following. They hiked for three or four furlongs before the pony reappeared. Then, with a struggle, they got Liam across its back and tied him on with the straps Rory had salvaged. That done, they hiked again, driving hard, sweat blurring their eyes, their legs burning with fatigue. They'd not have dreamed they could go uphill so far so fast. At least the forest was sparse here, with fewer blowdowns to bypass.

They went a mile, another, in little more than an hour. And always with a sense of pursuit. At last, on an overlook, they paused. Ahead, it was as far again to the divide. Behind—Behind something was coming, a pack of somethings, seven great wild hogs, led by a boar far bigger than the pony. "Megh!" said Rory, "get on the pony and ride!"

She stared at him.

Grabbing her, he half slung her up behind Liam. "*Now ride!*" He slapped the pony with the flat of his short sword, and it jumped forward, almost unseating the girl, who pale as milk, held on to the body of her brother as the pony went uphill at a hard-driving run.

Rory turned then, sheathed his sword and strung his bow. *I'll use the poison arrow first*, he told himself. *On the boar. He'll have the essence of the Dank Land's Soul. If I kill him, the others may take me, but they'll likely go no farther.*

Again the hogs came into view, their thick hair dark. No pony could keep pace with them; he doubted that other swine could, unpossessed. *O Forest Soul!* he thought, *help me if you can!* Then he nocked the corroded arrow.

They thundered on, disappeared again among some trees, then reappeared scarcely a hundred feet away, the hair along their spines a bristling ridge.

And stopped abruptly, actually skidding in the dirt. The towering boar stared at Rory, red-eyed, then looked past him, upward toward the divide, and Rory could hear his thought. "He is mine, this little one! And the others are mine! This is my domain!"

The answer was not in words, but Rory felt the message. *Not this time, evil one. Your master died long ago; two others of these halflings destroyed him. You have no source to renew your weakening strength now. Your days are numbered.*

The great boar snorted, pawed the ground, and, instead of turning back, charged at Rory. His arrow met it, glanced from its thick skull, furrowing the scalp, stopping in the shoulder hump. Then it was on him—and yet it wasn't, for it seemed somehow to pass through him without impact. Rory fell, not knocked down but overwhelmed. Then the boar wheeled, as if to try again, stopped, and fell over.

At once the other swine turned and thundered off downhill.

*   *   *

They were waiting with the pony, on the divide. Liam was lying conscious on the ground, his wounds bandaged with strips cut from shirt and breeches. When Megh saw Rory laboring up the trail, she ran to him, throwing herself into his arms.

"I was so afraid for you, darling!" she said.

"And I," he answered. They walked to Liam, arms around each other's waists. "How are you feeling, Mr. Maqsween?"

Liam grunted. "I'll live, *Mr.* Hoy." He paused. "If you're ready to go on, I think I can ride without being hogtied."

"I'm ready, Mr. Maqsween."

Liam chuckled. "Good. And on the way down, you can tell me what happened. I'll see what I can do with Da when we get back to Meadowvale. He'll be upset with you, but I've a strong influence on him. And the business is mine now."

They brought the dun and boosted him on.

When the wave of pain had settled and the grimace left his face, Liam looked down at Rory. "I know you took two fistfuls from the chest. That should be enough to pay down on Connorleigh's and buy a good keg of ale for the wedding. And still pay the Stoor his hundred crowns."

He chuckled then, and they started down toward the Mirrorudh.

Tiger Hunt

Introduction

The concept of this story came to me full-blown. It would be about Ron and Melody Cordero, who'd resulted from research in human genetics. Two very intelligent and otherwise gifted tailor-made humans. But inevitably there were some erroneous assumptions in the geneticists' understanding, and the "tailor mades" would live their lives sorting out and learning to deal with the results. "Tiger Hunt" is a cusp in the lives of Ron and Melody.

I tried to make this story as dirt-real as I could. I knew the approximate location from the start; studying topographic maps refined it. Then I called the county road department and talked at length with a surveyor who knew the terrain intimately.

When I'd finished writing it, it seemed to me I'd written something special, so I sent it off to Stan Schmidt at *Analog*. Stan said he would have used it, but he already had a story about a Pleistocene wildlife refuge, and didn't feel he should run another one soon.

Jim Baen published it in *New Destinies* and asked for a sequel, a novel. I'd already thought about that, and wanted to do it, but declined the invitation. I'd have had to spend time in Uruguay, knew no Spanish, and at any rate couldn't afford the trip.

* * *

The night was overcast, but not heavily, and there was a half-moon. Through the window of the little Beech Hoverhawk, Ron Cordero could make out hills, looking more barren than they actually were, their wooded patches mostly saplings whose leaves had fallen.

The IR finder was much more revealing than the window. The night was cool and still, and it hadn't rained for a week. Thus, 1500 meters below, he could see not only occasional large mammals, but faintly where they'd stood earlier to graze or browse, and more clearly where they'd laid down.

His practiced eyes even told him what species, in all likelihood, he was seeing. There was the Quadrangle AB-19 mammoth herd, *Neo-mammuthus primigenius*. He didn't trouble to count them; there'd be eight unless they'd lost a member, which wasn't likely. At the edge of the screen, in the Tin Can Creek drainage, he saw a band of hammerheads, wild horses, small and rough, growing shaggy in this season. And—

His attention sharpened. Something stalked the mustangs. Something large. He murmured into his throat mike, and the pilot banked the quiet little plane in that direction. Cordero locked the scanner on it, centered it, waited until they were nearer and lower, then keyed in the enhancer. And grunted his disappointment. Bear; a short-face. A few grizzlies had drifted into the Range, down the Teton and Marias Rivers, but that was a long way north. And this individual was too large for a grizzly. Male, too. Too big for a sow and there were no cubs or yearlings with it.

But bear wasn't what he was interested in.

He spoke to the pilot again, and they returned to their search pattern.

What he was looking for was a tiger of trophy quality, an over-the-hill male he knew of, declining in vigor, that he could justify having shot. One that didn't have many winters left to him. The Range let very few permits, and controlled closely what hunting it allowed.

Hyung wouldn't be too picky about condition; he'd hinted as much. "Just be sure the president gets his trophy, a good trophy, and don't take longer than three days." Which could require procedures they hadn't used before.

Loren Hyung, always the politician. He'd needed to be, when he'd been the boy wonder in charge of the old Pleistocene Genomes Institute. Fighting for credibility and funds, and adequate range. Fighting public uninterest, even parliamentary and bureaucratic hostility. Back when all they'd had was the 2,800 square kilometers of the Suffield Range, up in Alberta.

Back before the Yellowstone Volcanic Field let go. The eruption and the Red Plague, only months apart, had made half of Montana available.

Loren had really performed wonders then. Risking not only his job but his reputation, he'd gone to Washington instead of Ottawa. The staff, Cordero included, had thought their chief insane. But Loren had spellwoven key bureaucrats and politicians—it had taken magic more than science—and ended up with half the entire range seed stocks of the U.S. Forest Service and Bureau of Land Management. Then the BLM had seeded narrow strips across the desert of volcanic ash he coveted in Montana.

The Office of the President had also promised support for his central proposal—200,000 square kilometers in Montana for a Pleistocene Mammals Range.

Then he'd gone to Ottawa.

It wouldn't have flown at all, of course, if Washington and Ottawa hadn't already been holding exploratory talks on union. The Great Crash and three years of unprecedented Troubles worldwide, followed by the Plague and drastic depopulation, made things possible that otherwise would hardly have been conceivable.

Maybe Loren still needed to be a politician. With Kollar coming, it certainly couldn't hurt. But politics wasn't the sort of thing that Cordero, or maybe even Loren Hyung, cared for. It was hard to be sure about Loren. Though he'd been born in Vancouver, not in China, be was a difficult man to read.

Cordero hadn't known that Edward Kollar gave a damn about hunting. His trophies had been political. Maybe he was image-building now. There were people, a lot of people, who'd feel better about a president who hunted. Although the order had come down that there was to be no publicity.

* * *

The little plane doubled back on the next transect, and Cordero spotted a band of twenty or so giant bison, *Bison neo-latifrons,* lying up near a creek, no doubt chewing their cuds. And less than a kilometer from them, wooly rhinos, a female and calf. A little later he spied a pack of wolves—whether *Canis neo-dirus* or lobos, he couldn't tell—sleeping off a case of gluttony around the remains of a wild horse.

For some reason, Cordero tended to prefer the lobos—he didn't know why. The lobo was nature's own, while he'd dedicated most of his adult life to the products of genetic engineering. He was a tailor-made himself; he and Melody both were. With all that that entailed—the introversion, the sense of difference, the high IQs and longevity—all the minuses and pluses.

Finally he found his tiger. First, faintly, he saw its signature: where it had lain awhile on an open slope. Quickly he spotted the animal itself, lying up now within the edge of an aspen copse, its leaves fallen. By the edge of the copse, in the open, was the remains of a kill, a whitetail deer, aspen leaves scratched over it in a nominal effort to cover it.

Cordero was virtually certain it was the tiger he'd been looking for. It was too large for a female, and while he couldn't delineate territories with any accuracy, he was reasonably sure this was within the old male's.

In the morning he'd check him out on the ground.

Too bad the tiger wasn't closer to a road, Cordero thought. A saddle-sore president would be an unhappy president. Maybe Kollar would settle for a short-face; they were easier to find, and stuffed they wire awesome. Maybe he'd find the nerve to suggest it to him. Maybe the sun would rise in the west. The President of the North American Federation, Chairman of the Federation Party, Ed Kollar wasn't used to people suggesting he change his goals because they were awkward and inconvenient. Cordero told himself he'd be better off suggesting to the tiger that he move closer to the road.

Kollar wouldn't be arriving for a week. Maybe the tiger, in his wanderings, just might move closer to a road by then.

* * *

The next morning before dawn, Cordero was back in the air, this time in the stealth chopper. He relocated the tiger—it was still by its kill—and had himself put down to check the animal out. Put down on a hilltop two kilometers away. When applied to choppers, *stealth* is a relative term, and it was policy not to fly aircraft in such a way as to alarm the Pleistocene mammals.

After checking the wind—if he'd been other than downwind of the tiger, he'd have had the chopper move him elsewhere—Cordero started hiking toward it. The chopper stayed where it was. He carried zoom binocs with a lightweight collapsible tripod, and a *tracy* to talk to the chopper with. Should the tiger feel combative, Cordero also carried two skunk bombs, and as backup, an old .357 magnum S&W revolver that he'd never needed yet.

He jogged. It seemed to him he could detect the first hint of dawn. Best to be there early, and wait for light.

* * *

The sun was up when he got back to the compound. His wife was leaving for her job as principal clerk, when he came walking up the driveway toward the small government house they lived in. They paused briefly when they met.

"There are grapefruit sections in the fridge," she said. "And fried bacon. The rest is up to you."

He nodded. "I found the president's trophy animal."

She averted her eyes, not nodding. "I have to go," she said. "I'll be late." Briefly he watched her leave, then went in the house. After twenty years of marriage, he was used to the moods that settled on her now and then. When Kollar was gone, she'd be all right.

He found the grapefruit pieces and ate them at the sink, then took bran flakes from the cupboard, filled a bowl, added milk, and sat down at the kitchen table where the autumn sun flooded in. Afterward, the sharp corners of his hunger blunted, he fried eggs, made toast, and ate them with the cold bacon Melody had mentioned. He avoided coffee just now, drinking milk instead. He intended to go to bed for a few hours, and didn't want the caffeine.

As he did these things, his thoughts were on Melody. She'd always been subject to resentments, though the mood they engendered didn't usually persist the way this one had.

It had started when he'd told her that Kollar was coming, and that he'd be guiding him. He hadn't tried to find out why, specifically, it had upset her. He'd learned early that questions increased her resentment, fueled her mood. As if questions were accusations.

She'd never expressed dislike of Kollar in particular. He was the lowest profile dictator—well, semi-dictator—that Cordero knew of. But she sometimes expressed bitterness toward government, even though she worked for a government agency and was paid and treated well by it.

As with some other tailor-mades, things hadn't worked out for her. She'd been engineered to be a great singer, and her voice was a marvelous contralto, pure and rich. But somehow she had poor pitch, even with accompaniment. She could hear pitch but not duplicate it. As a little child she'd loved to sing, loved it more than anything, and poor pitch was usual in little children, no problem. But she hadn't outgrown hers.

She could have become a successful instrumentalist—she played the piano very well when she felt like it—but instead she painted. Which she also did well, but without enthusiasm.

The matter of sterility bothered her too. Lots of tailor-mades adopted. For one thing, having children in the house tended to disguise being tailor-mades. But Melody had been unwilling. In forty years, she said, we'd look younger than our foster children. We'd see them grow old and die.

He'd failed as a tailor-made too, but to him it didn't feel like failure. Because in his case the failure was of preference, not ability. The function he'd been designed for, he found distasteful. Instead he'd found something he loved, found it early and spent his entire adult life working at it, rising to the top. Occasionally, he wondered if Melody secretly resented his doing successfully what he truly loved to do. Above his present position were only administrative jobs. Desks and in-house politics, probably in the capital: Detroit-Windsor. He much preferred to spend the rest of his working life as senior field biologist on the Pleistocene Mammals Range.

They really did have a good situation here, both Melody and himself. There was little prejudice, though at least some of the people here knew they were tailor-mades. The Hyungs had to know, though they'd never mentioned it. The two families had known each other for twenty years, had seen each other almost daily. Since he'd arrived as a new graduate assistant at the old Pleistocene Genomes Institute at Medicine Hat, when Loren had been deputy administrator. In those twenty years, Loren and Lissa had aged twenty years worth, he and Melody perhaps seven or eight.

Their prospect of longevity was the thing the media had made the most of, back when Project Tailor Made had been exposed. And longevity was one reason some people resented them. Although in the Bad Old Days, the murders of tailor-mades had to some extent been inspired by certain television preachers. "Tailor-mades are not Children of God! They are blasphemies made by Godless scientists!" There'd been only—only!—three lynchings plus two assassinations. But there'd also been a dozen beatings, tortures and rapes; ugly, terrifying things, by packs. And half the victims weren't tailor-mades at all.

All in the name of God. Then churches from Catholic to Baptist, Unitarian to Islamic, had condemned the acts, and television had shown condemnatory dramas loosely based on them. All in all, new understandings had probably resulted, but scars had been left.

As exasperating as Loren could occasionally be, he showed no sign, even subtle, of prejudice. Nor did Lissa, who in fact was Melody's only woman friend, who could light a light in her and make her laugh.

Melody had never said so, but it seemed to him that she simply disliked government, and perhaps by extension Kollar, its boss now, because of Project Tailor Made. She considered herself a victim of it, and it had been a government project, initially secret, within the Agency for Special Studies.

Cordero washed his few dishes—Melody had cleaned hers—checked the sawdust-burning furnace, then sat down to brush his teeth in front of the television, taking his mind off his wife. After that he set the alarm clock, lay down across their bed, and went to sleep.

* * *

Every night until the day of the president's arrival, the Hoverhawk had been out to locate the sabertooth. The tiger's travels plotted as a very rough half-oval, and it had indeed moved somewhat closer to the highway.

On arrival day, a Marine Corps presidential security section had arrived before dawn—their H-67C Kommando was parked near the helipad when Cordero walked to work—and quietly, swiftly, they'd gone over the complex with various detection gear, looking for only they knew what. They'd also set up sentry equipment and fire positions.

No one told Cordero these things, but as he walked to the administration building and saw the personnel carrier with its rotors drooping, and its Marine Corps insignia, he knew in a general way what they must have done. What he'd have done, if he'd been in charge. It was just as well, he told himself, that they were eight kilometers from Great Falls here, and away from the highway. Obtrusive security could be poor PR.

He wondered if—the thought was both farcical and grotesque—he wondered if marines would shadow the president on the hunt.

Cordero was at his desk at 0755, his usual time. By 0950 he'd skimmed and read through the memos and reports there, dictating comments and replies to his computer as its silent printer turned his words into hard copy. Then he started scanning and reading through a backlog of technical journals and abstracts, entering keywords into his database. By noon he'd heard nothing about the president's arrival time, and went home to lunch.

Melody arrived before the tea kettle boiled. They made sandwiches from a tuna spread she'd mixed the day before, and sat down in front of ancient *Sesame Street* reruns, not saying a great deal. She wasn't disagreeable; simply quiet, preoccupied. The president's coming was on her mind, Cordero felt sure. When they left, clouds had blocked the sun, and a chilly breeze had come up.

Back at his desk, he continued his assault on the literature. He was browsing *Dissertation Abstracts* when his intercom interrupted him. Reaching for the receiver, he looked at his wall clock: 1412 hours. "Cordero," he said.

Loren Hyung's voice answered him. "Army One just called. They'll be on the pad at fourteen-thirty hours. Be at my office at fourteen-twenty."

"Got it. Fourteen-twenty at your office." Cordero's rectum had clenched at the message. As if he were going into battle, he thought wryly. Taking an old kitchen timer from a desk drawer, he set it for six minutes, then began reading the next abstract, a doctoral study from Laval University on the rate of snow accumulation on different parts of the Ungava Ice Sheet, and rates of perimeter extension. Peripheral firn fields, last winter's snow, reached south of the tundra now, into the taiga below latitude fifty-five! On the other side of Hudson Bay, the Keewatin ice had reached south of sixty. The opening phase of a new Pleistocene glaciation. It was as if the universe were responding to their reconstruction of the Pleistocene mammal genomes.

Whatever, he wondered, *became of the greenhouse effect?* Wondered facetiously, because with the solar constant down three percent, the climate had done just what you'd expect. The Yellowstone eruption, and the consequent two years of strongly increased albedo, had given the cooling a sharp boost, making a piker out of 1816, old "eighteen hundred and froze to death." But the solar "constant" was the real cause.

The timer dinged. Grabbing his jacket, he strode to Hyung's office near the front of the building. Hyung was putting on his jacket as Cordero arrived, and they went out a side door together. Occasional snowflakes drifted down the breeze as the two men walked to a shelter near the helipad, a shelter resembling a Winnipeg bus stop. Somewhere high, barely audible, a plane passed over. Probably loaded with electronics, part of presidential security, he thought, perhaps one of the old MVW surveillance planes.

When he heard the slapping of rotors, Cordero glanced at his watch: 1425:14. The marines were not in evidence, but they'd be watching. Intently. At 1429:23, Army One was on the pad, its rotors still. Steps extruded. A sergeant emerged, then a captain, both in field uniform, both wearing side arms, and stood at attention on the pavement on either side of the stairs. Hyung and Cordero stopped at the edge of the concrete slab.

Then a small man, also in field uniform, stepped out the door, paused, and started down the steps. For just a moment Cordero didn't recognize him. Somehow he'd always thought of the president as a larger man, not tall, but not so *short*. The president's eyes had found them from the door and examined them for a moment before he'd started down. They watched him to the ground, then Hyung started toward him, Cordero alongside, to meet the president halfway. Protocol? Cordero wondered. Hyung would know.

Cordero hardly noticed the Secret Service men, and the physician in army uniform, who'd followed the president down.

Up close, Ed Kollar might have stood 165 centimeters in jump boots, about five feet four barefoot. He looked hard and wiry; his eyes were pale blue, and Cordero wondered when last they'd flinched. But they were not fierce, not now at least, and the mouth half smiled as Hyung introduced Cordero to the president. The president's hand was large for his size, and when they gripped, its hardness disconcerted Cordero. Gripping it was like gripping a two-by-four.

Then they started toward the headquarters building, Cordero a pace behind, feeling swept along by the presidential wake. He wondered how much of the impact was the man and how much the office, or if differentiating meant anything.

Loren gave the president "the tour," starting with an introduction to the on-site staff gathered in the lecture hall. Kollar grinned at them—a grin so unexpected and so light, it startled Cordero all over again—said he was glad to meet them and that he admired what they were doing. Then the small entourage left,

Kollar still grinning. They looked into a couple of offices, visited the library and labs, then the huge vet clinic and necropsy room.

From there it was Loren who took the president to the gun locker to select a rifle for the hunt. And Loren who would drive the president to the rifle range, where he'd sight the weapon in for himself and get the feel of it. The Range insisted that their hunters use one of the "house" guns, four-shot bolt actions, so that in a moment of buck fever they couldn't spray bullets all over the place.

Normally the guides handled the hunter through the selection and familiarization, but Cordero had been glad to have Loren do it.

At 1640 they were back and in Hyung's large, utilitarian office: the president, the president's personal physician, one of the Secret Service men, Cordero, and Hyung. Another Secret Service man stood outside in the corridor, and a third was around somewhere.

"Ron," Hyung said, "give the president a rundown on your plans for the hunt. That'll give him an opportunity to ask questions and stipulate changes."

"Right," Cordero answered. "First though, sir, how many of your people will be going into the field with us?"

"None. It's you and me."

It was what Cordero would have hoped for, if it had occurred to him as possible, yet the answer both startled and worried him. It seemed to him he could smell the disapproval of the Secret Service man at this presidential edict. "Fine," he said. "We'll have a wrangler too, to keep camp and tend the horses. Our actual hunting will be on foot. I'd like to get an early start tomorrow—pick you up in front of the guest cottage at oh-six hundred. I've checked out a trophy-size male with an excellent set of tusks, and relocated him from the air last night so I know roughly where to look tomorrow. We can..."

The president interrupted him with a gesture. "Checked him out in advance? How do you do that?"

Cordero described the procedure—the ground approach, the zoom binocs. "If the tiger's in his prime," he added, "we pass him by. But if he shows signs of deterioration—grizzled muzzle, lost an eye maybe, especially anything wrong with his gait..."

The president stopped him again. "Suppose he doesn't get up and move around for you?"

"Once the light is adequate, if he isn't up and moving around, I shout at him. That always does it."

The presidential eyebrows raised. "Hnh! Which direction does he usually move then? Toward you or away?"

"So far, in the case of a tiger, he's always moved away, taking his own sweet time. Unless he's by a kill. In that case he'll pace around making warning noises—a sort of coughing sound—and maybe make a short rush to worry me. A saber-tooth is probably less dangerous than a Bengal. And in the case of any particular saber-tooth, he's probably never seen a human before, so I don't really worry him. Besides, there's likely to be a hundred meters or more between us, and he doesn't know how slow I am."

"What do you carry in case he does charge?"

"Well, first of all, even a short-faced bear isn't likely to make more than a bluffing charge. But if he keeps coming, we throw a skunk bomb his way. It makes a loud bang and puts out an oily cloud of mercaptans and butyl mercaptans—pretty much the same stuff as skunk spray. We've only ever used them—" He turned and looked at Hyung. "Four times, is it?"

"I think that's right. Yes."

"Four times in the field, that is. A lot more in enclosure tests, years ago. And it's always worked. Even rhinos back off. Even lions, and they tend to tolerate stinks better than most."

"No gun?"

"A sidearm. In my case a .357 magnum double-action revolver. Smith & Wesson. But the skunk bombs have never failed."

"You said lions. Any chance well meet any?"

"I'll almost guarantee we won't. We planted the lions in the eastern half of the Range and the tigers in the west, to let the tigers get well established before they had to compete. The original Pleistocene stocks coexisted for a long time, but we're not sure how well our reconstructions duplicate their behavior. An adult male *neo-atrox*—that's the lion—is a bit bigger than a tiger— about a fourth bigger than an African lion. But our biggest concern is that lions run in prides, and they can gang up on a tiger.

"The lions have spread a long way from their release points since then, but they're not this far west yet. Though it won't be long; maybe a year or two. Our annual survey, last month, showed one pride only about seventy kilometers east of where we'll be.

"As it turns out, there hasn't been any critical problem between the two species. There's enough horses and bison and muskoxen and pronghorn and deer that the prides apparently aren't inclined to tackle anything as dangerous as a tiger."

Cordero moved to wind things up. "By starting early, we can get close to our tiger by evening. Or—" He paused. "Or we can have an aerial spotter guide us to him by radio if you'd like."

The president flicked a glance at Hyung, who didn't react. "Is that something you do often?" Kollar asked. "Have a plane guide you to the animal?"

"Actually, it's something we've never done. But most of our hunters have a week to hunt in, if they need it, not just three days. And you *are* the president."

Kollar's eyes were steady on Cordero's, and he spoke wryly. "Let's do it the usual way. I didn't come here for a corral shoot, and my life won't be ruined if I don't get a tiger, this trip or any other."

Cordero nodded, blushing faintly. "Yes sir. And one other thing: I'm told you're an experienced rider."

"I was born in Moose Jaw, but I grew up on a working ranch in Cherry County, Nebraska. Rode saddle broncs on the rodeo team in college. These days I only ride now and then, but I should hold up all right."

"You said oh-six hundred. Would you rather start earlier? I'm willing, if you want to."

"No sir. Oh-six hundred is early enough."

* * *

The meeting broke up after a few more minutes. The president had specified in advance that no formal dinner was to be given for him, but he'd accepted an invitation for supper with Loren and Lissa. Considering Melody's feelings, Cordero was glad they hadn't been invited, and he felt drained from talking with the president, as if they'd wrestled. He'd have a quiet supper at home, check his hunting gear once more, watch TV for a little while, and go early to bed.

Melody was silent, before supper and while they ate. Afterward, while she loaded the dishwasher, Ron found an ancient *Laugh-In* rerun on television, and relaxed in his easy chair. Melody came in while Miss Ormsby was walloping the Dirty Old Man with her purse, and stepped between Ron and the set.

"Why you?" she said sharply. "Why didn't you assign some-one else? You're the senior field biologist! You could have had Richard guide him!"

Cordero felt himself, his spirit, slumping. He didn't need an upset now. "Loren chose me," he said. "He specifically wanted me to do the job."

"Why? Most of the others guide more than you do now!"

"I don't know why. I didn't ask; it seemed fine to me. And I know the beasties better, have more overall experience with them than anyone else on staff."

"I don't want you to go out there with that man! Call in sick! Say you have diarrhea! The flu!"

Her eyes were wild. Frightened.

"Sweetheart, I will not do that. I won't lie. Not without a compelling reason."

"Please, damn it! Please!"

"Melody, you're getting shrill."

She stopped. Then: "I'm your reason," she said. Quietly. Stiffly. "Don't I count?"

"You count," her husband answered. "More than anyone. And if you'd asked even yesterday, I'd have taken it up with Loren." He got up. "I'm going out. For a walk along the river. Come with me."

She stared for a moment, then relaxed and nodded. Going to the closet, he got their heavy jackets, gloves, the matched skating caps she'd knitted. Neither said anything. To his surprise, when they went out, the cloud cover had begun to break. In the west, Venus glinted through a gap, while Polaris was visible in the north. He felt her hand, ungloved, seek his, and he removed his own glove. It was a short distance to the Missouri, and they walked along the high bank on a bridle path, holding hands, while a breeze clicked the bare branches of cottonwoods.

"I'm sorry," she whispered. "I know I was—irrational. Just— don't let anything happen to you out there."

Happen to me. He squeezed her hand. "I'll do my best, sweet-heart," he said quietly. "I will."

* * *

The small hunter caravan headed southwest on what had

been I-15, in the chill half-light of an autumn dawn. Only one side of the old divided highway was maintained, a broken yellow line down its center. The president expressed surprise that the pavement was as good as it was. At some time within the last year or two, the breaks and potholes had been patched with macadam. Vehicular traffic everywhere was way down, of course. When the Red Plague had run its course, the world had had a little over a billion people left, of the eight billion there'd been four years earlier, just before the crash. In the North American Federation, the population had since recovered to 54 million, but they were concentrated increasingly in the Sun Belt states.

The caravan consisted of a AWD six-pack pickup, followed by a conventional AWD pickup with a horse rack, pulling a four-horse trailer. Cordero drove the six-pack, with the president beside him and two Secret Service agents in back.

At that hour they met only two vehicles, trucks, in forty-five kilometers. At the wind-picked skeleton of an abandoned village, they crossed the Missouri River, turning toward sunrise on a dirt road. After a time, the road ended at a routed wooden sign that read:

PLEISTOCENE MAMMALS RANGE BOUNDARY
TRESPASSERS WILL BE PROSECUTED
N.A.F. DEPT SCIENCE & TECHNOLOGY

They stopped there. Fifteen minutes later, Ron Cordero and the President of North America were in the saddle headed southeastward, followed at a little distance by their wrangler/packer, a loaded pack mule, and the bait nag. Cordero carried his .357 magnum on his belt, and in a long saddle boot, a .416 Remington Magnum. The rifle was to finish the kill if the hunter's four rounds weren't enough. Protection was the function of the skunk bombs clipped on Cordero's belt.

The president's rifle was a .375 H&H magnum with a muzzle brake to reduce recoil, and a three-round clip. It was less powerful, had less reach, and was less difficult to shoot than the Remington. But it was adequate even for *Bison Neo-latifrons*, and there was no hunting of mammoth, mastodon, or rhino on the Range.

The hills were mainly grassland, but scattered over them were copses of young aspen, mostly scrubby. The light cottony seed had ridden the winds from the mountains to the southwest. Where a seedling, delicate and frail, survived on the ashfall, it grew quickly, and was soon surrounded by clone mates that had sprouted from its widespreading roots. They grew where aspen had scarcely been seen for millenia, beneficiaries of the colder, wetter summers. The grass stood thicker and taller now too.

The president scanned the country around. "Nice," he said.

"It suits my tastes, sir." Cordero stopped his horse for a moment to let the wrangler catch up, but when the man saw this, he stopped too, keeping his distance. Cordero shrugged and rode on. Charlie Ruud had packed for him before, with other hunters, and had never hesitated to keep them company. He wondered if the wrangler was spooked by the president; it seemed out of character for Charlie.

As they rode, they talked. Cordero commented on how dour the Secret Service men had been in the pickup. Kollar chuckled. "I'm a trial to them; they don't like me out of their sight." He gestured upward with a thumb. "We're under surveillance right now, by people with good response time and plenty of firepower. But they're not satisfied with that."

Cordero glanced upward, not seeing anything, not sure that the president wasn't putting him on.

After that they discussed tigers—their habits, their relations with other species and other tigers. And how Cordero planned to conduct the hunt. From there, their sporadic conversations went to other species, both indigenous and "resurrected."

They stopped on top of a rounded ridge and got down to relieve themselves, then picketed their animals, took a quick cold snack of jerky and freeze-dried apple slices from their saddlebags, and sat down on the ground. Charlie Ruud still kept apart, holding his separation at sixty or seventy meters. From where they sat, they could see a group of mastodons, *Neo-mammut americanum*, browsing an aspen copse some seven hundred meters away, the first big game they'd seen except for a band of pronghorn. The genetically reconstructed mastodons were true to the original, including the shaggy red hair. "Even to the form of the cusps on the molars," Cordero said.

He grinned wryly at the president. "There was discussion of reconstructing the Neanderthal genome, but the powers-that-were were afraid of legal and ethical complications." He changed the subject then, realizing it could lead to talk about tailor-mades.

"Be all right if I ask Charlie to come over and sit with us? He's usually good company."

Kollar's head jerked a negative. "Let him he. He's following Loren's instructions. From me."

For a moment, the president's meaning didn't register on Cordero. Then a sense of...not fear but entrapment seeped through him. The president went on.

"You're an interesting person, Cordero. I want to know more about you." Uncertainty flashed in Cordero's eyes; a smile quirked a corner of Kollar's mouth. "I don't have execution in mind," the president added. "Or even persecution."

Cordero nodded woodenly, and somehow Melody's parting words came to him.

Again the president waited before saying more, giving Cordero a moment to settle out. "Dr. Hyung tells me you're the operational brains of this outfit," he went on. "That you're the one who came up with practically all the field management policies and procedures for this whole outfit." A muscular hand gestured eastward at the Range, the mastodons. "He says he's recommended you for a GS-13 Supervisory Biologist annually for years, and the DST has turned it down every time. He's quite sour about that. Says you ought to be at least a 14 by now, properly a 15, instead of a 12."

Again the eyebrow cocked. "A 15 would make you equal to him in grade, you know. Which is damned high praise from an administrator. Especially one with Loren's record of accomplishment." Watching for Cordero's reaction, Kollar tucked a slice of dried apple in his mouth, chewed awhile, then swallowed. "I've promised him I'll take care of it when I get back to the District. A lot of field people don't fully appreciate the fiscal crunches we have back there, but this sounds like a matter of justice too long denied."

He gave Cordero a chance to respond. *What*, Cordero wondered, *is he leading up to?* "Thank you, Mr. President. Loren mentioned a couple times sending up the paperwork, and that it hadn't gotten through. It's not something I've had a lot of attention on, but we'll be delighted to get it, Melody and I both."

The president didn't speak again at once, now giving Cordero a vacation from his steady gaze. His teeth engaged a stick of unsmoked jerky wearing it down, knotty muscles bunching in jaws, cheeks, temples. When he'd mastered it, he looked at the biologist again. "I'm not talking about a 15, you understand. A 13 this time and a 14 when you've satisfied the requirement of three years in grade. I'm not throwing regulation out the window, just getting action."

Cordero nodded. "Right," he said. Telling himself *this is not what he really has to say.*

Kollar seemed to read his awareness. "Maybe I should get down to the real reason we're talking here."

Once more he stopped, bit off a piece of hardtack and briefly chewed. "You've shown a lot of the talent you were engineered for, you know. More than just the intelligence."

So he knows I'm a tailor-made.

"You've shown the ability to analyze situations, take responsibility, handle things without the wrong kind of emotion, and create procedures that work. If you'd gone to West Point, you'd have been a general by now."

Now, Cordero thought, *were getting there.* "Thank you sir. But I respectfully submit that as a military officer, I'd have had a major shortcoming. I'd have been deeply unhappy in my career. And in a situation like that, my job performance would not have been satisfactory. Certainly not over time."

The presidential lips pursed, the presidential head nodded. "Not over an extended time perhaps." The eyebrow raised again. "I suppose you've never seen your personality profile."

"No sir. Never thought about it."

"I've seen it. Your profile, that is. And it's very unusual— extremely high, clear across the board. All the characteristics: *aggressive, appreciative, communicative, composed....*I don't recall them all. *Responsible* is one of them. The psych officer told me that psychologically you're either a frigging genius or a rare kind of psych case: someone so phony, the person himself doesn't know he's phony."

The president chuckled. "I asked him how I could tell which. 'By the person's accomplishments,' he said. 'By how well he does things.' And by your performance, Cordero, you're extremely able." He chuckled again. "The psych asked me how much money you make. Said that's the best single indicator he knew of. It'd be interesting to see what his profile looks like. Or maybe they don't reflect values."

The president got to his feet. "I'm ready to go if you are."

They unpicketed their horses, put the bits in their mouths,

and mounted. *So he's examined my personality profile,* Cordero mused. *In Detroit-Windsor, because he looked at it with a psych. What in hell is this about? Am I really that good? Or the complete phony? I'm sure as hell not rich.* Irritation flashed. *Cordero,* he told himself, *ignore it. It's probably bullshit.*

The president's voice drew him out of himself, and Cordero turned to him. "I suspect," Kollar said, "that talking about someone's personality profile is a good way to introvert him."

Cordero nodded, smiling slightly. "I guarantee it." He tapped his heels to his horse's ribs and started down the slope, scanning around as he did so, looking outside himself at his environment. The mastodons were still there; they paused in their feeding to watch the mounted humans. The sky was nearly cloudless. And somewhere a few hours ahead was a trophy-class *Neo-smilodon,* a sabertooth, waiting unknowingly for the president's bullet.

* * *

With the hours and a virtual absence of breeze, it became warm enough that they took off their jackets. They saw more wildlife: mostly hammerheads, but also numerous jackrabbits, once a coyote with three pups following her, and a band of about twenty pronghorn. Finally they came to a coulee, and after pausing to look, Cordero nudged his horse over its rim onto a well-beaten game trail that angled southward down its side.

In the bottom grazed a band of giant Pleistocene bison—a herd bull, four cows, and several yearlings and calves—perhaps a hundred meters ahead. He'd skirt them carefully, Cordero thought. There should be no problem. Herd bulls were dependably surly but seldom really truculent. Ruud knew well enough how to behave, and this president would too.

A shallow stream flowed along the coulee bottom, and a little way beyond the bison a young stand of cottonwood and balsam poplar accompanied the creek, their straight slender trunks clear of limbs for much of their seven-meter height. *They'll bear seed some year soon,* Cordero thought, *and we'll start seeing a lot more woods here.*

A vagrant puff of air brought a whiff of balsam poplar to his nose, like liniment on the breeze, and the bull snorted, snatching Cordero's attention.

A short-faced bear, *Neo-arctodus simus,* rushed from the cottonwoods as the bison turned and ran. In an instant the bear was on a calf, whose bleating lacerated the air. He clutched it, dragged it down, crushed its neck vertabrae with short, powerful jaws, and the bleating stilled.

The frightened saddle horses danced in the trail, their riders fighting them with reins and bits.

The bull had bolted only a dozen meters before stopping to face the bear. The other bison stopped when the bleating did, to mill around snorting. The bear's attention left his kill and went to the bull, which pawed the ground now, swinging its heavy head, its meter and a half spread of horns. The bull stood more than two meters at the shoulder, and Cordero guessed he'd mass at least one and a half metric tons, bone and muscle. The bear, designed for speed, might weigh a longlegged five hundred kilos—half a ton.

The bull started for the bear, and the bear for the cotton-woods. He'd come back for his meal after the bison had moved on.

All this had happened inside twenty seconds—the rush, the kill, the face-off, the departure. Cordero was holding his horse where it stood, not allowing it to turn. A glance backward had shown him the pack mule standing immobile on the trail while the bait nag roped behind it whinnied and jerked.

The bull reached the dead calf, sniffed its blood, raised his head and looked around. The bear was out of sight; the men and their horses were not. He turned and started toward them at a meaningful trot, head and tail both up.

Ron Cordero didn't wait for the huge beast to break into a gallop. He drew his revolver and fired, once. The bull fell as if axed.

"Jesus!" Kollar breathed.

"Okay, let's go," Cordero said, then gestured Ruud to come on, and urged his own, still-nervous mount down the trail. At the bottom he moved aside, making way for the president, and looked back again at Ruud. The mule hadn't moved; the bait nag had quieted, was probably trembling. The wrangler had let go their lead rope and was spurring up the steep bank to get behind them.

Cordero grinned and shook his head. "He's got a bullwhip. He'll have them down pretty quick."

Kollar gestured at the bull, which lay perhaps 30 meters away. "What do you do now? Call in a chopper to dress him out and salvage the meat? Or do we leave him here?"

"He's not dead. At least he shouldn't be, though I expect he's bleeding pretty badly. I shot him in the horn. Can you imagine what it would be like, a .357 magnum slug impacting a horn fastened firmly to the skull?"

"You shot him in the *horn*?"

"Right. I didn't want to leave this band without a herd bull to protect it. Although this one didn't do a very good job. He should have gone for the bear at first whiff."

At the gunshot, the cows and young had wheeled again and run farther down the coulee. Cordero crossed the stream, then waved Ruud and his animals past him and up the game trail on the other side. Finally he and Kollar followed, keeping one eye on the bull, which now had struggled sluggishly to its feet.

"You showed a lot of confidence in your marksmanship back there," Kollar said. "I'd have used a skunk bomb."

Cordero nodded. "You don't use a skunk bomb at that range without getting badly stunk up. Not when you're downwind. And it's really awful stuff, so I prefer not to, if I have a choice. Besides, the first time that guy back there gets challenged by some young bull, I wouldn't be surprised if his horn breaks where the bullet hit it. Then there'll be a new herd bull, maybe one that'll do a better job."

Ruud had stood by at the top of the coulee and let them pass. As they rode by, he commented with a grin on Cordero's marksmanship. Cordero laughed. When they'd reestablished their lead, he spoke to the president again.

"It sounds as if you vetted me personally. And thoroughly. I'm curious why."

Kollar grunted. "What do you know about Uruguay?"

"Uruguay?" The seeming non sequitur took Cordero by surprise. "That's...I get Uruguay and Paraguay mixed up. Uruguay...Let's see. The capital is Montevideo, which is a seaport, so Uruguay's the one on the Atlantic between Brazil and Argentina. But that's all I really know about it." He'd used the old, conventional names: Brazil and Argentina no longer existed as political entities, but their successors were numerous and changeable.

"Beyond that I can only guess: Southern Brazil is grassland, and so is a lot of Argentina, so I suppose Uruguay is grassland too, probably cattle country. And it's far enough south of the equator, it should have winters of a sort: a cool season. Which probably also means it had heavy European immigration, like Argentina. And it wasn't in the news to any extent, in the days when we had lots of international coverage, so it probably had fairly stable government. Back before the Collapse and the Troubles. But I've heard something about fighting there in recent years."

The president grinned broadly. "You get an A-plus on reasoning from limited data. Population before the Collapse was about 3.4 million, with a high literacy percentage and a decent standard of living. After the Plague, probably a couple hundred thousand were left. Twelve years ago, General Mazinni sent an army in and annexed it to Argentina del Norte.

"There's been a series of resistance actions against the Argentinians ever since, plus military incursions from the north, by the Republic of Rio Grande do Sul. Like most of South America, services—medical, transportation, education, utilities—are pretty much back to the levels of the eighteen hundreds—all right for now, maybe, but not when the population grows back to a couple million. Especially with Argentina or Rio Grande do Sul looting the place in the name of taxes and reparations."

Kollar had turned serious again. "What I'm going to tell you now is covered by the Official Secrets Act, and it's highly classified. If you talk about it to anyone not cleared for it, you're in serious trouble."

Cordero's guts tightened. "Maybe I don't want to hear it."

The president ignored him and seemed to change the subject. "Except for the occasional chinook," he said, "the winters here average what these days? Near zero now in Fahrenheit terms, eh?"

"Minus fourteen Celsius at Great Falls for January, the last ten years. That's including the chinook days."

The president nodded. "And the summers are cooling too."

"Seventeen Celsius for July," Cordero answered. He thought of the new pocket glaciers in the Bitteroots, south of Missoula. Still small, measured in hectares or fractions of hectares, but twenty years ago they hadn't been there at all. In spite of himself, Cordero was intensely interested now in what the president was getting at. "And its going to get a lot colder before it gets warmer," he added. "The bigger the Canadian ice fields get, the faster they'll grow. Positive feedback."

"Right. So a few of us have been considering warmer real estate."

Cordero had realized that from Kollar's interest in Uruguay. But why was *he* being told?

"Specifically," Kollar continued, "the North American Federation is considering the invasion and conquest of Uruguay; taking it away from Argentina del Norte. Mazinni's having trouble keeping his own nation together in the face of ambitious district governors and occasional warlords."

"Why should the Uruguayans like NAF rulers any better than Argentinian rulers?"

"For one thing, we won't loot the place. And we'll offer the government to the leader of their own resistance movement: Eustaquio Aguinaldo. All we'll ask—insist on, actually—is that we be allowed to land immigrants. Technical people and farmers, mainly, from Canada and the northern tier of states. All of them with a cram course in Spanish."

While superficially it sounded plausible, Cordero was unconvinced. But instead of pulling on the strings that bothered him, he brought up an ancillary issue. "Uruguay's pretty small, as I recall. Can you move enough people there to do much good?"

"The land is good: soil, climate, people. And—" The president paused, shrugged, went on. "Just to the north is Rio Grande do Sul, their recent invader, a country about twice as large as Uruguay. Like Uruguay, it's good grazing land, with a potential for extensive irrigation. And across the Uruguay River to the west, there's Entre Rios and Corrientes-Misiones, states of Argentina del Norte. They're all pretty heavily depopulated. With a total area about like the Federation east of the Mississippi and south of Kentucky. But more fertile. We'll take them too."

Ed Kollar wasn't looking at Cordero now. He might have been looking at problems, or possibly his horse's neck.

"Mr. President."

The eyes raised, met Cordero's. "Yeah?"

"Pandora's box."

"Uruguay? All of them? They could be, easily enough. We'll need highly skilled on-site leadership. And good, hard-nosed officers willing to keep their troops from abusing and insulting the local civilians. And luck. A certain amount of luck."

"A lot of luck," Cordero said, "or it'll turn into a great bleeding ulcer that'll be hard to let go of and terrible to keep."

Kollar said nothing, and they rode without talking again till Cordero called another break. This time they sat down on an outlook facing east.

"Mr. President, why did you tell me all that?"

Kollar's eyes turned to him, direct and meaningful. "Before the McArdle administration killed it, Project Tailor Made engineered six people for political leadership and four others for military leadership. Ten all told. There wasn't much difference in the specs for the two types. They were to be 'the great leaders of tomorrow.'

"I don't have to tell you that tailor-mades didn't work out as intended. In general they met the physical specs but often not the mental and mostly not the psychological. Of the ten designed for leadership, six survived the Troubles and the Plague; damned high survival. You're the most promising. To be the on-site leader of the Uruguay Project. And that's beside the fact that you grew up speaking and reading Spanish in your foster parents' home."

"On-site leader of the Uruguay Project?"

The president nodded.

"You know a lot about me, Mr. President. I suppose you know that my foster father put a certain amount of pressure on me to attend West Point. And couldn't even get me to do a full ROTC in college. I'd seen enough of the army, and heard enough, growing up on army bases." He smiled wryly. "What I grew up liking was the mountains and wild country around Fort Huachuca and Fort Richardson."

"Right. You did do two years of Army ROTC out of respect for Colonel Cordero, but only two. Four would have entailed a hitch in the army afterward. I'm not talking about making you a general though. The army'd have a harder time swallowing that than what I have in mind. No, I want you to be my personal representative, my minister plenipotentiary in charge of the project on the ground. I wouldn't expect you to take actual military command, but you'd be the top man in strategy and policy—and my personal representative. If you needed to order the generals, overrule them, you'd have the authority.

"First you'd get trained and tutored out the kazoo; it'll be three years at least before we make our move. By that time you'll know as much about Uruguay as Leroux does, Mazinni's viceroy there."

Cordero's body quickened as the president talked.

"I don't foresee any extreme difficulties in military operations," Kollar went on. "Uruguay's neither mountainous, forested, nor swampy, and the Argentinians there aren't well armed or disciplined, or particularly well led, though they are seasoned fighting men. The hardest part will be not antagonizing the Uruguayan people. Any more than the minimum that goes with an uninvited army on someone else's soil."

"Mr. President, my name is Ron Cordero, not Jesus Christ or Abraham Lincoln."

Inwardly, Cordero found himself excited by what Kollar had told him, which made no sense to him at all. He tried to shake it off. "I'm sorry, sir, but—the answer is no. It's not something I'm—willing to do."

"I don't want your answer now, Ron. I want it when the hunt is over. After you've had a chance to sleep on it."

You mean you don't want a no answer, Cordero thought. *If I'd said yes, you'd have jumped on it and called it a contract.*

The offer, and his inexplicable internal response to it, had shaken him. What was it Melody had said? "Don't let anything happen to you out there?" And it was happening, or trying to.

* * *

At 1415 they reached the draw the tiger had been following twelve hours earlier, but they were to intercept him at a point twenty-five kilometers farther north. He'd hardly have doubled back north; that didn't fit his foraging pattern, nor that of any other large predator that Cordero knew of. He might have left the drainage and moved to another, but the best bet was that he hadn't. Judging by his usual rate of travel, he'd pass through late that afternoon or in the evening—unless he made a kill somewhere along the way.

Cordero moistened a finger and held it up. It cooled toward the west; what little breeze there was had shifted around from the south. The tiger wouldn't be afraid of men—he'd probably never seen one till that early morning a week ago—but their odor would be strange to him. It might spook him, or conceivably cause him to circle round to investigate them from the rear.

So they crossed the draw to be downwind of him. In the bottom, in the narrow strip of young cottonwoods, they stopped to water their animals and fill their canteens. Then, after leaving the draw again, they left Ruud, the saddle horses and the pack mule, well away from any cover. Ruud was to make camp there and wait, his tracy on to stay in touch.

Cordero and Kollar hiked along the rim on foot, leading the bait nag. A couple of kilometers north, Cordero saw a promising setup. The slope was mostly open, the bottom cottonwood. Near the top was an aspen copse about ten meters in diameter.

They hiked down to the copse's lower edge, and leaving the president there, Cordero led the bait nag another forty meters downslope. It lay down on command, as trained, and Cordero threw quick hitches around the left legs, front and rear, leaving it unable to rise.

Then, after relieving himself, Cordero walked back up to the copse, and the two men made themselves as comfortable as they could, back just within the fringe of the saplings. They weren't actually screened from below, but their outlines were obscured, and the dry aspen leaves in the copse would warn them of any approach from behind.

"Now comes the hard part," Cordero whispered. "We may have to sit here till tomorrow, and one of us needs to be awake at all times. Now's a good time to relieve yourself, back in the thicket aways. The odds of the tiger coming along will keep getting higher until he gets here."

"I took care of that while you were working on the nag."

"Okay. If you need to eat or drink, keep your movements slow and even. You probably grew up hunting whitetails; the same things apply.

"And you can figure he hears better than we do, so if there's anything we need to say to each other, the sooner the better."

The president nodded, saying nothing.

The afternoon went slowly. The breeze was slight and the sun warm for men in down jackets. It was hard not to doze. When he found himself nodding, Cordero nudged the president, caught his eye, made sure that Kollar was truly awake, then slowly lay back on the leaf-covered ground and napped. To be nudged awake in his turn.

When it was he who watched, thoughts drifted through his mind. *Why me!?* was one. *I've got no military experience, no diplomatic experience. No leadership experience, beyond being the senior field biologist over eleven other field biologists scattered around who don't need much supervision.*

The answer, of course, was: the government, at considerable expense, had genetically engineered people for leadership.

According to the psych tests—whatever they were worth—he was the best of them, good enough to suit Ed Kollar. And in three years he could learn a lot.

Another question was *why am I interested? My God! All the while I was growing up, there was one thing I knew for sure: I wanted nothing to do with the military. Now—if it weren't for Melody, I might have said "yes" back there.*

The answer to that was ready, too, as if he'd known it all along: From infancy, he'd heard his foster father's occasional comments to his foster mother on the politics—the cronyism, backbiting, back *stabbing*—within the officer strata.

These comments, when he had them, would be voiced at the end of the day, while hanging up his blouse and tie, to he elaborated over the ritual cocktail that followed. To Al Cordero, these things did not ruin or drastically degrade the military experience. They were simply something he found distasteful. Dishonorable. He eschewed such behavior himself, fulfilling his duties proficiently and responsibly, using his training, experience, and common sense as far as regulation and policy allowed. And covered his ass only when it didn't infringe on his sense of honor.

Retiring with no regrets, respected. And a bird colonel, a rank attained by few.

Nonetheless, it had been those comments and stories that had turned Ron Cordero against a military career. It had not been pacifism, or unwillingness to exercise authority, or disdain for patriotism. True he'd never liked the idea of living his life within the constraints of military regulations, orders, and demands. But the force behind his attitude had been a childhood reaction he'd never examined before. Now, sitting in an aspen copse in a Montana afternoon, waiting for a sabertooth tiger, he realized this.

So. And what lies behind the attraction of Kollar's offer? he asked himself. The Federation planned to invade a foreign country that neither threatened nor offended it. Three foreign countries eventually. Where was the ethics in that? Why should it attract him?

Kollar would say that Uruguay was already ruled by foreigners, plundered by them. Ruled by one and raided by another. The scene resembled somewhat that in China a century and a half earlier: Arrogant foreigners plundering. Disorder and death. The Federation had the potential to improve the situation dramatically for the people there.

If they'd accept them. *A helluvan if.* And Kollar considered him the best chance for getting it done! If there was a chance. The challenge outranked any other he could think of.

Except, he insisted, *I'm not going to do it. So once more then: What is there about it that attracts…* It struck him then. *I had a purpose, a reason for being, and it was poisoned for me. So I looked around for something else, and found this.*

And now there was Melody, and an oath. "To love and to honor, to have and to hold, in sickness and in health, till death do us part."

These thoughts, these discourses, did not control Cordero's attention. He heard the tiny rustling when a vole or deermouse moved about in the dry aspen leaves. Heard a raven croak overhead, to be answered by another off north somewhere. Occasionally the breeze puffed harder, rattling the few adhering aspen leaves. Now and then the bait nag snorted softly, and once it struggled to get up.

Both men pulled their hat brims down to shield their eyes as the sun lowered in front of them, gilding the bands of clouds there. The light had begun to fade a little, and carefully, quietly, Cordero took the night sight from his pack, fixing it to his Remington. When that was done, Kollar did the same for his rifle. The clouds reddened to vivid pink, to rose, then faded to gold-trimmed purple. The two hunters relied more and more on their ears.

For a while they were not sleepy. Then the president nudged Cordero and lay back to nap. Cordero seemed to shift into a higher state, one he could not recall experiencing before. He was keenly alert, and no thoughts drifted into his mind. He could hear the brook muttering a hundred meters down the slope. The soft even breathing of the man beside him. The increased rodent activity. There was a tiny squeak, in a pitch barely discernible to his ears; it seemed to him that a shrew must have killed somewhere ahead in the grass.

After a time the condition faded, and eventually he poked Ed Kollar, who sat up silently, his face featureless in the darkness, to look at him. Cordero lay back and went to sleep.

* * *

And awakened to a sharp jab! He sat up, senses abruptly keen. It seemed to him that just before he'd wakened, he'd heard the bait nag snort, but just now there was nothing.

Or—*there* was a sound, soft, undefined, off to his left. Another to his right, and another—and another at the rear of the copse: paws tentatively pressing leaves.

He knew exactly what caused the sounds, unlikely as it seemed. They'd moved in from upslope, from the east, and smelled hunters and horse; had come to investigate and make their kill. His hand slipped not to his rifle—it wasn't the weapon for a close quarters melee—nor to a skunk bomb, but to the Magnum on his belt. Then—

He yelled! Abruptly! Wildly! and jumped out of the copse, pistol in hand. In every direction, lions grunted, crouched, or bounded a few uncertain leaps. A lioness charged low, and he fired point blank, saw her skid headlong; heard the ear-blasting wham of Kollar's heavy, high-velocity rifle; something massive slammed into him from behind, sending him sprawling, crushing him down. Huge, heavy, foul-breathed, with muscles jerking powerfully in death. He heard another rifle blast, and the jerking stopped.

After a few seconds he decided he wasn't injured. He wriggled his way free, and on hands and knees, turned to see. A male lion, enormous-looking this close, lay inert beside him, head massive, mouth sagging open, teeth not *Nea-smilodon's* sabers but impressive enough. Suddenly Cordero's heart was thuttering.

"Are you all right, Cordero?"

The lions, he decided, had almost surely fled. "I think so, yeah. Yeah, I'm all right." The slight pain in his chest, he realized, was the tracy in his shirt pocket. He'd fallen on it. Standing up, he scanned around. The bait nag was struggling to rise. Nothing else moved. He stepped into the copse, picked up his Remington, and stepped back out, holding it in his hands instead of slinging it.

"The place for us is in the open," he said, "in case they come back. We can forget about the tiger tonight. We'll try again tomorrow."

The president grunted. "To hell with the tiger. This guy'll do." He poked the lion with his boot. "Now that I look at him, I wish I hadn't had to shoot the big, beautiful sonofabitch."

Cordero nodded. Chances were, the big male had had good years ahead of him, of hunting and siring, of sleeping in the sun in summer and holing up in snow drifts in winter. It weighed, he felt sure, better than three hundred kilos—far bigger than anything in Africa—and its soft coat was thick and warm.

"You want to ride back in the chopper with the trophy?" he asked. "Or on horseback?"

"The chopper. And I want you to come out with me."

Cordero reached inside his down jacket, brought out his *tracy*, and switched it on.

"Charlie, are you there?"

"Yeah. I heard the shooting. The H&H, right? Did he get his tiger?"

"Not a tiger, Charlie. A pair of lions, one of them a trophy. A whole pride was stalking us, and we didn't know it till they were all around us. The president saved my ass; I had to crawl out from under the big male he shot.

"Look. They may decide to visit you. If they do, they'll be excited, wound up. Pump up your Coleman and light it. Then make sure the picket pins are driven all the way to China, and be ready to do some shooting. To scare them. Don't shoot to kill unless they press the issue.

"When the lamp is lit and you're satisfied with the picket pins, get on the M-3 and call headquarters for the chopper, with men to load the lions. "Got that?"

"Got it."

"Also have them bring out someone to ride back in with you. Per policy. The president and I will fly back in the chopper.

"And Charlie, don't say anything about what happened. Tell them we've got two lions to take out with us, and that everything's fine. No use getting Melody all upset, or the Secret Service guys either."

"Right, Ron. That all?"

"That's it. I'm off the air but wearing my plug."

Cordero put the *tracy* back in his shirt pocket, leaving the ear button in place. "Too bad your tiger didn't come along first."

"Ron, I didn't really come out here for a tiger. It was the last step in vetting you. Call it a job interview. And a chance to see you work. It was too important to leave to someone else."

Cordero looked hard at him. The president gestured at the big male lion. "You know what, Cordero?" he said. "You owe me. You know that. You owe me and so does Melody."

"Mr. President, that is a lousy goddamn point of view."

Kollar laughed. "I got that, Cordero. But it's also the truth.

And having told me off that way, you look better than ever for the job."

Cordero brushed aside the compliment. "Mr. President, it may be true in your mind that I owe you. But what counts is, is it true in mine?"

He said little more then, just squatted by the lion and waited. Thinking. About Melody and a lot of things. About the kind of president that would do what this one had, in the past and in the future. An hour later he heard the chopper and called it to give the pilot a location fix. Minutes later it was on the ground. While the president helped the crew load the two lions, Cordero talked to the man it had brought out, an old cowboy and sometime logger, telling him where Charlie was. He was to take the bait nag with him. The chopper would follow, in case the lions got interested.

Then Cordero got in the chopper with the president. Two Secret Service men were there; Cordero ignored them. "Eddy," he called to the pilot, "hold off on the racket a minute, okay?"

"Sure, Ron. Tell me when."

"Mr. President," Cordero said. "I'll admit you've got my interest. But there's no way I'd even consider it unless you—we— can convince my wife. Which will take some doing if it's possible at all. And I mean *convince* her, not bulldoze her. She's got to feel all right about it."

"Fair enough."

Cordero raised an eyebrow at the president's casual reaction. "She may get a little fierce."

"I'm prepared for that. Loren and I talked about things when he was in the District week before last. And we brainstormed it with Lissa last night after supper."

Cordero stared at him. Christ! I'll bet you did at that. Well. If you want me that badly, and if Melody agrees, and if I decide to do it, I won't be shy about demanding things my way.

"Okay, Eddy," he called, "any time."

The starter whined. The rotors began to turn, gained speed, and after a minute the chopper lifted. Cordero felt a brief emptiness, a sense of leaving a life behind.

Whoa there! he said to himself. *You haven't decided to do it yet.* But it seemed to him he had. If Melody agreed. If this life was over for him, it was because he had another to go to, the one he'd been born for. And that, it seemed to him, was something Melody would understand, given a little time.

The Ides of September

Introduction

In *Ellery Queen's* or *Alfred Hitchcock's* mystery magazine, I forget which, I once read a short story about a Cajun sheriff in the Louisiana bayou country, and very much liked the ethnic flavor. I'd already decided to try my hand at mysteries, and an ethnic rural sheriff seemed a good way to go.

A few decades earlier I'd worked in the Lake Superior region, and loved it. Especially Upper Michigan, partly for its natural beauty, and partly for the flavor of its ethnic colonies, most of them Finnish. (The old colonization projects had settled immigrants in ethnic groups, which have since intermarried a lot, greatly reducing the ethnicity.)

So I wrote "The Ides of September," setting it in a fictional, backwoods Upper Michigan county at the beginning of the 1980s. Matti Seppanen, its Finnish-American sheriff, is the central figure. I hoped it would turn into a series. *The Saint* mystery magazine promptly bought it and asked for more.

I'd realized from the git-go there was a problem with setting a detective series in a sparsely populated backwoods county. There might be two murders in a decade, neither of them requiring much investigation. But by creating a concentration of lakes in the western part of the county, lakes with considerable resort development, and outsiders with money to fuel their vices...

At the end of the story I'll add a few comments about the principal characters—after you've gotten to know them.

* * *

Mary Eberley sat at the kitchen window nursing her breakfast coffee, which now was merely warm. The white-and-blue porcelain clock said 7:40, the Ojibwa County courthouse was less than a ten-minute walk away, and the sheriff wasn't due there until eight. Outside the window, the lawn was white with frost. Mrs.

Perttula was in the living room talking loud Finnish to her aged mother, who was hard of hearing.

I might as well start, Mary decided, and got up. The new jeans were stiff on her legs, the hunting boots unfamiliar weights. A gray twill shirt lent a touch of manliness to her slim, unmanly torso. After shrugging into her green twill jacket, she picked up her new lunch pail, the first she'd ever owned, and walked to the front door.

"Good-bye, Mrs. Perttula," she said.

"Good-bye, Mary."

"How do you say good-bye in Finnish?"

"Näkemiin."

Mary turned to the grandmother. "Näkemiin, Mrs. Herronen."

The old lady beamed up from her rocker. "Näkemiin, tyttö," she said, and there was more, which Mary didn't understand.

"She says it's nice to have a young person living here again," Mrs. Perttula translated.

The autumn morning was crisp and pleasant as Mary walked down the maple-lined street. So close to the great lake, the leaves were just starting to turn. Boarding with the Perttula's promised to be a new experience in itself. And living in a small town through an Upper Michigan winter.

The sheriff wasn't evident when she entered the office. She'd met him the day before, after arriving across the square at the White Pine Hotel, where the reception desk doubled as the bus station.

A middle-aged deputy sat pecking deliberately at an elderly typewriter, filling out his watch report. He looked up, his index fingers poised.

"Can I help you?" He had an accent, like everyone else she'd spoken with here.

"I'm Mary Eberley. I'm here to see Sheriff Seppanen."

"He ain't in yet," the man said, returning to the report. She sat down. *I wonder what they think of having a sociology student spending a year up here on her graduate research,* she thought. Her appointment as a deputy was a legal formality, not a salaried job. It made her research possible.

Two minutes later Matti Seppanen walked in. Physically, he was almost a stereotypical back-country sheriff. Seemingly in his fifties, he was about five-feet-ten and beefy, with remarkably big shoulders. His face was clean-shaven, his brown hair crew-cut. But the stereotype ended at his eyes, which declared a direct simplicity and calm self-certainty.

"Good morning, Mary. Good morning, Eddy." The deputy looked up again. "Mary," the sheriff said, "I'd like you to meet Deputy Nisonen. Eddy has the midnight-to-eight shift. Eddy, this is Mary Eberley, the young lady we've been expecting."

Nisonen nodded. "Nice to know you," he said, then turned and pulled his report from the platen.

"Anything I need to know about?" the sheriff asked him.

"Yeah. Hjalmar Tallmo phoned about ten minutes ago. He found Bill Skoog dead alongside the Stormy Lake Road, by Icehouse Lake. Looked like somebody shot him."

The sheriff picked up the call-in report from the dispatcher's desk—the dispatcher was in the cell block, feeding the few prisoners—then radioed the day deputy. "The sheriff calling sheriff three. Pete, where are you now?"

"I'm on 67 heading south out of town for Icehouse Lake, to check out the murder report on Bill Skoog."

"Good. I'll get there about ten minutes after you." He turned to Mary. "Let's go."

She almost had to trot to keep up with him as he strode to his pickup truck. *How many murders would Ojibwa County have in a typical year?* she wondered. She'd overlooked that item in her background study. Surely less than one. The county had barely 9,000 people, more than 3,000 of them here in Hemlock Harbor, the rest scattered over 1,500 square miles of back country. The population was predominantly Finnish-American, especially the rural population, with Swedes second and the rest assorted American. Hemlock Harbor was the only actual town. The other eight dots on the map included two resort villages on Lake Superior, three on concentrations of inland lakes, and three tiny crossroads places where farmers might stop to buy a six-pack. Her atlas identified the farmer villages as "Tamarack," "Makinen," and "Oskar."

She'd ridden through Makinen and Tamarack on the bus—each had five or six frame buildings, a pair of gas pumps, and a beer sign. Oskar was probably the same. She wondered how a town ever got named Oskar.

When the pickup topped the forested hill south of town, she could look out over the cold blue of Lake Superior, stretching sea-like to a distant horizon. A few miles offshore, a long barge was being towed toward the harbor by a tug. Probably from Canada or Minnesota with a cargo of spruce logs for the paper mill.

She turned her attention to the sheriff. "You people talked as if you knew the dead man."

"Bill Skoog is a deputy game warden."

"Um. Is there a lot of bad feeling between local people and the game wardens?"

"Not much. A little bit here and there, now and then."

The radio squawked. "Sheriff one, sheriff one, this is the dispatcher. Over."

They didn't even bother to use the ten-code, Mary thought.

"This is sheriff one. What have you got, Marlin?"

"A Roy Olson just phoned in that he had a calf stolen last night. On the Wolf Creek Road. You know the place? Over."

"About three miles east of the Oskar Road. Where's the calf missing from? Barn? Pasture?"

"Pasture. Olson said he heard a shot about three this morning. Thinks maybe a headlighter shot it for a deer and then hauled it anyway."

The sheriff grunted dubiously. "Okay. One of us will be over later today, when we finish at Icehouse Lake. Is that it?"

"That's it."

"Okay. Sheriff one out." The sheriff hung up the microphone on the dashboard.

"Do you think it really was a poacher?" Mary asked.

"That killed the calf? Could be. Or could be a bear. Cows' eyes aren't the same color in a spotlight as a deer's, and poachers are usually in bed by midnight."

He pushed the heavy pickup hard through gently rolling forestland—broken at intervals by clusters of small farms, their buildings mostly small and neatly painted, their yards largely bare of trees, as if to let in as much sun as possible in winter. After half an hour, the deputy in sheriff three called for an ambulance. He'd found the dead man.

Five minutes later the sheriff left the blacktop for a graveled road, turning west into the national forest, the woods now unbroken save for an occasional small lake or bog. Shortly afterwards, they turned north, and saw two vehicles parked beside the road— one a white sheriff's department sedan, the other a green pickup. Matti Seppanen slowed and pulled off behind the sedan.

The deputy walked over, clipboard in hand. He was still young, and wore his blond hair in a white-sidewalls style.

"Pete Axelson, Mary Eberley," the sheriff said curtly, then walked directly to kneel by the body. His thick fingers opened the dead man's forest-green uniform jacket; the blood that had soaked it was congealed and crusted. Mary heard a muttered Finnish expletive. Seppanen rolled the body over, pulled up the shirt in back, and examined the bullet's exit hole.

"Look at it, Pete. What do you see?"

"A small hole. Couldn't have been a soft point slug."

"Right. I doubt it was even a rifle. Now look where he was laying. What does it look like to you?"

Mary watched the deputy's eyes narrow, his lips pursing.

"Judas," he said, "there ain't much blood there, for somebody whose jacket is all soaked with it."

"Right. Maybe about as much as might drain out if he got put there after he laid dead awhile."

The sheriff walked to the game department pickup that stood with its door still open. "Take a look here," he said.

Axelson peered in thoughtfully. "Uh—the headlight switch is on. Does that mean anything?"

"It could. He might have left them on to light something." Matti strode off past the body in the direction the lights would have shone, Mary and Pete following, about twenty-five yards, to squat beside a pile of entrails.

"What do you see here?" he asked, looking up.

The younger man frowned. "Deer guts. And whoever killed it didn't know what's good. Left the heart and liver."

"All right. How many deer guts did you ever see?"

The deputy grinned. "Quite a few."

The sheriff took a jackknife from a pocket and slit the bulging sack-like rumen, which drew open, displaying its contents. There was a smell like fermented grass, like a cow's breath.

"Anything more to say?"

Axelson whistled silently. "Did you know what was in there?"

"I had a pretty good idea. So what have we got here?"

"It's full of grass and either clover or alfalfa. I don't..."

Seppanen silenced him with a gesture and looked at Mary. "What does this tell you?"

She looked around. There was only forest—dark maples with

more autumn color than in town, a few darker hemlocks, scattered golden-barked birches, and along the ditch bank some young firs. Only along the road was there grass, and no clover she could see.

"Would you expect it to be full of grass and clover here?" she asked.

"You got it." The sheriff smiled up at her, wiped his knife blade on some roadside grass and stood. "Grass maybe, but not a lot of clover. And for damn sure there'd be a lot of browse— leaves, needles, twigs." He turned to his deputy. "The first thing that hit me, they didn't look right for deer guts. I think we'll find they came out of a calf. And there's a Roy Olson over east of Oskar that had a calf stolen last night. So what do you make of this?"

Axelson concentrated. "It looks like—like someone killed a calf and brought the guts here to make it look like Bill caught some headlighters with an illegal deer, and got shot by them. After they really killed him somewhere else and brought him."

Seppanen nodded abruptly, strode back and dug in the dead man's pocket, coming out with keys on a ring. "It looks like he parked here himself. Otherwise they'd either be missing or in the ignition." He stood again. "Pete, bag the rumen for the game department to examine. Then stay here and wait for the ambulance. Follow them to town. Tell Doc Norrlund I want his best estimate of what kind of bullet killed Billy, and about what time. And check his jacket for any sign of powder burns."

He turned to Mary. "Let's take a walk." She nodded. After he'd clipped a walkie-talkie on his belt, they crossed the dry roadside ditch. An inconspicuous trail, made years past by a tractor dragging logs, entered the forest, carpeted now with last year's moldering leaves. They followed it, the sheriff's eyes watching the ground.

"What do you see?" Mary asked. He shook his head. Two hundred feet from the road lay a lovely lake, and they stopped beside it. It was round, perhaps three-eighths of a mile across; she would not have hesitated to drink from it.

"Icehouse Lake," Matti said. Heavy forest came down to the shore all the way around, except for a segment to their left, where a large, lodge-like summer home stood in a circle of lawn, with a boathouse and other outbuildings nearby. A dock extended some fifty feet into the lake behind it. For a moment the sheriff contemplated the buildings, then raised the belt radio.

"Pete!"

Several seconds lapsed. "Yes, sheriff?"

"Radio Marlin and have him phone the Forest Service. Find out the nearest logging camp around here, the closest to Icehouse Lake." He clipped the radio back on his belt. "Time was," he said to Mary, "there was little gippo camps scattered all over the woods. When I was young. Now the loggers mostly live at home and drive to work."

She nodded. "Why did we come down to the lake?"

"Bill would have parked where he did for some reason. Maybe to come in on this trail." He looked across the lake. "That's a long dock."

"What did you think we might find here?"

He shrugged massive shoulders. "I thought we might see sign of a body being dragged. On a tarp maybe. But I didn't." He looked toward the summer home again, then they walked back to the road. Pete Axelson was sitting in his patrol car with the microphone in his hand and an open mapbook on his knee. After a minute or so, the receiver sounded.

"Sheriff three, this is sheriff's dispatcher. There are two loggers, the Waananen Brothers, batching on a pulp job only about three-quarter miles northeast of Icehouse Lake, on the east side of the Stormy Lake Road. That's in the northwest quarter of Section 17, Township 47 North, Range 39 West. Their shack is back in where you can't see it from the road, but you can see where they drive in. They've put a culvert in the ditch, with gravel over it. You want me to repeat that?"

Pete had penciled an X on the map page. The sheriff took the microphone from him.

"This is Matti. I'm with Pete. We'll find it; I can hear their saws." He gave the mike back. As they went to his pickup, Mary could hear the distant sound of a chain saw, joined a moment later by a second. A truck approached from the north, loaded with logs—the rough black of sugar maple, smooth gold of yellow birch, gray of basswood and others. It slowed as if to stop at the cluster of official vehicles, then drove on. Pete had covered the body with a square of white plastic so it wasn't exposed. The sheriff started the motor.

"If the truck driver had known there was a dead man here, do you think he'd have stopped?" Mary asked.

"Might have. People around here are more interested than in

places like Milwaukee or Chicago. Or Ann Arbor. The residents, I mean, not the summer people." He looked at the young woman beside him. "I'll try to mention the kinds of things I think you might want to know, but don't hesitate to ask questions. I'm surprised you ain't used the tape recorder more," he added, referring to the small instrument hanging from her shoulder.

She smiled into the big square face. "I'm lucky. I can sit down later and play back the day from memory. That's one reason I had a 3.87 grade point average as an undergraduate."

"Um. If you ever want a real job as a deputy, let me know."

They climbed back into Matti's pickup and headed in the direction of the logging camp. The road dropped into a broad flat, the hardwood forest giving way largely to spruces, firs, and other conifers. The sheriff slowed. There was the culvert, and he crossed it to follow wheel tracks back in among the trees. Soon, they came to a small, battered travel trailer with a propane tank and a small, prefabricated metal shed. The chain saws were much nearer now. The sheriff shifted into four-wheel drive and pushed on. They heard a tree fall. The nearer saw slowed, to begin a series of alternate idlings and snarlings as the operator began sawing off limbs.

Matti parked beside the logger's jeep and they walked toward the noise, the woods becoming swamp. Moisture from the spongy moss-covered ground darkened their boots. The woods became open, the larger trees lying now as piles of small logs along a tractor trail, backed by delicate green saplings that would grow to take their place. The smells were new to Mary; she decided she liked them.

Yes, the cutter told them, he'd heard a gunshot the evening before, some distance off, probably about 9:15. He'd looked at the clock at 8:50 when he'd heard a low-flying plane, and the gunshot was some while after that. He'd gone to sleep about ten.

He wasn't sure what direction the shot came from. It was hard to tell when there was only one, but he thought it was from the south.

Back in the pickup, Mary mentioned that she'd gotten the interview on tape. "I noticed," Matti said, and began the slow bouncy drive back to the county road.

"So how does it stack up now?" she asked.

"Hmm. I might as well tell Pete and headquarters while I'm telling you. Hold the mike for me; I need both hands to drive here."

He summarized his conversation with Waananen, the logger. "It was interesting what he said about the low-flying plane. That dock at the lodge is awful long for two or three private boats; more like a seaplane dock. And we know there's quite a bit of drugs dealt in the Stormy Lake and Kekebic resort areas.

"So just to speculate—suppose Bill Skoog is patrolling along, watching for headlighters—poachers that hunt deer at night with spotlights. And suppose he sees a plane start down to land on Ice-house Lake and gets curious. It ain't really any of his business, but he parks and goes down to the lake to watch. And then, instead of doing the smart thing—heading back and mentioning it to us the next day—suppose he walks around the shore to snoop a little. Maybe peeks in a window. You might have noticed his boots were wet, as if he'd got in some wet ground."

"Umm. Everything fits, doesn't it?"

"What we've got fits. What there is of it."

They passed the patrol car and green pickup, turning west a short way farther on. Another quarter mile brought them to a wide driveway, blacktopped against dust, that curved in through timber to the large house on Icehouse Lake. Matti drove in and parked behind a black, four-wheel-drive pickup standing high on large tires. He radioed in his location. Then they went up the wide front steps to the wrap-around front porch, where he pressed the door-bell. Chimes sounded inside. When there was no response, the sheriff sauntered out to the black pickup, Mary half a step behind and feeling watched, exposed. He peered over the tailgate, then circled the vehicle.

They heard a window open, a slight sound pregnant with threat. Under other circumstances it would not have been noticed. Seppanen raised the radio to his mouth and spoke casually but not quietly. "Sheriff three, this is the sheriff. There's a black pickup parked here, Illinois plates 1PK378. The box looks freshly scrubbed, the rest just hosed off."

He put the radio back on his hip. "To discourage anyone from shooting us out the window," he murmured. "And maybe get them looking backwards, thinking what they should have done, instead of frontwards, planning."

Briskly then, he walked to the incinerator behind the house. Opening the front, he carefully explored the ashes with a poker leaning there. "Sheriff three, this is the sheriff. There are fragments of heavy polyethylene in the incinerator, like it could have been a plastic tarp. Also some charred blue denim fragments, a zipper like off a pair of pants—and someone just came out the back door. Sheriff out." He turned and waited for the man.

"Can I help you, officer? I'm afraid I was sleeping late this morning."

He was in his late twenties, possibly thirty, his brown hair frowzy, supporting his statement.

"Is that your pickup?" asked Seppanen.

"Yep."

"You're not from Illinois. You're from somewhere around Lake Superior; I can tell from how you talk. You live around Finns."

The man grinned at him. "Takes one to know one. I lived in Hibbing, Minnesota till I was nineteen. I guess it never totally rubs off." He thrust out a hand. "My name is Jim Connelly." They shook. "What can I do for you?"

"Did you hear any shots last night?"

"Yes, matter of fact, I heard two. One around nine o'clock. The other was at 9:20, because I remember looking at the clock and thinking that the poachers must be busy. I have to admit, it reminded me of fall in Minnesota."

"Kind of looks like poachers. We had a game warden killed last night, just over there by the road. There was a pile of guts nearby, as if he caught someone dressing out a deer, and they shot him."

Connelly shook his head. "The hazards of being a north-country game warden."

"There's something that bothers me though." Matti's eyes were steady. "Murder is a serious felony; shooting deer is a misdemeanor. Why would someone commit murder to get out of a $200 fine?"

The man became studiedly casual. "Well, sheriff, you know how clannish these Finn farmers can be. No offense, but they don't much care for non-Finns butting into their affairs." He shrugged. "That's the way it was back home, anyway. What you need is to have Finn game wardens."

Seppanen's quiet eyes threatened to see through the man. "You got a point there. Mind if I look around?"

Connelly's gaze hardened. "Just stay out of the house, unless you've got a warrant. I tried to be helpful, but I don't appreciate being accused of some crime." He turned and walked stiffly to the house. Matti watched him through the door, then raised his radio again.

"Sheriff three, we've got a suspect. White male, six feet, a hundred seventy pounds, brown hair, closed-clipped dark beard, range accent. Got that? Calls himself Jim Connelly. Says he's from Hibbing, Minnesota. And he's got a scar below the left eye."

"Okay, I got that. Sheriff, the ambulance is just pulling in."

"Right. I ain't done yet. Connelly lied to me. Said there were two shots, about nine o'clock and 9:20. Which fits the way things were set up to look but not the way they were.

"So I want you to get any fingerprints off Billy's wallet and badge case, also the right front door and headlight switch of his truck. Steering wheel too; the killer might have touched it."

There was a brief silence, during which Mary could visualize the deputy scribbling rapidly on his clipboard, a sort of long-distance stenographer. "Right, sheriff. I got it."

"Okay that's all for now." Seppanen clipped the radio back on his belt.

A backwoods Sherlock Holmes, thought Mary. *He doesn't miss a thing.* "What's next?" she asked.

"Let's just look around." He walked directly toward the house, stopping outside a back window to examine the flower bed beneath it, its frost-killed plants shriveled and brown. A dozen yards away, the bed had been spaded and freshly raked. He went to it, and from a pocket took a plastic specimen bag and filled it with soil. Then he examined the wall, and with his pocket knife dug something from it. Silently he showed it to Mary—a somewhat flattened slug.

The back door opened, and they looked up into the muzzle of an automatic pistol.

"What did you find, sheriff?"

Seppanen simply looked without answering.

"Back away with your hands up." Connelly came down the steps and gestured toward the door. "In the house. Move!"

"No thanks."

"I'll count to five."

"Pull the trigger and it'll be heard. I've called in a description of your truck and you. Right down to the scar beneath your eye."

The man stood, undecided, his mind racing.

"Tell you what," the sheriff said. "Let me handcuff Mary for you. Then let her run off in the woods over there"—he gestured westward—"in the direction away from my deputy. When she's got a three or four minute start, I'll take the battery out of my truck so she can't come back and drive it or use the radio. Then you can handcuff me and take me with you."

"Matti! He'll kill you!"

"I don't think so. He'll drop me off in the boonies somewhere. And if he kills me, that's better than both of us getting it. I'm sixty years old, while you're—what? Twenty-five?"

Connelly stared at him suspiciously, then decided.

"Handcuff her," he said.

Matti manacled her wrists in front of her, then leaned forward and kissed her cheek. "Just in case I don't see you again, have a good life."

"Okay," said Connelly, "get out of here. That way." He pointed, and reluctantly she started, then, at fifty feet, began to run. She'd just reached the forest's edge when the pistol boomed. She turned, saw Matti on the ground, and screamed. Connelly half pivoted, his feet not moving, and tipped over, falling without trying to catch himself. Her second scream cut short as she saw Matti start to get up, and she headed back to him.

When she arrived, he was on one knee by the gunman, who lay on his side with a knife hilt jutting out at the breastbone.

"How?" she asked.

Matti got heavily up. "In the old days, some Finns were what they called *puukkojunkkari*, knife fighter. When I was a kid, I learned to throw a knife. Like this." He raised his hands above his shoulders, then abruptly doubled forward, his right hand flashing to his collar in back, then flashing forward. "I used to practice that when I was a teenager. Then, when I joined the sheriff's department, I started carrying a knife between my shoulder blades. For thirty-three years I never needed it. Then, he turned his head to see where you'd gotten to, and that gave me my chance."

The sheriff took a deep breath. "You know, that's the closest I come to getting killed since Italy in 1944."

* * *

At the end of the shift, Matti, Mary, and Pete stopped at the bar in the White Pine Hotel, settling down from the day.

"Why did you want me to fingerprint Bill Skoog's wallet?" Pete asked.

"Connelly said Skoog wasn't a Finn. Why would he think that? Actually he was a Finn; it's just that, like quite a few Finns, he had a Swede name. I figured he must have looked in Bill's wallet and seen the name and knew it wasn't Finn." Matti raised his glass then, swirling the amber whiskey and clear ice cubes, watching them pensively.

"A penny for your thoughts, Matti," Mary said softly.

"I was just wondering. If maybe I shouldn't have killed him. He might have let me go, you know?"

"No, you done right," Axelson said. "He killed Bill; he probably would have killed you."

"Yeah, I'm not regretting. But Pete..."

"Yeah?"

"He let Mary go. Too bad I had to pay him back like that."

Afterword

By the time I'd finished "Ides," it seemed to me that Matti and Mary had to have a June and November romance, and marry. And when Keith Bancroft, *The Saint's* editor, suggested the same thing, that settled it. The second Matti Seppanen story made their mutual attraction clearer. But sad to say, after a few issues, distribution problems sank the resurrected *Saint*, so I didn't follow through on the project.

However! In 1990 I wrote a novella, set in about 2010, featuring a young detective in L.A., where there are all kinds of crimes. His name is *Martti* Seppanen, son of Matti and Mary. The novella dealt with a very science-fiction crime, so it appeared in *Analog science fiction/science fact* for April 1991. In October 2001, Martti resurfaced in a Baen Book, *The Puppet Master*. A futuristic detective trilogy in one volume.

Matti and Mary would have been proud of Martti. And as his literary grandfather, so am I.

Coming soon from
Silver Dragon Books

The Aethereal Sea By Marguerite Mullaney

Turn of the Wheel By Jennifer Oberlander

High Rage By Jim Burk

Black Roses By Christine Morgan

The Elfland Affair By Terry Bramlett

John has been a soldier (1944-46), merchant seaman and logger; and after belatedly attending college, district forester. Later came a doctorate, and 17 years as a research forest ecologist. Next came several years primarily as a casual laborer and free-lance editor in L. A., while trying to break into screenplay writing. Finally he settled into SF. Besides assorted short fiction, he's had 25 novels published—the most recent being *Soldiers* and *The Puppet Master*. The *Helverti Invasion* and *The Second Coming* will be out in 2003 from Baen Books.

Printed in the United States
926900006B